"I have a confession to make."

She touched her lower lip with her tongue and took a shaky breath. "I didn't wear this dress just to distract Ralph. I also wanted to knock your socks off."

Whoa. If she could be that honest, so could he. "You succeeded. My toes are kinda curled, too."

"I also wanted you to know that I'm not a Pollyanna."

The jury was still out on that one, but he knew what he was supposed to say. "I got the message, loud and clear."

Her smile was faint. She didn't move. God, he'd only thought her laugh had made him warm. The *kiss me* look was smokin'. It was also an invitation and he decided to take it. "Wondering," he asked softly, "just how much further you can go and still be safe?"

She blinked. "What makes you think that?"

"It's what I'm wondering."

Dear Reader,

Most of us look forward to October for the end-of-the-month treats, but we here at Silhouette Special Edition want you to experience those treats all month long—beginning, this time around, with the next book in our MOST LIKELY TO… series. In *The Pregnancy Project* by Victoria Pade, a woman who's used to getting what she wants, wants a baby. And the man she's earmarked to help her is her arrogant ex-classmate, now a brilliant, if brash, fertility expert.

Popular author Gina Wilkins brings back her acclaimed FAMILY FOUND series with *Adding to the Family,* in which a party girl turned single mother of twins needs help—and her handsome accountant *(accountant?)*, a single father himself, is just the one to give it. In *She's Having a Baby,* bestselling author Marie Ferrarella continues her miniseries, THE CAMEO, with this story of a vivacious, single, pregnant woman and her devastatingly handsome—if reserved—next-door neighbor. Special Edition welcomes author Brenda Harlen and her poignant novel *Once and Again,* a heartwarming story of homecoming and second chances. *About the Boy* by Sharon DeVita is the story of a beautiful single mother, a widowed chief of police…and a matchmaking little boy. And Silhouette is thrilled to have *Blindsided* by talented author Leslie LaFoy in our lineup. When a woman who's inherited a hockey team decides that they need the best coach in the business, she applies to a man who thought he'd put his hockey days behind him. But he's been…blindsided!

So enjoy, be safe and come back in November for more. This is my favorite time of year (well, the beginning of it, anyway).

Regards,

Gail Chasan
Senior Editor

Please address questions and book requests to:
Silhouette Reader Service
U.S.: 3010 Walden Ave., P.O. Box 1325, Buffalo, NY 14269
Canadian: P.O. Box 609, Fort Erie, Ont. L2A 5X3

BLINDSIDED
LESLIE LAFOY

Silhouette®

SPECIAL EDITION®

Published by Silhouette Books

America's Publisher of Contemporary Romance

For Garrett
Who picked up a hockey stick eight years ago
and changed the course of our lives.
Thank you, Son.

 SILHOUETTE BOOKS

ISBN 0-373-24716-8

BLINDSIDED

This edition published by arrangement with Harlequin Books S.A.

® and TM are trademarks of Harlequin Books S.A., used under license. Trademarks indicated with ® are registered in the United States Patent and Trademark Office, the Canadian Trade Marks Office and in other countries.

Visit Silhouette Books at www.eHarlequin.com

Printed in U.S.A.

LESLIE LaFOY

A former high school history teacher with wide ranging interests, Leslie collects antique silver and loves to work with stained glass. She admits to being one of the last women in America who considers sewing a recreational activity. And home rehabbing—major, major fun. She's married—twenty-one years—to David and they have a teenage son who plays hockey and lacrosse.

In her spare time <g>, Leslie has written nine historical romantic suspense novels and one novella. She's now adding contemporaries into the writing mix just for the fun of doing something different.

The Girls' Guide to Hockey

There are four basic types of hockey players.

The Goalie. He's the guy standing in front of the net and looking like the Road Warrior version of the Michelin Man. Under those pads is a man who has the single-mindedness of a medic dragging a wounded soldier to safety. **Off ice...** They can be a bit oblivious to what's going on around them. If you want their attention, try tossing a puck across their seemingly blank stare.

The Center. Speed. Drive. Confidence. Loads and loads of confidence. While these tendencies can be a bit off-putting off ice, it is possible to drop his jaw. **Off ice...** Just sweetly move around him and go on like he isn't there. They're so not used to that that they'll come after you out of sheer curiosity.

The Wingers (Left and Right). They're every bit as good as the center; they just don't usually get the spotlight. Which is fine by them. It's not that they lack confidence, it's that they prefer to play strong supporting roles. **Off ice...** Invite the whole team over for dinner and ask him to help. He'll adore you forever.

The Defensemen. aka The Rescuers. They charge into the fray and put not only their bodies, but also their hearts and souls between the puck and the net. They're usually the most unassuming guys on the ice. "It's no big deal. It's just my job." **Off ice...** They live to be needed. Just don't gush publicly over their rescue exploits. **Privately...** Everyone likes to be appreciated.

Prologue

That had gone as well as could be expected, Catherine Talbott decided as she watched the team's now former general manager storm out of the office. The door could probably be put back on the hinges. And if it couldn't, she could live without one. She'd lived without a lot lately. She was actually getting good at it.

John Ingram—he who had just joined the ranks of disgruntled former employees—was somewhere in the administrative office shouting about Cat pretending to have a penis when Lakisha Leonard sauntered in through the mangled doorway.

Cat's assistant flipped her assortment of beaded braids over her shoulder and arched a glitter-spangled brow. "He's not happy."

The understatement of the year. "People who get fired usually aren't," Cat pointed out, organizing the pile of bills on the desk in front of her and trying not to fixate on the huge, red PAST DUEs stamped on them.

"Carl isn't going to be happy, either," Lakisha said warily. "The two of them go way back together."

"Yeah, well," Catherine countered, setting aside the neat stack of bills with a sigh, "if I could find another coach willing to work for stale peanuts and flat beer, they could go forward together, too."

Lakisha drew back slightly, puckered her lips and wiggled her nose back and forth. In the month since Catherine had inherited her brother's hockey franchise, she'd seen Lakisha's "rabbit look" often enough to know that there was something to be said. "What?" she asked, her pulse racing. "You know a decent coach who can be had cheap?"

"I didn't want to mention it right off," Lakisha began, looking like she really wasn't all that excited about mentioning it now. "Your plate being as full as it is and all. You've barely had time to get your feet under you."

"But?" Catherine pressed.

"Your brother was working on a plan."

Of course he was. Tom had always been working on The Next Big Thing. All the intricate details of his various plots to take over the economic world had been scribbled on napkins from one end of his office to the other. Putting them together to actually understand the grand plan was proving to be a bit difficult, though. "I must have missed that particular note," Catherine quipped, eyeing the pile on the credenza. "Do you happen to know which restaurant he had the brainstorm in?"

Lakisha selected a braid and rolled the beads between her fingers. "He said the time wasn't right."

"What, he was going to wait until the players filed pay grievances and the power company shut off the lights?"

"No." The secretary abandoned her hair to consider the palm tree motifs on her impossibly long acrylic nails, then shrugged and turned away, saying, "I guess I could get you the file."

"That would be nice," Catherine muttered. She leaned back into the massive leather chair and closed her eyes. "It would have been even nicer a month ago."

Tom might have owned the team, but the plain truth was that Lakisha Leonard was the one who made the machinery run. And turning the controls over to Tom's baby sister wasn't something she'd been willing to do without certified proof of competency.

It had been a grueling thirty days. But somewhere between hauling her life across two states, the endless meetings with the league's governing board and getting the new season started, she'd somehow managed to assure Lakisha that Tom had indeed been of sound mind when he'd drawn up his last will and testament.

Of course Lakisha was the only one who believed it. Cat sure didn't. The vote of the governing board was still out. The players, while terribly respectful, were openly uncomfortable. Carl Spady always called her "Little Lady" in a tone that implied that she really ought to be home baking a cake and doing the laundry. John Ingram had called her "Sweetie Pie." Well, until she'd fired him for nonperformance and then Sweetie Pie had morphed into a power-hungry bitch.

And she could understand how he'd come to feel that way. He'd been the Warriors' GM for the last ten years. But, as far as she could tell, he'd stopped putting any effort into it somewhere around the sixth. Tom had never called him on it. She had. Not because she could—as John had claimed—but because she simply hadn't had any other option.

It was done, though. She'd put a man out of work. There was no going back, no point in wishing things were different. The franchise was on the financial rocks and what had to be done to save it had to be done. There was no one else to do it. It was the responsibility of ownership. She owed it to the players. To the fans. It was business. And while every bit of it was absolutely true, none of it made her feel any less guilty. Nice people didn't make other people unhappy.

The dull click of beads announced Lakisha's return and Cat opened her eyes just as a fat, brown expansion folder landed on top of the past due bills.

"There you go," Lakisha announced, already on her way out again. "You read while I go make sure John doesn't steal my only decent stapler. Replacing it could bankrupt us."

That wasn't all that much of an overstatement. Catherine sat forward and turned the folder around. Across the flap, written in Tom's characteristic block lettering, was a name: Logan Dupree.

She slipped the band and pulled the contents out—a stack of papers, pieces large and small, of yellowed newsprint and glossy magazine and photo stock. The top one was a clipping from a long ago sports page. Lord, what a smile the kid had. Wide and bright and full of life. Eighteen-year-old Logan Dupree, the caption said, had been signed to play center for the Wichita Warriors, the minor league affiliate for the Edmonton Oilers. Tom had written at the bottom of the article: Des Moines. July, 1984.

Catherine mentally ran the math. Over twenty years ago. The kid wasn't a kid anymore. He was almost into his forties. And two years younger than she was.

She flipped the clipping over, moving on to an eight-by-ten color publicity photo of Logan Dupree in a Wichita Warriors' jersey. Sweater, she corrected herself with a quick wince. They called them sweaters. Pants were breezers. She had to remember those sorts of things. Like that the *C* on his left shoulder meant that he'd been the captain of the team. A manly man among men.

She skimmed Tom's recruitment notes. At eighteen, Logan Dupree had been six foot two and weighed an even two hundred pounds. He shot left and had a slap shot clocked at eighty-seven miles an hour. Catherine grinned. Tom had failed to note that Logan Dupree had thick, dark hair, a chiseled jaw, cheekbones to kill for and the kind of deep brown, soulful eyes that could melt panties at fifty paces.

She worked her way down through the stack of newspaper clippings, photos and magazine articles, through Logan Dupree's life. She read about his being called up to the majors, about his success there, the trades, the big money contracts, the houses, the cars, the beautiful women.

And she watched him, from picture to picture, change over those years. His shoulders broadened and his chest thickened. The angles of his face became even more defined, more ruggedly handsome. He developed a sense of presence, too; an in-your-face sort of confidence that made his good looks even more dashing, more dangerously appealing.

But it was his smile that changed the most. What had been wide and bright became studied and controlled. Genuine and real were replaced by superficial and plastic. The price of success had been his happiness. The sacrifice of himself. It was so sad.

"Get a grip," she grumbled as she flipped through the photo spread from *GQ,* past a picture of Logan Dupree in a tux and seemingly unaware that he had a Hollywood starlet draped around his neck. "You don't even know the man."

She gasped and recoiled, then slapped her hand over the picture, unwilling to see any more of the gory details than she already had. The caption was sufficient. An accidental high stick. A freak injury. The sudden end of his playing career. Of his hopes for Lord Stanley's cup.

And at the bottom of the article, highlighted in yellow, was a quote. "I'm not interested in coaching. If I can't play, I'm done." And beside it, in the margin, was a simple note in Tom's handwriting: *Ha!*

Chapter One

Logan Dupree didn't need more than one eye to tell him that the woman in the navy blue suit was a problem looking for a place to happen. He took a sip of his scotch and racked his brain, trying to put her into a place, into a group of people. And couldn't. Which didn't necessarily mean much. Long stretches of his memory were nothing more than a chemical-induced blur.

The boat beneath him rocked on the wake of a vessel slowly leaving the yacht club marina. The motion brought him back to the moment and the curly-haired blonde standing on the floating dock. She was shading her eyes from the Florida sun with one hand and studying the stern of his ship. In her other hand she clutched a battered leather bag.

He skimmed her from head to toes. Navy skirt, navy blazer, navy pumps with barely a heel. Run-of-the-mill stockings. A simple white blouse with the first two buttons left open. On a woman who had decent cleavage it would have been sexy. On her… She wasn't a supermodel; that was for sure. Or a model, period. She was too short, too plain. Not his type at all. She looked more like a—

He dragged a slow, deep breath into his lungs and considered her again with narrowed eyes. A reporter? No, reporters almost always had a photographer in tow. A lawyer? Yeah, that was the more likely possibility. She was wearing the uniform. Logan thought back, ticking through the calendar and the parade of women who'd knotted his sheets over the last year. There weren't that many of them; his stock had plummeted the day they'd announced that he'd never again meet the NHL's vision requirements.

But in the years before that there had been a hell of a lot of women. Most of them without names that he could recall on the spur of the moment. Which was about as clearly as he could recall the particulars of their encounters. Safe sex was automatic, though. Even when three sheets to the wind. If this woman was here to threaten him with a paternity suit…

Good luck, lady, he silently challenged as he watched her move farther out on the floating dock. She was halfway between the stern and the gangplank when she managed to get her heel caught in the space between the dock boards. He winced as it brought her up short, smiled as she frowned down at it and then wrenched it free with a little growl. She shoved her foot back into her shoe and immediately started forward again. And without looking around to see if anyone had seen the graceless moment. He took another sip of his drink and decided that he had to give her points for that.

"Good morning," she said brightly as she came to a halt at the base of the gangplank. "I'm looking for a Mr. Logan Dupree. Would that happen to be you?"

She had to know damn good and well who he was. She wouldn't have found him if someone in corporate hadn't pointed her this way. But that realization paled beside another that swept over him in the next second. She had the bluest eyes. Bright blue. With the hair and the "kiss me" mouth… God, put her in a frilly little costume and she'd look like one of those dolls off the Home Shopping Network. "Maybe," he answered. "It depends on who you are and what you want."

She smiled. "May I come aboard?"

He wanted to say no. He really did. Instead, he shrugged, dredged up a smile he hoped passed for polite, set his drink on the table beside him, and levered himself up out of the deck chair. She didn't wait for him to step over to the railing and offer her a hand up the ramp, though. No, she vaulted up the narrow walkway all on her own and without catching her heel and toppling over into the water.

Logan released the breath he'd been holding as she gestured to the other chair on the deck and asked brightly, "May I have a seat?"

He nodded and watched as she lowered herself into it with an easy, confident smile, smoothing the skirt over the curves of her hip and backside as she did. They were really nice curves, he had to admit as she put the bag down between them.

She waited until he'd taken his own seat again before sticking out her hand and saying, "Allow me to introduce myself. My name is Catherine Talbott."

The name meant absolutely nothing to him, but he politely shook her hand and replied, "Ma'am," while bracing himself to remember a string of names followed by *Attorneys at Law.*

"Tom Wolford was my brother."

The fact that he'd guessed her wrong was hammered into oblivion as the past slammed forward, crisp and clear. Tom Wolford, standing in the shadows and exhaust clouds of the Wichita bus station, a vending machine ham sandwich in one hand, a can of pop in the other. The big man lumbering forward to throw a welcoming arm around the shoulders of an already homesick kid and lead him off into the world of minor league hockey. The pair of plaid polyester pants, white belt, white shoes, the hat with the crimped crown and the narrow brim… The half cigar that was never lit but always clamped in the corner of his mouth….

Tom Wolford. Daddy Warbucks. The old days and the first foot in the door. It had been a long time since Logan had looked that far back. Now that looking forward wasn't an option, maybe he could afford the luxury of reminiscing every now and then. It had been, what—almost five years since they'd last spoken? He should call Tom and— Logan blinked and frowned. "Did you say *was*?"

She nodded ever so slightly and her smile looked tired. "He passed away a little over a month ago. A heart attack."

"Unless he'd changed a lot in the last fourteen years," Logan said as his throat tickled, "it couldn't have been an unexpected one."

Catherine Talbott's smile faded on a sigh and shrug of her slim shoulders. "No, it really wasn't. Still…"

Logan silently swore and kicked himself. "I'm sorry," he offered sincerely. "I can be a real clod sometimes. Tom was a decent man. I owe him a lot and I'm sorry he's gone."

Tucking her hair behind her ears, Catherine Talbott managed a slightly brighter smile. "I was hoping you'd feel that way."

Duh! his brain groaned. The memorial plaque. The endowment of some fund for underprivileged kids' sports. He'd been tapped for such things before. It came with making the pro ranks. He knew the drill from beginning to end. "Oh, yeah?" he drawled, wondering how much she had in mind. "Why?"

"Tom left me the team."

As responses went, it didn't even come close to his expectations. "You own the Wichita Warriors?" he asked, having a hard time getting his brain wrapped around the image of Shirley Temple sitting behind Tom's huge metal desk.

"Yes, I do."

The assurance didn't help one bit. "What does Millie think of that?"

"Well… She's…"

The obvious hesitation sent a cold jolt through his veins. "Millie's not dead, too, is she?"

"No, no," she hurriedly answered. "My sister-in-law is very much alive." She hesitated and took a noticeably deep breath before she added, "But she has dementia. There are good days and there are not so good days."

"I'm sorry to hear that," he offered again, thinking that he was beginning to sound a little too much like a parrot. A socially retarded parrot. He used to be a lot better at this sort of thing.

"It's one of the risks of growing old," she went on. "You don't have much choice except to deal with what life gives you. Tom provided well for her, though. Millie doesn't want for anything now, and there's money to see her through even a long decline. She's not going to be pushing a grocery cart around town and eating out of Dumpsters."

Millie eat out of Dumpsters? Never. Not even demented. Where Tom had been the loud impresario, Millie had been the perfect princess. "That's good to know. I can't tell you how many Thanksgiving, Christmas and Easter dinners I had at Millie's house. She always made sure that we weren't alone those days."

"She still does the bring-all-your-friends spreads. With a little help now, of course. We did a backyard brat and potato salad affair when all the players came in for the new season."

God, it was so small-town, so Wichita. So incredibly minor league. "I'll bet everyone had a real good time."

She nodded and then her smile faded on another sigh. "Until Tom collapsed."

Oh shit. He should have seen it coming. The nod followed

by the sigh was the tip-off. He couldn't offer apologies again. He just couldn't. He'd choke to death if he even tried. "So," he ventured, then cleared his throat as subtly as he could. "How are the Warriors doing these days?"

"Well," she drawled, "that depends on your perspective, I suppose."

Uh-oh. Evasion was never a good sign. She was working up to something. The something that had brought her halfway across the country. And odds were it wasn't to hit him up for a memorial contribution. "You're a month into the season. What's the win-loss record?"

"Two wins, ten losses," she supplied with a little grimace.

Bad. Really bad. "Why are they losing?"

"I wish I could tell you, Mr. Dupree, but I don't know anything about hockey."

Gee, there was a surprise. "What are your GM and coaching staff saying?" he pressed.

She seemed to chew the inside of her cheek as she stared off over the water. "That it's not their fault," she finally answered. "That Tom didn't spend enough to get the talent necessary to win."

Yeah, it was usually someone else's fault. And dead guys made perfect scapegoats. "Is it true?"

"Looking at the books," she replied, still staring off, "I'd have to say that he spent all that he could. And then some."

And then some? There it was. The Warriors were in financial trouble and as the club's poster boy for Big Dreams, he was the logical choice for White Knight, too. "Let's cut to the chase, Ms. Talbott," he said firmly. "Why are you here? What do you want from me? A bailout?"

Her gaze came back to his with a snap and a blink. "Well, yes. In a—"

"How much to take the ink from red to black?" he demanded, not caring that he sounded irritated. He was irritated.

"I don't want your money, Mr. Dupree," she challenged as she squared her shoulders and her blue eyes flashed icy fire. "I want your talent. And I'm willing to pay you for it."

She couldn't afford to pay him so much as a nickel on his NHL dollars. "My talent at what?"

"I've had two offers for the franchise. Both of them reasonable and fair considering the shape it's in."

How had they gone from him bailing out the team to her selling it? Talk about conversational whiplash. "You should signal left turns before you make them," he growled.

Another sigh. "I know. I'm bad about that." Another little heave of her shoulders. Another pointless effort to tuck her curls behind her ears. "Here's my thinking on it all," she said, holding her hands in front of her like a balance scale. "I could sell tomorrow and walk away with a lot more than I have now. But if I did, I'd be selling out Tom's hopes and expectations. I have a problem with that on a personal level. I'd feel much better about it if I could improve the franchise before I let it go. Tom couldn't be disappointed then. Does that make sense?"

It did. But in the most dangerous sort of way. If that was the full scope of her reasoning, the woman was playing a high-stakes game listening to her heart, not her head. And that was a guaranteed way to fail. He looked away from the big blue eyes that were so earnestly searching his. "Do you have experience in running any kind of business?"

"I've organized several successful charity events."

He waited for her to toss out the next item on her résumé. All he got were the sounds of the marina. "That's it?"

"I have a master's degree in Sociology," she offered brightly. "And I'm an expert in robbing Peter to pay Paul. No one does it better."

What the hell had Tom been thinking? Millie, even with her marbles rattling loose, could do a better job than this little socialite. Had Tom lost it, too? "Let's go back," Logan said tightly. "What do you want from me?"

"I understand that you're something of a legend in the minor leagues."

Yeah, he was a legend there. In the majors, too. But not for the reason he wanted. In two years the only memory of him was going to be the moment when his eye tumbled out of its socket on national television. "Nail the point, Ms. Talbott. What do you want from me?"

"I want you to coach the Warriors this season."

He gripped the arms of his chair, trying to keep himself from falling out. Step back twenty years? Start all over from nowhere? He'd never in his life wanted to coach. "You're kidding."

"No, I'm not."

She certainly seemed sane. And sober. "Give up kicking back in the Florida sun and surf," he posed dryly, "to spend the winter riding a broken-down bus across the windswept, frozen prairie with a bunch of third-rate hockey players. Would you go for an offer like that?"

"Actually," she said, with a fleeting, weak smile, "if you don't, I'm going to have to."

"Come again?" he asked, stunned and even more appalled. "You know nothing about hockey but you think you can coach?"

"The sea of red ink is deep. Really deep," she explained, her eyes darkening. "I've already let John Ingram—the GM—go and taken over his responsibilities. The office staff has been pared down to one. Looking at the team's record so far, I figure no one can do worse than Carl Spady when it comes to coaching. I'll promote the current assistant coach and play his second for no pay. And when we get back into black, I'll leave the bench and hire the best I can to replace me."

His head pounded. "You're nuts."

"Maybe," she allowed. "Mostly, I'm determined."

"The men won't play for a woman."

"They're not men. They're boys," she calmly countered. "The average age is twenty-three. And their choice is to play for the Warriors or go home. I may not know much, but I do know that we're the bottom rung of the professional hockey ladder."

With her at the helm and on the bench…? The publicity would be incredible. The minors' first female coach of a men's team. The tickets to the freak show would go like hot-cakes. She'd make money out of it. Hand over fist. But the players… God, being relegated to an unaffiliated team in the Central Hockey League was humiliation enough for them. Adding professional pity to it… Thank God it wasn't his problem. His smile was grim and tight and he both knew it and didn't care. "You have a lot to learn, Ms. Talbott. You might want to start with a copy of *Hockey for Dummies*."

"I've read it from cover to cover. Twice," she assured him. "And I bought myself some books on practice drills, too. They don't make all that much sense at this point, but they will eventually."

He'd bet the boat that she'd never even laced up a pair of skates. The poor bastards. All the Warriors wanted was to make a living playing a game they loved. It wasn't much of a living and as dreams went it was a long shot at best, but… Jesus F. Christ. Did they have any idea of what was coming down the ice at them?

"Carl Spady pulls down a hefty five-figure salary," she said, interrupting his nightmare. "I'd rather pay it to you."

And he'd rather give up his good eye. "I'm making a solid seven-figure one sitting right here in this deck chair."

"So I've heard."

She'd said it softly, but there was an edge to her tone that made it ring like an insult. He held his breath and tamped down the instinct to charge squarely into the challenge. It took a of couple seconds and a conscious effort to unclench his teeth, but he eventually managed a fairly even, "Oh?"

She didn't reply. Instead, she leaned down and flipped open the leather bag at her feet. "Here's my card," she said in the next second, straightening to hand him a fuzzy-edged card. "Please consider the offer and let me know what you decide."

He looked down at the business card. Pink. With some fancy, feminine font. Pink! "There's no thinking to be done, Ms. Talbott," he declared as he tossed the card on the table beside his drink. "The answer's 'no thank you.' I'm not even remotely interested."

"Well, if you're sure…" she said while she rose to her feet.

Logan gained his own, reached down, snagged the handle of her briefcase, and held it out to her saying, "I am."

She had to tilt her head way back to meet his gaze. For a long second she seemed to be considering him, chewing on the inside of her cheek as her eyes darkened. Then the boat shifted slightly beneath them and she rocked back, unbalanced. Even as he reached out to steady her, she righted herself with a tight smile and turned away.

His arms fell back to his sides as she put the briefcase on the seat of the chair and opened it again. From it she drew a thick, brown expansion folder. Handing it to him with both hands, she explained, "Tom built this file over the years. Since there's no reason for me to keep it, I think he'd probably want you to have it."

He looked down to see his name scrawled across the front flap in black magic marker. The thing was stuffed to the gills and weighed a ton.

"Mr. Dupree?" She waited until he looked up. "If you change your mind…"

"Not going to happen," he assured her blandly, plunking the file down on the table.

"Just the same," she went on as she closed her case and took it in hand. "I'm on my way to the airport. My son has a 'Hockey in Focus' class tonight and I promised to have locker room treats for everyone afterwards." She moved toward the walkway, adding as she went, "You can reach me on my cell after six. I'll either be at home, making brownies, or at the rink, handing them out."

Brownies. Probably with little pink sprinkles on top. Did she make them for the Warriors, too? Did she send them out on the road with little care packages tied up with pink ribbons? She probably put notes inside reminding them to eat sensibly and to remember to brush their teeth.

"May I ask you a personal question, Mr. Dupree?"

He brought his attention back to the marina. She stood on the floating dock, shading her eyes with her hand again. He shrugged his permission and refrained from mentioning that he considered an answer optional.

"My son is twelve. The first time he ever set foot in an ice rink was the day after Tom's funeral. The hockey bug seems to have bitten him just as he stepped inside the door. As a man who played the game, can you give me some idea of what the odds are that it might be nothing more than a passing interest?"

Twelve? If he was remembering right, that made the boy a Pee Wee. The second year kids were allowed to check. Having to learn to skate while getting hammered into the boards meant that the kid was either a masochist or had found a passion. Given that his mother was an obvious loony tune… He decided to give the kid a break and yank Mama's chain. "I hope Tom left you some stock in CCM."

She arched a brow. "CCM?"

God, she really was beyond clueless. "It's a company that

makes hockey gear," he supplied. "Along with others like Easton, Bauer, and Itech. Just to name a few. Didn't you notice the names when you bought him his equipment?"

"I didn't buy it. The Warriors outfitted him with their old stuff and hauled him out onto the ice. I was too busy worrying about broken bones to pay any attention to the labels."

What a typical mom. Logan chuckled and shook his head. "Hockey players will do anything to bring another guy into the fold. Does the kid nag you about getting to the rink on time?"

The look on her face was answer enough. His own mother had often worn the very same exasperated expression. "He starts in two hours before we have to leave the house."

"It sounds to me like he's been pretty well bitten. Brace yourself," he warned, grinning. "It's a long, hard, expensive haul."

"Thanks," she muttered, rolling her eyes as she turned away.

The question came out of the blue and tumbled off his tongue before he could even think to stop it. "Why did Tom leave you the team?"

She paused and looked over her shoulder to meet his gaze. "I normally charge ten bucks for the story," she said, her eyes twinkling. "But if you'll take the job, I'll tell you for free."

Damn, she was cute. In a pink, fuzzy, kid sister sort of way. The cameras would love her behind the bench. Is that what Tom had been thinking? "I can live with the mystery," he countered, knowing that he wasn't being completely honest about it.

With a quiet laugh, she walked off, waving and calling back, "Have a good one, Mr. Dupree. Talk to you soon."

Hopefully she had enough good sense to stop holding her breath before she passed out and went face-first into a bowl of brownie mix. Shaking his head, Logan watched her make her way along the floating dock and up the steps to the parking lot. As she climbed into the driver's seat of a bright red Taurus, he smiled and turned back to the chair and his now watery scotch. She had a nice swing. Not that he wanted it in his backyard, of course. And she did have killer legs—especially considering how short they were.

Logan polished off his drink in one quick swallow. Rolling the empty glass between the palms of his hands, he eyed the expansion folder she'd handed him. There was no reason to open it up and go through it; he knew what was inside. Tom had kept a file on every one of his players. On "his boys."

With a bittersweet smile, Logan wandered his memories. The Warriors had been Tom's family, their accomplishments his greatest source of pride. Every morning ten copies of the *Wichita Eagle* had been delivered to the front office and Tom would cull the sports page, carefully cutting out the articles. One copy was always stapled to the bulletin board by the ticket counter. Another copy went into the individual files. Another was always mailed to the player's parents with a note from Tom about how pleased he was for the opportunity to know such an outstanding young man, such an outstanding human being.

Being a good person had been important to Tom. Being a good hockey player hadn't mattered nearly as much to him. He'd insisted that every man on the squad pick a social cause or a community organization and give it at least ten hours a week of volunteer time. It had been part of the playing contract and Tom had made the rounds, checking to make sure the players were where they said they'd be and when. No one had ever gotten away with shirking their charitable commitments. For Tom, giving back had been important.

And when the local paper mentioned the good works, Tom had posted, filed and sent those clippings home, too. Logan's mother had saved them all. He and his sisters had found them in a box in the bedroom closet after her funeral. Along with them had been cards from her bridge club ladies congratulating her on having raised such a good, caring, talented man.

Logan swallowed down the lump in his throat and rose from the chair. He needed another drink, he told himself as he headed for the liquor cabinet below deck. He didn't need to feel guilty or the least bit obligated about a damn thing.

Chapter Two

There was the good, the bad and the ugly. And then there was the Wichita Warriors. They had exclusive claim to the deepest pit of god-awful that Logan had ever seen. He gazed out over the sparse crowd, mentally calculating the gross. Unless the concession contract was a good one, Catherine Talbott was going to be paying expenses out of her own pocket this week. What did it cost her per game to rent the Kansas Coliseum these days? Public venues seating nine thousand didn't come cheap. It had cost a fortune when he'd played here and odds were the rent hadn't gone down in the past twenty years.

Arena rent, office rent and overhead, hockey equipment, insurance, travel expenses... Add in the player salaries. Minor leaguers—especially those in the west—didn't make huge amounts of money, but considering the Warriors' performance in tonight's game, hell, if they were pulling down five bucks an hour they were being overpaid.

The ref brought the puck to the face-off circle in the Warriors' own end and Logan watched the players slide into position. Wheatley, the center and a left-hand shooter, stood at the dot with his back to the goal. Vanderrossen and Stover fell in on either side of him and opposite the Austin Ice Bats' wingers. Andrews and Roth, the Warriors' defensemen, slipped in behind their teammates, checking over their shoulders to make sure they weren't blocking their goalie's view. Rivera nodded and set himself at the outside edge of his crease.

The ref did his quick visual check with the linesmen, and Logan drew a breath and held it. The puck dropped. It was still in midair when Vanderrossen flung his stick and gloves to the ice and himself at the opposing winger. Stover did the same on the other side. The whistle came in the next second—but about a half second after the puck ricocheted off Andrews's shin guard and wobbled through Rivera's wide open five hole.

The Ice Bats bench didn't put up much of a celebration for the goal. Apparently the previous ten had pretty much used up all their enthusiasm. The players on the ice were too busy trying to de-sweater and break each other's noses to notice the score. The fans obviously didn't care that the tally had just gone to eleven-zip; they'd come for the fights. And to jeer the refs, Logan decided a few seconds later as the officials sent all four of the brawlers to the locker room with ten-minute game misconducts.

Logan glanced at the clock suspended from the arena ceiling. Three minutes, eighteen seconds left in the third period. An eternity by hockey standards. The way things were going, the Ice Bats could easily double the score before the final buzzer. There was no hope for the Warriors in that amount of time, though, and everyone knew it. What there was of a crowd was running toward the exits while the players set

themselves up for the face-off at center ice and the Ice Bats'
goalie did push-ups in his crease.

With a hard sigh, Logan scrubbed his hands over his face
and closed his eyes. He'd been insane to even come look, to
so much as entertain the notion that coaching the Warriors
might be a more productive use of his life than drinking the
days away on his boat and feeling sorry for himself. So much
for nice thoughts. Basking in the sun and polluting his liver
was a slow road to hell. Coaching the Warriors would be like
getting there on the bullet train.

Logan checked his watch. Ten o'clock. They'd already
rolled up the ramps and shut down the airport for the night,
so he was stuck until the first morning flight to civilization
at six. How to kill eight hours in the middle of a Wichita night
had always been a problem and from what he'd been able to
tell on his trip from the airport to the Coliseum, no one had
come close to solving it in the fourteen years he'd been gone.

The options tonight were the same as they'd been from
October through April for almost all of his adult life: go back
to the hotel, drink in the bar until they closed it down, leave
a wake-up call request, crash a couple of hours and then
stumble to the terminal gate with a raging headache so he
could do it all over again the next night in another town. The
beauty of his boat was not having to do all the stumbling between point A and point B.

Snagging the overpriced, too glossy program from the cement floor, Logan rolled it into a tube, shoved himself up out
of the hard plastic seat and headed toward the exit just as the
final buzzer sounded. He paused and turned back to check
the scoreboard—12–0. He was thinking that the Ice Bats had
shown the Warriors some mercy when his gaze slipped past
the scoreboard to the sky boxes along the east wall.

Only two were lit. One was the press box with a pair of
announcers undoubtedly trying to wrap up a dismal show.

The other contained a single, slim figure with blond curly hair. Catherine Talbott stood alone in the owner's box, her arms folded across her chest and her head bowed as though she were praying for a miracle. She needed one, he knew. Just as he knew that he wasn't going to be it.

Logan shook his head and was turning away when his conscience squirmed. With a wince, he stopped again. He'd already given her offer way more time, money and consideration than it deserved. And he'd told her yesterday before she'd walked off his boat that he wouldn't take the job, that he didn't want or need it. There was no reason for her to hear it again. It would be cruel to go up to that sky box. It'd be like rubbing salt in an open wound; she had to feel bad enough already.

Cool reasoning didn't settle his conscience. It prickled and then clenched tight like some long neglected, suddenly over-exercised muscle. With a growl, Logan eyed the sky box again, wondering just what the hell he could say to her that might be anywhere near encouraging or optimistic. *Hey, at least you didn't have to call an ambulance. Cheer up, they won two of the fifteen fights. Lady, if someone wants to buy this loser franchise, sell it!*

Logan blinked, and in that same second the lights in the owner's booth winked out. The scoreboard went dark in the next. He considered the now silent arena and the scarred, shaved ice below. Wichita had never been a great hockey town; it was too far south, too far north and nowhere near cosmopolitan enough to bring in transplants from the parts of the country where hockey was a way of life. It didn't matter how bad or how good the Warriors were; it had never made a difference and never would.

Tom Wolford had spent his life swimming against the tide. And from the looks of things, he'd been pretty well swept out to sea for his effort. If Catherine Talbott didn't know that the odds were stacked against her, then someone needed to be bluntly honest about it. It didn't have to be him. It wasn't like there was some big ledger book that said he owed her anything.

Aw, hell. Who was he kidding? Getting the hard stuff done had always been his job.

Cat leaned back against the grille of her ancient Jeep and crossed her ankles. The team's just as ancient bus idled on the far side of the private parking lot, its running lights glowing bright orange in the crisp autumn night, the storage doors open, the driver standing beside them, smoking a cigarette and waiting for the team to file out and board. A good fifty feet separated the bus from the rear doors of the Coliseum. Cat considered the space, wondering what she should say to the players as they passed. *Good game!* probably wasn't going to cut it. Even she knew that tonight's game had been beyond pathetic. Telling them they'd win next time wasn't something she thought she could choke out. At least not sincerely. Chewing Carl Spady up one side and down the other might cheer them up for a while. Or not. Most of the players had been on the team long enough to know that their coach would react by making their next practice a revenge-fest.

Of course she could just jump in her car and drive off before she had to face them. Cowardly, yes, but it would spare them all the awkwardness of trying to be upbeat. But it would also leave the players with nothing to counter Carl's infamously nasty potshots. Why Tom hadn't dumped him years ago was a mystery she hadn't been able to solve. There had been nothing in the scribbled-on napkins to give her so much as a clue.

She was wondering about the therapeutic value of a good cry when the rear door of the arena squeaked on its hinges.

Putting self-indulgence on hold, she stared down at the gravel just long enough to summon a smile and then lifted her head to give it to the man coming through the doorway.

The smile evaporated the instant the shape of the dark silhouette registered in her brain. The player had changed into his street clothes; they all did before boarding the bus. Always. And they always had their gear bags over their shoulder and their sticks in their hand as they went that way. Except this time, this player. He'd left his gear behind. God, was he quitting the team? Were they all packing it up and leaving it behind?

"You can't!" she cried, vaulting off the front of her car to stand in the path of the player made featureless by the dark. "As long as you play, there's hope. If you quit, it's gone."

"Empty hope doesn't count for much."

She knew the voice. Her heart actually fluttered, just before it shot up into her throat and cut off her air supply. "Logan Dupree?" she croaked out, her oxygen-deprived brain suggesting that she throw herself into his arms and kiss him senseless.

"I'm surprised I'm here, too," he drawled with a lopsided smile as he stopped in front of her.

God, even in the dark he was so damn good-looking. And so tall. So broad shouldered. Throwing herself into his arms would require a running leap. The automatic half step back sparked some common sense. Swallowing around her stupid heart, Cat leaned back against the grille of her car and asked as nonchalantly as she could, "Do you want the free story now or later?"

"Never will be fine," he replied, settling in beside her and crossing his arms over his chest. "There isn't enough money in the world to get me to sign on to this disaster you call a team."

Her heart dropped like a lead weight into the pit of her stomach. He wasn't here to be her knight in shining armor.

"Please lower your voice," she said, desperately trying to anchor herself and hoping she didn't sound as dizzy and queasy as she felt. Thank God she hadn't done the grateful damsel routine. "The players will be coming out and they don't need to hear themselves being run down."

"They're not stupid," he pointed out quietly. "They know they suck."

The choice was between crying, throwing up, or going on the defensive. "Well, they don't need to hear anyone else say it," she countered, lifting her chin. "That would be mean. And I happen to believe—contrary to what Carl thinks—that you don't get people to improve by focusing on the negatives."

"If you don't look at the negatives, there's no way you'll ever turn them into positives."

"But where's the motivation to improve if there's never a word of praise for the things you do right and well?"

"Okay, I'll give you that one." The shrug that went with the concession said that he considered it a very minor one.

God, she didn't want to ask, but she had to. Just had to. "Do they do anything right or well?"

"Well," he said slowly enough that she knew he was searching, "they can all skate."

"Big deal," she grumbled.

"Actually, it is. No hockey player is ever any better at the game than he is at skating. The two go hand in hand. Your boys could stand some fine tuning, but they're not send-'em-packing bad."

Yes, they were her boys. And they had heart. They went out and took the beatings night after night. If they were willing to step up and keep trying, then she couldn't do any less. Her stomach settling and her brain coming back to earth, she stared at the idling bus and asked, "So if they can skate, why don't they win?"

"Consultants make big money, you know."

His voice was light, his words edged with amusement. He wasn't going to hold out on her. Cat smiled. "And the owners of struggling minor league teams don't have big money. Could we work out a trade of some sort?"

"What are you offering?"

Her body if it were twenty years younger. "Dinner and drinks?" She sweetened the offer by adding, "At the best sports bar in town."

He turned his head and grinned at her. "Toss in the ten dollar story and you've got a deal."

"Deal," she said, resisting the urge to stick out her hand by shoving both of them in the hip pockets of her jeans. "So tell me why they don't win."

"They don't play as a team."

She waited, watching him out the corner of her eye. He seemed fascinated by the lighting on the water tower over at the Greyhound Park. "And?"

"That's the biggie."

"For dinner, drinks and the story, I want the smallies, too."

He frowned. "Are you still thinking about stepping behind the bench and coaching?"

And he'd complained about her not signaling unexpected turns? "Let's just say that the possibility is looming large," she replied. "You've seen what Carl Spady's got going. Do you think I could do any worse?"

"Probably not," he allowed as a smile slowly tipped up the corners of his mouth. Still studying the water tower, he said, "You've got two sets of problems going on out there on the ice. The first is in the technical aspects of the game. Players are often out of position, they don't have a plan for salvaging a busted play, the lines aren't set up to maximize skills and styles, shift changes are rough, and they're running a playbook that was outdated ten years ago. Those are the most glaring problems, by the way, not the only ones."

Lines. She'd read about those. Something about the five guys on the ice together. She'd look it up again and figure out how it went with what he'd told her. "What's the second set of problems?"

"Attitudes," he supplied, a steely edge to his voice. "You have Glory Boys, Grinders and Goons. As long as they see themselves and each other as being only one or the other, they'll never play together as a team."

She was trying to remember if she'd ever heard the terms before and wondering where she could get a decent definition when he added, "Hell, I actually saw Wheatley strip the puck from his own wingers three times tonight. Vanderrossen and Stover would rather take a penalty than a pass. And your third line didn't take a single shot on goal the entire game. All they did was D—badly—to give the first and second lines a rest. Which, quite frankly, they hadn't earned."

She blinked, stunned at how thrilling she found his passion for the game. Found *him.* "D?" she asked lamely, hoping the response would take long enough for her to gather up a few of her scattered wits.

"Defense," he replied, grinning. "Keeping the puck out of your own net."

Oh, yeah. She knew that. "Can the problems—both sets of them—be fixed?"

His smile disappeared. "It would be a long, hard haul."

That was the second time in two days she'd heard the expression. "Seems to be a standard description of the game," she observed.

"Accurate, too."

He cleared his throat and took a deep breath in the same way she did when she was getting ready to say something necessary but unpleasant. Not wanting to hear it, she deliberately cut him off. "But these boys aren't new to hockey.

They've been playing the game all of their lives. They have the grit to change, don't they?"

He slid her a sideways glance and sighed. "Some do, some probably won't," he answered, going back to his study of the water tower. "They each have to weigh the coach's expectations against their own and figure out if they want to give the coach what he needs. Some will hang up the skates and others will lace them tighter."

"Is there any way to know who's going to do which?" *Please God,* she silently added, *let the hanger-uppers be the expensive ones.*

"The Glory Boys are going to be your toughest sell. They have the biggest egos, and they tend to view themselves as God's gift to hockey."

Ah, a definition. She knew which ones he was talking about. She called them The Swaggerers. Glory Boys was more descriptive. And much easier to say. "It's occurred to me," she admitted, "that anyone playing hockey in Wichita, Kansas, isn't God's gift to anyone or anything."

"You might want to remind them of that," he said coolly as he looked into the distance. "Especially when they threaten to take their razzle-dazzle to a more appreciative team. If they do, offer to help them pack their bags. You'll be better off without them. Nothing poisons a locker room faster than an out-of-control ego."

If he saw her nod of agreement, it didn't give him pause. "Your Grinders will be the next hardest. They don't have any self-confidence. They've got to take some shots thinking they can actually score the goals. And the Goons are going to have to be put on leashes. You played an entire twelve minutes at full strength tonight. Your penalty killing unit was exhausted before the end of the first period and your power play unit never went out."

More stuff to look up. More things to think about and figure out. But since she had such incredible expertise at her fingertips… Well, figuratively anyway… "Why hasn't Carl fixed these things?"

"Good question," he conceded with a slow nod. "Have you asked him?"

"I've asked him why we don't win. He told me it was because they were no-talent bums who don't want to win. Tom did all the recruiting, in case you're wondering."

"He did back in my day, too." He turned his entire body to face her and unfolded his arms to stuff his hands in the pockets of his khakis. "And in case you're wondering, there's decent talent on the team. It's just not put together in the right combinations and pointed in the right direction. As for wanting to win…. They have to think they can. Believing is nine-tenths of winning." He smiled. "Don't you know about the Miracle on Ice?"

"1980," she supplied. "Lake Placid. The American kids beat the mighty Russians. I was eighteen and cheered my ass off in the family room. And for the record—I'd never watched a hockey game before that. I didn't know squat except that those boys were wonderful. And exciting. And worth cheering for."

"Nothing's ever been as exciting as that game. Nothing ever will be." He hesitated, then shrugged one shoulder. "Well, except for maybe being on the team that wins the Stanley Cup. They say there's nothing like that feeling."

She hadn't been able to look at the pictures in the magazine article Tom had saved, but she had read the story. And done a bit of Net surfing afterwards. The Tampa Bay Lightning had been in the running for Lord Stanley's cup the year Logan Dupree had been injured. The sportswriters had all predicted that losing him would end the Bolt's chances. And they'd been proven right. As a player, Logan Dupree had lost his chance to have his name placed on the Holy Grail of hockey. Talking about the cup with him would be right up there with asking Mrs. Lincoln about the play.

But she'd read an article on the history of Lord Stanley's little trophy and knew that players weren't the only ones whose names went on it; the coaches' did, too. His chances weren't completely over. Odds were that if he could see problems, he could fix them, too. "You'd make a good coach."

"No, I wouldn't."

She winced, realizing how self-serving her comment must have looked to him. "I wasn't talking about the Warriors," she assured him. "And how do you know you wouldn't be any good? Have you ever tried it?"

"Yeah," he retorted dryly. "We went winless the entire season."

"Tom didn't have any clippings of that adventure," she said, suspicious. "When exactly did you do this coaching? Where?"

"Long Island. Ten years ago," he supplied crisply. He smiled and leaned back against the car again. "My girlfriend at the time had a seven-year-old. I was trying to earn points with her."

A kids' team? "Man," she drawled, trying not to laugh, "if you can't coach a bunch of Mites to a win…. I'm afraid that I have to withdraw my job offer. No hard feelings, okay?"

He gave her a smile that could have powered the East Coast for a week. "I'll live. Where are we going for dinner?"

Dinner? Who cared about food when she was being dazzled by perfectly even teeth and crinkly cornered, twinkling eyes? "Hero's in Old Town," she answered, really sorry that she hadn't met him years ago. "It's just a ways up the left side of that street straight across from the Eagle building on Douglas. Just head downtown, you'll see the cars packed in there. You can't miss it."

"How about if I follow you?"

How about if he gave her time to recover from that smile of his? "It's going to be a bit before I head that way. I always wait and talk to the boys as they go to the bus. If they come out to see that I've bolted on them, they're going to feel lower than they already do."

"Then I'll wait with you."

"You don't have to."

"I know, but women out on the roads alone at night isn't a good idea. Not that you couldn't handle anything that might happen, but still…"

Cat nodded and stared at the water tower. When was the last time a man had inconvenienced himself for her? Willingly?

She was back to high school and still searching when he said, "If we've run out of things to talk about, it's going to be a very long dinner."

Cat smiled. Since she couldn't see him being pleased about any nomination for Knight of the Year, she went in another direction. "If you don't mind me asking, why did you come to see the game tonight if you had no intention of taking the job? It's a long way to travel for bad nachos and even worse hockey."

"Old time's sake, I guess. I got to thinking about Tom and remembering the years I spent here. I didn't have anything else going on, so…" He shrugged. "Whoever said you can't go back home was right."

"Did you ever really think of Wichita as your home?"

"Naw. It was just another stopping point along the way to fame and fortune on ice."

"Where is home? Des Moines?" she pressed.

"It used to be." He sounded sad. "But my parents are both gone and my sisters moved away after they got out of college. There's nothing there now to call me back."

"So Tampa's home?"

He shook his head and folded his arms across his chest again. "It's just another of the stopping points. It's no more special than anywhere else."

Rootless in Tampa. Not only was it a lousy movie title, it had to be a miserable way to exist. She was about to point that out when the door of the Coliseum opened and the first of the players followed the shaft of light into the parking lot.

Off the hook, Cat stepped away from the car. "Hi, Matt," she called out, recognizing the shorter than average shape heading her way.

Matt Hyerstrom barely managed a smile and shifted the weight of the bag on his shoulder. "Hey, it's over," Cat said kindly. "You have to shrug it off and go on to the next one."

"Yes, ma'am."

Cat could tell that he didn't believe a word of it. She pivoted as he went past and then called after him, "We're going to modify the lines, you know."

He stopped and turned back. "Really?" he asked. "When?"

"Tomorrow morning at practice sound good to you?"

With a huge grin, he turned back toward the bus, saying, "Sounds perfect, Mizz Talbott."

"We're changing up the lines?"

She looked back to find Jason Dody coming her way. "Yes, Jace, we are," she assured him, hoping that they were indeed talking about the same thing. "I figure it couldn't hurt. Which line do you want to play on?"

"Anyone's except Wheatley's," he answered quietly as he walked past her.

"Well, we'll just see what we can do about that. Give your dream line some thought tonight and we'll see how it works."

He lifted his sticks and called back, "Will do, ma'am."

Two for two. Hey, she was on a roll. She greeted the third player crossing the lot. "Georgie, if that lip of yours gets any lower, you're going to step on it. There's no reason to add injury to insult tonight." He lifted his head and grinned. "Ah, that's much better," Cat said. "You're so good-looking when you smile. Girls can't resist a smile, you know."

"Yeah?" He stopped in front of her and planted the tips of his sticks in the gravel between their feet. "What are you doing later?"

Cat laughed outright. "I'm old enough to be your mother, Georgie. Get on the bus."

His grin even brighter than before, he did as he was told, leaving her to watch the next man heading for the bus. Her smile faded as the team's Goliath came near enough for her to see the contours of his face. "Oh, damn, Ryan," she said softly, taking his arm and stopping him. She angled his face into the orange glow of the bus's running lights. A line of black stitches held together a jagged tear that ran over a huge lump above his right eye. "That has to hurt. What did Doc Mallory say?"

"That he had one helluva time getting the needle through the scar tissue, ma'am."

As always, the gentle voice coming from such a burly body melted her heart. "Maybe we need to think about fighting a lot less and playing a little more, huh?"

He gave her a weary smile. "Coach says I need to get better at the fighting."

"Consider his directive countermanded."

"Huh?" His attempt to cock a brow ended in a wince.

"I own the team, Ryan," she said, "so I get to make the rules. I say less fighting, and I'll make sure Carl understands that's what I expect. When you get home, put some ice on that."

"Yes, ma'am," he promised as she released him and gave him a little pat in the center of the back. She had to reach up to do it.

There wasn't anyone else right behind him. Cat sighed in

relief and stuffed her hands back into her pockets. Four for four. Now all she had to do was make good on her promises.

"You're good."

She smiled at the man leaning against her car, both amazed that she'd forgotten he was there and pleased by his approval. "Thanks. Wait until you see me behind the bench."

"That's a whole different world," he countered. "You're good at parking lot cheerleading. You'd be smart to leave it at that and not push your luck."

Yeah, well, she'd spent way too many years of her life not pushing and, with one notable exception, she had nothing to show for it but regrets. "Hold on to that thought, I'll be back to it in a few," she said, eyeing the round, decidedly bald silhouette coming through the arena door. She went to meet him halfway, calling out, "Carl! If I could have a minute with you, please."

He paused, barely, turning sideways as though he would walk off at any moment. His smile was the one he always gave her. The I'm-tolerating-you-only-because-you-sign-the-checks smile. The one that set her teeth on edge every time she saw it.

"It'll have to be quick, Mrs. Talbott," he informed her as players moved around them. "The bus is waiting."

"And it'll sit right there until you get aboard," she pointed out. "I'd like for you to change the lines starting with tomorrow morning's practice. Obviously they're not working as they are now."

"It won't make any difference. You can't make a silk purse out of a pig's ear."

Sow's ear, she silently corrected. "I don't care. I want the lines changed, Carl. And while we're making changes, I've never been a fan of either boxing or professional wrestling. I'm tired of our games being more a contest of fists than finesse. The fighting needs to be stopped."

He gave a thumbs-up sign to one of the players walking past while telling her, "Fights are what the fans come to see."

"Yeah, all six of them," she countered dryly. "Maybe if we actually played hockey a few more people might be interested in coming to the games and helping to pay the rent." At his snort, she put her hands on her hips and looked him square in the eye. "And your salary, Carl."

He stopped smiling. He leaned close. "Look, Little Lady. With the exception of Wheatley, this team doesn't have the talent to play the grand and glorious kind of hockey you've been watching on ESPN. Those guys are the pros. These guys are the ones who couldn't make it. They're bottom of the barrel."

Bottom of the barrel? The boys took beatings for this man? Cat had to count to ten before she could unclench her teeth. "Let me ask you something, Carl. If you have such a low opinion of the boys, of their abilities and their chances, why do you bother to coach them?"

"I like seeing the country," he answered, edging away from her with a sneer, "from the window of a stinking, belching, rattling bus."

Cat stepped directly into his path. "I'm serious, Carl. Why do you coach them if you don't believe in them?"

"I dunno," he snarled. "Maybe it's because I don't have any other hobbies that I can make good money at."

"A hobby?" she repeated, furious. Passing players stared, but she was too mad to care. "You consider coaching the Warriors a *hobby?* For these boys, it's life. It's their dream. How dare you blow them off!"

He tried to step around her again. Cat planted herself in his way, said, "You're fired, Carl," and stuck out her hand, palm up. "I'll have the keys to the office and the rink, please. You can clean out your desk in the morning after Lakisha unlocks."

He reached into his pants pocket and yanked out a key ring. "You got it, lady. We can talk about my severance package then, too."

Standing with her hand out, she watched him find and separate two keys from the others. "This isn't exactly a spur-of-the-moment decision and I've read your contract, Carl. There's no severance provision. You'll draw this month's salary and that's it."

He slapped the loose keys into her hand, asking, "Your boyfriend over there sweet talk his way into my job?"

Logan. Oh, God. She'd forgotten him again. What would he think when he found out she'd fired Carl? That she was trying to manipulate him into taking the job? How was she going to convince him otherwise when she'd gladly give him anything he wanted if he'd sign on? Oh, wasn't that going to be a scene and half. She'd rather set herself on fire.

"In the first place, Carl, he's not my boyfriend," she said as she stuffed the keys in her pocket. "And in the second, he's not interested in coaching."

"You're not going to find anyone who'll be willing to take on this bunch of losers. You know that, don't you?"

Losers? The son of a bitch. She walked away, refusing to give him so much as a backward glance as she called over her shoulder, "And the horse you rode in on, Carl!"

Logan chuckled as she blew past him, "I take it Spady isn't all that enthused about the idea to mix up the lines."

She wasn't in the mood to face the truth squarely or to tap dance around it. Not right now. She needed time to cool down and figure out a plan of some sort. "What Carl Spady thinks doesn't matter," she declared as she yanked open the driver's side door. "I'm starving. Do you need a lift to your car?"

He came off the front end, his amusement replaced by a look of wary assessment. "I'm parked right over there," he said, making a vague motion in the direction of the lot out-side the chained off area.

"Then I'll see you at Hero's," Cat announced, practically throwing herself into the seat and pulling the door closed. She turned the ignition over and snapped on the lights in the next second, all too keenly aware of Logan Dupree's frown as he walked away.

"God," she groaned, as she sagged into the seat and closed her eyes. "I hate frickin' roller coasters. Just hate them."

But there was no climbing off now and she knew it. Tom had belted her in and shoved the lever into Go! She had a cou-ple of minutes before Logan got to his car. With a hard sigh, she opened her eyes and reached for the *Dummies* book in the passenger seat. "Lines," she muttered, flipping through the index. "Definition and composition of."

Chapter Three

All right, he was a fair man; he could admit a mistake when he made one. He'd been wrong about Wichita's nightlife being the same now as twenty years ago. In the old days, downtown after dark had belonged to raggy winos and the homeless with their shopping carts. These days the drunks were younger and much better dressed. And the Safeway-mobiles had been replaced by Beemers and Infinitis. Yes, downtown had definitely gone upscale.

Which meant that Catherine Talbott's very old Jeep stuck out like sore thumb. Logan stood in the public parking lot and considered it. God, what year was that thing? White and boxy, it had to be from the early nineties. It was missing a strip of door trim on the driver's side. There was piece of duct tape holding the driver's mirror in place. And the fact that she was walking around to lock each of the doors by hand told him that the automatic controls didn't work anymore.

The engine apparently ran well, though. She'd flown down the highway, powered through half a dozen ramp curves like a NASCAR driver, and sailed through downtown with green lights all the way. She'd hit the brakes only twice—to slow down just enough to keep it on four wheels as she made the turn in to the parking lot and then to stop the charging beast after she'd whipped it into the tiny spot between a late model Yukon and a Suburban with a temporary tag. Did she drive like a bat out of hell all the time? Or had she been driving off her "Come To Jesus" Talk with Spady?

He'd made a mistake about her, too, he admitted while she locked the back hatch with the key. Well, sorta, anyway. Yeah, she wasn't a model, super or otherwise. He'd gotten that part right. But she wasn't a kid sister, either. Especially when she stuffed her hands into the hip pockets of her jeans. Lord, what her too big shirts had hidden up until that moment. Like the fact that Catherine Talbott had curves. Really nice curves. In all the right places. The kind of curves that made for perfect handholds. And handfuls.

She dropped her keys into her purse, slung the saddlebag-looking thing over her shoulder, and came toward him with an easy smile. Logan smiled back and asked, "Who taught you to drive? One of the Andrettis?"

"The choke sticks," she answered as he fell in beside her and they headed up Mosley Street. "It's either pull off the road and shut it down for ten minutes, or hang on tight."

"Why don't you get it fixed?"

"Because mechanics don't take rubber checks."

Good reason. "You have a brake light out, too. Left side."

"Always," she said with a groan. She looked over—and up—at him to add, "Thanks. I'll put a replacement bulb on the parts list. Maybe Santa will be good to me this year."

She owned a semi-pro team. Why didn't she have a company vehicle? Something that wasn't falling apart. Was the franchise that poor? A coach's five-figure salary would buy a new car. A nice one. Maybe he should take the job but not the paycheck. No, he corrected as they turned off the brick paved street and headed toward the door of the bar. He was going to get on the plane in the morning. With a totally clear conscience. He'd already given Catherine Talbott some free advice. *Excellent* free advice. He'd give her some more over dinner, and all of it combined would be contribution enough. He didn't owe her—or Tom—any more than that.

He took a half step to get out in front of her, to make sure he got his hand on the door pull before she did. She looked up at him, obviously shocked by the courtesy. For about a half second. Then she grinned her thanks as she slipped past him. Nobody's eyes could be that naturally blue, he thought as he let the door close behind him. She had to be wearing colored contacts. And God Almighty, whatever perfume she was wearing smelled good. Eat-me-up-with-a-spoon good.

"Two," she said to the hostess at the podium and over the low roar of a packed house.

Logan half watched the hostess make her notes and then snag a couple menus. As long as he was in a mood to admit mistakes… Catherine wasn't quite as short as he'd thought, either. He was used to moving around in a world of giants; hockey players under six feet were few and far between and the women who crossed his path came close to that mark more often than not. But compared to the hostess who led them to a table, Catherine wasn't any midget. Maybe five-five, five-six, he guessed as he held the chair for her and she smiled her thanks up at him again.

The smile, though…he'd been right on about her smile. Logan sat down across the table from her and hid behind his menu, determined not to let himself get dazzled again by wide and bright and completely genuine. So she didn't seem to have one coy little bone in her curvy body; it wasn't as if he was going to stick around long enough to enjoy the novelty.

"Iced tea, please."

Logan looked up from the menu to his blind side. Yep, a waitress stood there, pad and pencil in hand. "Molson," he said when the server met his gaze. She shook her head and he made a second guess. "Labatt's?" She nodded and walked off, writing it down. He glanced after her. The wiggle in her walk wasn't nearly as sexy as the one he'd followed to the table. Inviting, yes. But with a deliberate effort that didn't make for appealing.

He considered his menu. "What do you recommend?"

"Everything. It's all good."

Big help. "What are you having?"

"My usual, the Cobb salad. Caesar. Hold the croutons and tomatoes." She folded her menu closed and laid it aside as she smiled at him and added, "I avoid unnecessary carbs whenever possible."

She was one of those Protein People? Why? He stared blankly at the plastic covered folder in his hands. It couldn't be to lose weight. She wouldn't blow away in a stiff wind, but there was something to be said for having some meat on the bones. Better healthy-looking than looking like some junkie. He still hadn't figured out her purpose when the waitress returned, set their drinks on the table in front of them, and asked if they were ready to order.

Logan laid his menu aside. He had a usual, too. "The lady will have the Cobb salad."

The waitress glanced over at Catherine and asked, "Caesar and hold the carbs?"

"Please," Logan said with a nod. "I'll have the large K.C. Strip, medium rare, baked potato, blue cheese, load her carbs onto mine, and I get the check."

"He does not," Catherine protested as she sat up straighter. "I get it."

The waitress looked between them. Logan smiled and met the blue-eyed gaze across the table. "Wanna arm wrestle me for it?"

"No." She looked up at the server. "We'll work it out before the time comes and let you know."

The waitress gave him a quick nod that told him her bet was on him and then walked off. Logan snagged his beer, leaned back in his chair and settled in.

"We had a deal and it was that I buy your dinner," Catherine reminded him.

"Put what you're saving tonight into the new car account," he countered. "And the other part of the deal was the story of why Tom left you the team." He angled the mouth of the beer bottle in her direction and winked. "I *will* hold you to that offer."

She had promised. Cat reached for her tea and wished she could get away with a simple "because he knew I needed it." But, as stories went, it wasn't much of one and certainly not worth any ten bucks. No, she had to pour out the whole thing. It was only fair. "Tom was actually my half brother," she began, setting down her glass. "Same father, different moms. And twenty-four years apart. No surprise that we weren't really all that close when I was a kid. But Dad died when I was twenty-eight and Tom and I sorta connected at the funeral."

The waitress arrived at the table and set a salad plate down in front of Logan. He started—ever so slightly—and reached for his napkin wrapped silverware in an obvious and not-so-successful effort to hide the fact that he hadn't known the server was there.

Cat picked up her silverware, as well. His right eye was the blind one, she recalled. As she laid her napkin in her lap, she quickly closed her right eye and checked her field of vision.

And understood how things coming from that side could be such a surprise for him. Poor man. The least she could do was give him some sort of sign that something was coming at him so he didn't spend his dinner getting blindsided time after time.

"Anyway, because I was in Dallas and Tom was here," she went on, "we had a distant, three-four times a year 'hey-what-you-been-doing' kind of thing for the next ten years. But he was there for me when the big stuff happened. He and Millie came to my wedding and they set up a college savings fund for Kyle when he was born."

The man across the table cocked a brow. "Kyle's your son."

Cat nodded. "Tom was always my big brother. But Millie really got into being the doting aunt for Kyle. She's always spoiled him absolutely rotten."

He swallowed a bite of salad. "And then?"

She adjusted the alignment of the forks beside her imaginary plate and forced herself to take a breath, made herself meet the gorgeous brown gaze square on. "And then my husband had a massive midlife crisis."

"He left you."

"High and dry," she admitted, grateful that Logan Dupree hadn't let her flounder around in the telling. To the point. That was Logan's style. But gently. Kindly. That was nice of him. "I thought I was doing real well with the coping," she explained. "I climbed on the back of the Harley. I didn't say anything when he traded his Town Car for the roadster. I didn't laugh when he had the hair transplants or when the face lift made him look kinda Chinese. I took the scuba diving lessons and I packed my bags for a 'second honeymoon' on the Mexican Riviera." She sighed and put on a smile that she hoped didn't look as strained as it felt. "Unfortunately, he decided to take his administrative assistant on the honeymoon instead."

"Shit."

Bless Logan for the wince. "Yeah," she agreed. "It was a late afternoon flight. I spent the morning double-checking the babysitter and getting all that kind of stuff set. He spent it selling his Harley and the roadster and cleaning out the bank accounts. Which was the last of the liquidating as it turned out. The week before he'd cashed out both our IRAs and 401(k)s."

Across the table, Logan snapped his jaw closed and then frowned. "That's illegal. Your accounts are yours, not his."

"That's what my attorney said and the divorce judge agreed with him. But having a judgment and enforcing it are two different things. It's like Ben's disappeared off the planet."

"Ben's the ex?"

She nodded, tucked her hair behind her ears, and continued with the story. "I put on a big act for Kyle, of course. Told him that everything would be all right. That Mom could hold it all together. I was three weeks into the private oh-my-God-where-am-I-going-to get-money-for-groceries part of it all when Tom called for one of his regular check-ins. I lost it big time on the phone. I mean, I just blubbered."

"Understandably."

Oh, yeah, right. Like he would have sobbed and gone incoherent on his big brother. "Tom and Millie drove down that same night," Cat went on. "They begged me to move up here. Tom offered me an administrative job with the team. And yes, it was generous of him and it would have been a smart thing to do, but I couldn't do it to Kyle. His dad had left him, too. I couldn't upend what was left of his world. I couldn't haul him away from his friends, his school, the only house he'd ever lived in. I just couldn't."

"So you stuck it out in Dallas," he summarized as he pushed away his half-eaten salad.

She shrugged. "Ben was the dean of students at a private

tech college. As the dean's wife, I took care of the social schmoozing that goes with the job. All volunteer, of course. But I had connections from the years I spent in the trenches. I pulled myself together and called in the chips. A friend of a friend hired me to help plan charity events. It wasn't big money, but it was enough to keep us going."

He lifted his bottle in a salute of sorts and said, "You get points for grit."

"Thanks." Grit points were a small consolation. They didn't offset the tally on the big scoreboard. Not only had she been dumped for a twinkie half her age and ripped off in the process, she hadn't seen it coming. Hadn't even suspected. Naive and stupid and old. Yeah, earning a bit of respect from Logan Dupree was nice, but it didn't make the reality hurt any less.

"Do you still have the house in Dallas or have you sold it already?"

And he got points for his effort to keep the conversation going, to keep her from the usual slide into the same ol' wallow. Bless the man for that, too. "A month before he liquidated the retirement accounts, Ben borrowed against the equity. To the point where it would have taken another ten years of appreciation to break even. I didn't have much choice except to give the keys to the bank and walk away."

"Ouch."

Aw, he seemed genuinely pained by it all. What a sweetheart. At the edge of her vision she caught sight of the waitress coming toward them with their dinners. Cat deliberately turned her head that way and smiled in satisfaction as Logan Dupree did the same.

"Actually, it was a relief to have the six ton gorilla off my back," she assured him after the server left and they'd taken their first bites. "And we were ready to move on, anyway. When Millie began slipping, Kyle and I started making regular trips up here to help out with her team social functions. Wichita had become a second home to us, so after Tom passed away… Well, moving wasn't the awful thing it would have been right after Ben took off."

"It was nice of you to help Millie out like that."

"It was the least I could do. If they hadn't anchored me when I desperately needed to be, Kyle and I would be living in a Maytag box under some overpass."

"I doubt that."

"Seriously. I was a mess for a long time."

"You seem okay now."

"Yeah, I think I'm over the worst of it. My fantasy life has gotten fairly tame in the past year, anyway. That has to be a good sign." At his cocked brow, she explained, "Oh, the standard thing. The bimbo-ette gaining a hundred and fifty pounds overnight. Ben's transplants failing and his face sagging back to real. That sort of stuff."

He grinned. "You're so vicious."

Yeah, her attorney had pointed that out, too. But not so kindly, and certainly not with a smile and a twinkle in his eyes. "He is Kyle's dad."

"If he walked through the door right now, would you take him back?"

"Not on a bet," she answered firmly even as her gaze instinctively darted to Hero's front door. Just in time to see the last of six of the Warriors come through it. She reached for her tea and desperately tried to wash the panic down. God, they had to know she'd fired Carl. He wouldn't have kept quiet about it. If they saw her and came over to talk about it… Damn, damn, damn.

"Tom didn't exactly leave you a gold mine, you know."

Her heart racing faster than the engine on her Jeep, she swallowed hard, begged fate for one huge favor, and replied, "The Warriors have potential. You said so yourself."

"When?" he demanded, a bite of steak frozen halfway to his mouth.

"In the parking lot behind the Coliseum. Not quite an hour ago."

He popped the bit into his mouth, chewed and shook his head. He swallowed and picked up his beer. "That wasn't exactly what I said."

Relieved that the players had moved straight to the bar without a glance in her and Logan's direction, she countered blithely, "Doesn't matter. It's what I heard and what I believe."

He lowered his chin and leaned slightly forward. "Well, the guys have to believe it, too. And they don't. They put on smiles for you, but they don't for a minute think they have a prayer of ever being any better than they are."

Yeah, but... She stabbed a chunk of hard-boiled egg. "Carl's done a number on them, that's all."

"It's frickin' genetic," he said as he sagged back into his chair with a half stunned, half amused look on his face.

God, he was handsome. And especially when he smiled in that lopsided way of his. The dimple in his cheek was positively darling. "What is?" she asked, kinda stunned herself.

"Your I-can-fix-anything approach to things," he said as he rolled his eyes and went back to his steak. "Tom was the exact same way. His theme song should have been 'Ain't No Mountain High Enough.'"

It had been. Millie had had it played at the funeral. Along with a whole bunch of other Motown hits. It had definitely been an odd service, but everyone had left with a little spring in their step, so all in all... But Logan didn't need to know about any of that. There was a larger point to be made and she wasn't about to pass up the chance to make it. "How'd you wind up in Wichita, playing for Tom?"

His gaze snapped up to meet hers and she saw his mental

wheels whir. "I ended up here," he said slowly and oh-so-grudgingly, "because no one else wanted me."

She had him and they both knew it. "But Tom believed in you, in what you could do. And he was right, wasn't he?"

"I'm the exception, not the rule," he countered. "And besides, the game's way different now than it was when I went in. Twenty years ago, you didn't have to fight the Europeans for a chance in the majors. Now you do, and they're damn good."

His appraisal was hard and all but growled, *Gotcha*. Like that was going to slow her down. "So, because the chances of making it to the big leagues are slim, every minor leaguer should pack up their dreams and quit trying? They should just accept that they can't ever improve? That they can't be any more than they are today?"

He looked away and sighed. "It'd be the rational thing to do."

"But?" Cat pressed.

He chuckled softly. "Hockey players aren't hardwired to be rational. The whole game's based on the fact that you have to be a few sandwiches shy of a picnic to play it."

Goal to Catherine Talbott. But she could be gracious. "I think the same could be said for owning a minor league team."

"In Wichita, for sure," he agreed. "Have any of the prospective buyers mentioned the possibility of moving the franchise somewhere else?"

Interesting that he remembered that bit of conversation from yesterday. And that he apparently hadn't accepted her reasons to hold off the sale. "We didn't get that far in the discussions. I've given it some thought, though. Not that I have any idea of where that somewhere else might be."

"Anywhere would be better than here." He looked up to meet her gaze as he added, "Selling the franchise now would be an even better idea."

"Maybe down the road," she half promised as a movement on her left sent her heart into sudden overdrive again. "But not right now." *Right now, Matt Hyerstrom's about to ruin everything.* She reached for her tea and wished she'd ordered a margarita instead.

"Hi, Mizz Talbott."

"Hi, Matt. I'd've thought you'd be too worn out from the game to even think about going out on the town."

The young man's grin was as sheepish as his shrug. "There's more than one way to work out the aches, ma'am, and…well…" He shifted his weight from one foot to the other. His gaze slid to the other side of the table as he squared his shoulders, stuck out his hand, and said, "Mr. Dupree, my name is Matt Hyerstrom. I'm left wing, third line."

Logan took the offered hand and gave it what looked— to Cat, anyway—like a solid, sincere shake. "Nice to meet you, Matt."

"I can't…" Matt looked over his shoulder toward the bar and then back. "*All* of us can't tell you how great it is to know that we've got a real coach now. To be honest, we thought Mizz Talbott was nuts for firin' Carl tonight, but now… We'll do anything you ask us to. Anything."

She'd never known that brown eyes could look icy and sharp; icicles had nothing on Logan Dupree in that moment. Jesus. Amiable and pleasant to ugly and lethal in a second flat. And without giving her a chance to explain. She reached out, touched the young man's arm and brought his attention to her. "I'm afraid that there's been a misunderstanding, Matt. Mr. Dupree is here strictly as a consultant. I don't have a replacement for Carl yet."

"Oh." His shoulders slumped and he gave both her and Logan a weak smile as he edged backward and his face turned a bright red. "Well, it was a nice idea while it lasted. Sorry I broke into your dinner."

"It's all right, Matt. Really. I'll find someone else you'll be just as pleased with." His nod was weak, but it would have to do. She turned back to Logan. "I'm sor—" The rest of the apology died on her tongue. Ice had gone to fire. Raging, barely controlled fire. What did he have to be mad about? She'd nipped it. Beautifully. Smoothly.

"Hyerstrom!" he barked, his gaze locked with hers.

"Yes, sir?"

Cat heard hope in the young voice, could see him frozen at the edge of her vision. She held Logan's gaze and silently promised him Holy Salad Throwing Hell if he crushed the kid.

"The team needs to have new laces tomorrow morning," he said calmly, crisply. "Pass the word."

"Yes, sir!"

Cat frowned, repeated the words over in her mind, and considered them along with the pulsing jaw of the man glaring at her. The conclusion seemed reasonable. And impossible, too. "Did you just agree to coach my boys?"

He tore his gaze from hers and practically attacked his steak. "Only until you can find a decent replacement. When were you planning to tell me that you'd fired Carl Spady?"

An honest, direct question. Which required the same kid of answer. "Never. I figured that if I did, you'd see it as a form of blackmail."

"You figured right."

God, it was hard to breathe. And something was wrong with the heater in Hero's; the place was like an oven. She was dizzy. Queasy, too. And a little voice in the back of her head whined to go home. Another little voice suggested that she tell him to pack up his suspicions and go to hell. She opted for middle ground. "Then don't sign on. No one's twisting your arm. I can handle it perfectly well without you."

He looked up just long enough to growl, "Yeah, right."

Cat laid her fork down, her appetite gone. "I don't want you coaching my boys thinking that you've been boxed into doing it," she said while she tucked her napkin under the rim of the salad bowl. "They deserve a coach who's taking them on for the right reasons. They deserve someone who believes their dreams are worth something. If you don't, then you're not the right man for the job."

"What time is practice and where?"

Did he believe in them or had he not heard a word she'd said? Or had he heard and just not given a damn? Did it matter which right this minute? She was past tired; she was flat wrung out. If she had to go at it all again... No, not tonight. Tomorrow. She'd be sharper tomorrow, after she'd had some sleep. "Practice is at the rink, 6:00 a.m."

"What rink? The Coliseum?"

Yeah, like she could afford arena ice for practice. In his dreams. "The city ice rink," she answered. A bit more testily than she'd intended.

His hands stopped and his gaze came up from his plate. He studied her for a long moment. The edge of his anger seemed to dull a bit. "They didn't have one the last time I was here. Where is it?"

"Just west of McLean on Maple. Across the street from the baseball stadium."

"How long is practice?"

"An hour and a half."

He cocked a brow. "Get us double that until I tell you otherwise."

Who's paying for the extra time? she silently demanded. *You want me to rob a bank on my way home?*

"Who unlocks?"

"I do," she answered tightly. "At five."

"It's going to be a short night," he announced as he laid down his silverware. He glanced over at her barely eaten salad, at her napkin beside it, and apparently came to the conclusion that she was as done as he was. He rose to his feet, saying, "I'll walk you to your car."

It crossed her mind to tell him that she was perfectly capable of finding it on her own, but she bit the words back as he stepped to her chair and put his hand under her elbow to help her rise. Damn him and his timing. She slung her purse over her shoulder as he tossed two twenties on the table. Just when she had a really zingy comeback, he got chivalrous. It took all the righteousness out of the being snarky.

"Pack it in, gentlemen," she heard him say from behind her as she headed toward the door. "Tomorrow's going to be a long, hard day."

Yes, it was, Cat admitted to herself as they moved toward their cars. Her agenda had been full before she'd fired Carl, before Logan Dupree had shown up out of the blue. Maybe it wasn't such a good idea to wait until daylight to make sure things were set straight. Sleeping on problems never helped; they just made the bed lumpy. She fished the car keys out of her purse and tried to think of what to say, of what questions she needed to ask, what answers she needed to collect. And if they were the wrong answers… Geez Louise, how did you fire someone you hadn't really hired? How did you question motives and tell someone they weren't as perfect as you'd thought?

She stopped at the back of the Jeep, took a deep breath to steady herself and looked up at him. "Look, Logan. I—"

He shook his head, took the car keys out her hand and walked up the side of the Jeep. She watched him, her jaw dropped. No one had ever unlocked a car door for her. Not ever. Good God. He really was a gentleman. She'd always thought of them as being right up there in the Real Department with the Tooth Fairy and the Easter Bunny. But against all the odds, one had—

She started and winced as he opened the driver's side door. The sprung door whose front edge popped the front quarter panel every time it swung open or closed. And not quietly, either. The sound made climbing in and out an acutely public declaration of poverty. On good days she could smile about it and tell herself that a car wasn't anything more than a way to get from one place to another, that the Mommobile ran and it was paid for. On bad days, though… The Junkmobile was rolling, clattering, baling-wired proof of just how badly she'd failed at life.

She glanced over at the shiny black Lexus Logan had rented and then back to her Jeep. Today had been lousy pretty much all the way around. She'd had enough. So the bed was lumpy. She couldn't remember the last time it hadn't been.

Cat went up the side of the car, accepted the keys from him and slipped into the driver's seat with a "Thank you," that sounded every bit as exhausted as she felt.

It wasn't until she'd cranked the engine over that he said, "I'll see you at the rink at five sharp," closed the door with a huge pop and walked off toward his own car.

Tired, embarrassed, and not at all certain whether Logan agreeing to coach was good news or bad, Cat backed out of the space and headed for the street. A quick check in the rearview mirror relieved her conscience. His headlights were on and his car was moving; he wasn't stranded. She turned west and checked the rearview again as she stopped for the red light at Emporia. No Lexus headlights, no Logan behind her. Just a battered old pickup truck. Good. She was so ready to be alone.

The light turned green and she pressed the accelerator. The Jeep went nowhere. With a sigh, Cat slammed it into Park and turned the ignition off and then on again. The engine roared back to life, the choke wide open. She closed her eyes, clenched her teeth and tried to kick the revs back down into the normal range. As always, it didn't work. The pickup truck driver honked his horn. The tires of the Jeep squealed as she put it in drive and shot forward. They squealed again as she took the corner at Douglas and Main and headed for the highway.

And again when she careened into the empty parking lot of the downtown library. The brake pedal mashed all the way to the floor, the Jeep came to a sliding, engine-roaring halt. With trembling hands, Cat cut off the engine and then collapsed back into the seat. Ten minutes. In ten minutes she could go on and everything would be just fine. And while she waited, she'd calm down and think. Try to figure out why Logan Dupree had taken the job and why he was angry with her about it. Or maybe not, she admitted as the tears welled in her eyes and rolled down her cheeks.

Chapter Four

Nope. The man looking back from the mirror didn't have a clue either. Logan sighed, dumped the contents of his pockets onto the hotel room bureau and then sat on the side of the bed. The man in the mirror didn't *look* stupid.

"Appearances don't mean shit," Logan growled, falling back onto the mattress. His head cradled in his hands, he stared up at the ceiling. It was all just a blur. One minute he'd been thinking about how well Cat was handling the divorce thing and then—wham!—he was the coach of her team.

It wasn't like he'd been boarded, though. Not if he was being fair about it. There had been warning signs; he just hadn't paid any attention to them. Hyerstrom standing there… God, his mom would have said the kid looked like a new copper penny. All that hope. And then Cat… Smooth as silk and saying she'd get someone to coach who they'd like even better than him.

Better. Yep, that's where the edge had gone out from under

him. There'd been a flash behind his eyes, a little voice in the back of his head snarling, *Who's better than me?* and then it was a done deal. He'd committed himself. He'd come to town just for a quick glimpse into the fiery lakes of hell and ended up buying property. On the water's edge.

He should have his head examined. A good shrink could probably get him out of it. So could a good airline pilot. All he had to do was get on a plane. Let his answering service screen his calls. Eventually Cat would quit calling.

Logan frowned. Cat wouldn't call. She'd die before she picked up the phone and even so much as asked him about the weather. Begging him to come back... No way. Threatening him with a breach of contract suit... Never. Even if she had the money to hire a rottweiler in a three-piece suit. Which she didn't. She didn't have enough to make a payment on a no frills little car. Naw, she wouldn't track his ass back to Tampa and make him feel guilty. She'd just lift that little chin of hers, sniffle in a quiet, ladylike way, try to tuck her hair behind her ears and then put on a smile and do a cheer for the team. She'd go on doing her best to make it all come right. And not even come close.

Logan closed his eyes and groaned. Damn his ego. Damn his pride. And while he was at it, damn his good sense for not having saved him from the other two. He was stuck. In Wichita. For the next five months. Six if they made the conference play-offs. If they actually managed to play for the title it would be—

"A damned miracle," he grumbled as he sat up. He sighed. Five months was doable. No one could honestly expect him to pound the Warriors into a play-off caliber team. Not at this point. Yeah, if he'd had them since last fall, or even the end of the last season, it would be a different story. But he hadn't, and just getting them to the final season buzzer with a win average above fifty percent would impress the hell out of anyone who'd seen them play at the start of it.

Five months. Logan considered the carpet between his feet. There was so much to do…. He checked his watch and added an hour for the time difference as he pulled his cellphone out of the holster. Okay, so it was after one in the morning back in Tampa. On a weekday. He scrolled to the number and hit the button. He owed Dominic Parisi a middle of the night phone call. Several, actually.

It took five rings before a groggy-heading-toward-pissed voice snarled, "Do you know what time it is?"

"Yeah," Logan answered, grinning, "sure do."

A grunt of recognition. "You sound too happy to need bail money, Dupree."

He sounded happy? Well, yeah. At the moment. "Consider this payback for San Diego."

"What about Edmonton?"

Ah, Nic was smiling; Logan could hear it. "It's down the road yet. So are New York and St. Louis."

The rustle of sheets. "God," his friend groused on a strained breath. The click of a light switch. "It's a bitch getting old."

"Like that's news," Logan countered, chuckling and stripping off his tie. "I need a big favor, pal."

"Like at one o'clock in the morning *that's* news. What's up?"

"I need you to go over to the apartment first thing in the morning," Logan explained, opening the collar of his shirt, "pack up my gear and some of my winter clothes and ship it to me."

There was silence on the other end of the line. Logan could well imagine the look on Nic's face, the way his dark brows were drawn together at the bridge of his nose. The nose that had been broken half a dozen times and never straightened because Dominic Parisi was absolutely convinced that women found it irresistible.

"Okay," Nic finally said, "I'm paying attention now. Where the hell are you?"

Logan laughed and looked out the hotel room window at the prairie night, at the flat blanket of lights and the sea of black that surrounded it. "The middle of fricking nowhere."

"Must be ice there or you wouldn't need your gear. And where there's ice, there's a rink twink."

Catherine Talbott a rink twink? Shirley Temple in spandex and sleeping her way through the team? "There's no twinkie," he assured his friend.

"Hey, I'm already awake. The least you can do is make it worth it. Is she a blonde or a brunette?"

Logan reminded himself that that was just the way Nic was. One track off ice. One track on. "It's not that kind of a deal. You'll just have to believe me. And whether you do or not, I need you to ship my crap to…" He frowned and yanked open the nightstand drawer. "Hold on, let me find the address."

"You don't know where you are?"

With the phone cradled between his ear and shoulder, he pulled out the phone book and tossed it down on the bed. "I don't know the address of the team office," he said as he flipped through the yellow pages.

"What team?"

H. H-O. Hockey. "I kinda got roped into something and…" *Wichita Warriors.* Interesting. The Warriors' office was at the ice rink. Same address for both. And the only two listings. "You ready to write?"

"Yeah. Roped into what?"

Logan read him the address slowly and made him read it back because he liked his skates and didn't want them to end up in Timbuktu. It took forever to break in a new pair.

"Wichita," Nic said. "You're in Wichita?"

"Yeah. And you don't have any idea of where it is, do you, Mr. Big City?"

"It's somewhere in flyover country and that's as much as I want to know. What have you gotten yourself into?"

"I'm coaching my old farm club team," Logan supplied. "Except they're not affiliated anymore. The job came up and there's no one else to do it and…" He shrugged. "Ah, hell, I'm not doing anything else, so why not."

"How's the woman come into all of this?"

God Almighty. "Listen to me, Nic. There is no woman."

"Oh, c'mon, Logan. There's always a woman. Is this one a redhead?"

"Just send me my gear and my stuff," Logan replied. "And, hey, leave Mrs. Brands a note on the fridge, will ya? Tell her that I'm going to be gone for the season and that she can have any of the stuff in the kitchen that she wants to haul out of there."

"Okay, man. You got it. You want it all overnight, right?"

"I want it yesterday, but the next flight in will have to do." He glanced down at the yellow pages. "Apparently the rink has a pro shop. If it's a decent one, I may be all right for a day. If not, I'll be coaching from the damn box."

"I had a coach one time who did that. Turned out he couldn't skate."

"Could he coach?" Logan asked, closing the phone book and pitching it back into the drawer.

"I thought so at the time, but then I was only six, so you know…" Nic paused and Logan could practically see him shrug. "This team of yours… They any good?"

"There's some potential."

"Oooh, code for they suck."

"Pretty much," Logan agreed. "It's gonna be a long season."

"She must—"

"Give it up, Nic. I'm not doing this for any woman."

"So why *are* you doing it? I distinctly remember you saying that you'd skate in hell before you stood behind the bench. What's changed?"

The man was a damn pit bull. Digging in the corner for a puck, it was a good quality, but outside of that... "I looked back, okay?"

"Huh?"

He could probably explain it, but only if there were rubber hoses, hot lights and an electric chair involved. "If you'd get that stuff on its way, I'll send you a Kansas shot glass for your collection. A couple of them."

"Not doing shot glasses anymore."

Logan cocked a brow. "Oh, yeah? Did you hit a magic number or something?"

"Five-twenty-two. But that's not it. Last girlfriend took 'em as souvenirs."

"All of them?" he asked, stunned. "How the hell did—"

"She was pissed and I was out of town," Nic supplied blithely. "I'm collecting Porsches now."

Logan could so see where this was going. "How many you got so far?" Logan asked, playing along.

"Yours'll be the first. Feel honored?"

Logan laughed and shook his head. "Don't hold your breath, pal."

Nic laughed, too. "I'll take care of this end for you. You take care of that one."

"Will do, Nic. Thanks for everything."

"Until, man."

Logan punched the end button and closed the phone. He had his gear and a basic wardrobe on the way. Two things off the list. The two most important. Someplace to sack out that didn't have a Gideon Bible in the nightstand was next, but that would have to wait until daylight and regular business hours. Dominic Parisi was one thing, a Realtor picked from the phone book was another. In the meantime...

Logan checked his watch again. Just under four hours before he had to be at the rink. He could try to catch a few hours of sleep. He could turn on the TV and see what crisis was now threatening the survival of mankind. Unfortunately, short sleeps that rejuvenated some people only made him surly and there was nothing he could do about saving the world.

He shoved himself off the bed, went to the desk and pulled out the hotel stationery and the complimentary cheap pen. Dropping down into the chair, he allowed himself one hard sigh, and then began to list the names of the players. His players. His team.

Not Cat's. She owned the team, she wrote the checks, yeah, but that was the extent of it. Regardless of what Nic thought, this wasn't about getting a curly-haired blonde with an hourglass figure, perky smile and totally groundless optimism into bed. Or even making her happy while standing upright and fully clothed out on some public sidewalk. No, this was all about paying back debts. He owed Tom. He owed it to The Dream and to The Game. The fate of the world was out of his hands, but the Warriors' wasn't. By God, they were going to play decent hockey or go home.

And if Catherine Talbott, Mother Hen and Team Cheerleader, accused him of being a big, bad meanie and tried to step in…. Logan moved the Realtor down a notch on the to-do list. First things needed to go first.

Cat sat slightly forward in the overstuffed chair and squinted at the haze trapped between the two panes of glass on the family room's sliding glass door. The hermetic seal was obviously gone and the resulting cloud of condensate was—just as obviously—*not* in the shape of Elvis. Or Matt Damon. Or Madonna. Not the one from New Jersey or the one from Judea. So much for the hope—faint though it had been—of using admission money to pay for ice time. Which was probably just as well; people who charged for that sort of stuff were even more pathetic than the people who came to look at it. Like that man, years ago, who had had the potato shaped like the head of Richard Nixon. Of course it had gotten him on TV with Jay Leno. Or had it been Letterman? Didn't matter who, actually. It had been the exposure that mattered. She could use some of that right about now. How to get it, though. How to get people to buy the tickets so she could pay the bills?

The grandfather clock in the front foyer chimed 2:00 a.m. Cat read the news scrolling along the bottom of the TV screen, noting that it was the same as it had been for pretty much the last hour and a half—there was a wildfire in California, a hurricane headed toward Florida, unemployment was up, housing starts were down, someone was going to outsource two thousand jobs, the stock market was flat, and everyone had an opinion on what the Fed ought to do at its next meeting.

In the big scheme of things, her problems weren't even a blip on the radar. Well, the national radar, anyway. On her personal scope, things were about to go down in flames. And it wouldn't take any FAA caliber agency to figure out what had gone wrong, either; she'd reached big and gotten what she'd hoped for. If only she'd anticipated the potential down side of convincing Logan Dupree to sign on.

A flutter off to her right. She turned her head and smiled as her sister-in-law emerged from the hallway and advanced into the family room. How the almost seventy-year-old woman could look so good, so unmussed, after four hours in bed… God, not a single silver strand of hair was out of place.

"You're up late," Millie said, as she smoothed her robe and sat in the companion chair.

Cat nodded. "I didn't wake you, did I?"

"Oh, heavens, no. I hardly sleep anymore. One of the…" She pursed her lips for a moment and then looked at Cat with an arched brow. "Following things?"

"Consequences?" Cat guessed.

"Yes. Of getting old." She glanced at the television. "Is anything interesting happening in the world?"

"Just the usual stuff," Cat supplied. "Wind, fire, rain, plagues of locusts."

Millie's attention came back to her. "Which one of them has you worried?"

It showed? Since there was no lying to Millie and Cat knew it, she started at the top. "I fired Carl Spady this evening."

"Good for you," Millie replied. "Tom was planning to do that. He's pleased, I'm sure."

Well, that was good news. It would have been better if Tom had actually done it, but what the hell. "The trip to Tampa paid off," Cat went on. "Logan Dupree showed up at tonight's game and, over dinner, agreed to coach the team."

Millie blinked at her. "And that's upsetting?"

"Well, yeah."

"I can understand that. You certainly aren't the first woman sent into a whirl by Logan. I assume he's still as handsome as ever?"

Millie thought she was sleepless over some man? Not since junior high. Well, okay, she'd had some long nights over Ben, but only after the rat bastard had taken off and taken all her money with him. "Some men wear the years well," Cat offered diplomatically. "Logan's one of them."

"Has he ever married?"

Oh, God. Millie was thinking of playing matchmaker? This needed to be nipped in the bud. "Not that I know of. But I'm not interested in him that way, Millie. He's out of my league for one thing. And, more importantly, my life is complicated enough at the moment. I don't have the time or the energy for a man."

Millie nodded and looked back to the television. "Maybe you should make time and find the energy."

Cat reminded herself that her sister-in-law was from the generation where being attached to a man was a woman's sole source of identity and security. There was no changing Millie's perspective and so no point in trying. "If I'm going to make anything," Cat countered, "it's got to be money."

Again Millie looked back at her. "Do you need me to cash in some...broker things?"

"Stocks," Cat supplied. At Millie's nod, she smiled and shook her head. "Thank you for offering, Millie. I really appreciate it, but the team has to make it on its own. If it can't, it's time to fold it up and pack it away. Stuffing money down a rat hole is stupid."

"Tom did it for years."

Oh, jeez. "I didn't mean to—"

"I know," Millie interrupted sweetly. "But to Tom the team was about more than profit. Or loss, as the case may be."

"For him it was the care and feeding of dreams." She winced at the cynical edge to her voice and wished that she could call the words back.

"Dreams are important, Catherine," Millie gently chided. "They should never be given up or allowed to wither. Without them, there's no reason to go from one day to the next."

Yeah, Cat silently countered, *but it's a helluva lot easier— and a lot more fun—to dream when money is no object.*

"You're not believing me, are you?"

Cat managed a weary smile. "Oh, I believe you, Millie. It's the paying for the dreams that has me depressed at the moment. I asked Logan to coach without thinking about how he might change things and how I was going to pay for it all."

"Such as?"

"He wants to double practice time. Which is a logical and no doubt necessary thing to do given how awful the team is at this point. But I'm barely managing to pay for the hours we've already got slated. Times two…" She sighed and massaged her forehead with her fingertips. "Any ideas?"

"Tom auctioned off the players one time."

Auctioned? Was that really the right word? Cat slid a look at the older woman. "Come again?"

"It was a long time ago," Millie explained. "As I recall, it was very successful. There was a dinner affair at the Petroleum Club with tickets sold for admission. Expensive enough to make it only for the upper crust, of course. The Petroleum Club doesn't allow riffraff. The boys wore tuxes and did a fashion runway presentation and the women bid on an evening out with a player. With decorum, of course. The team paid for their dinner and the movie out of the proceeds. And, as I remember, the boys were rather flattered by all the attention."

Cat could see it. And so many other possibilities. "The team as a charity," she muttered, glad to have her brain back. And in working order, too!

"Is it that bad, Catherine? Are we really a charity case?"

"Not yet," she assured her. "I have lots of ideas. I know how to do charity fund-raisers. Why I didn't think of approaching it from this direction, I don't know. Thank you!"

"You're just tired," Millie assured her. "You simply can't think well when you've met yourself coming and going for months."

"It has been a little intense."

"You really ought to slow down a bit, you know. Sleep does wonders for a person."

Cat absently hummed agreement. The auction would be even more profitable if she did some smaller events first. Get the boys' faces out there so there was something of a drool factor to drive ticket sales.

"And I'm sure Logan will be more than happy to assist any way he can," Millie added. "He was always such a nice young man. Very polite and…" She frowned and Cat waited, unsure of what word she wanted, but couldn't find. "He said thank you often. And meant it."

Ah, appreciative. And gallant, too, she admitted, remembering all the little courtesies of the evening. "He's still a gentleman."

Millie sighed softly. "There are so few of them in the world these days. Have you noticed that?"

"Yes. Yes, I have."

"An intelligent young woman wouldn't let one get away simply because he didn't appear at just the right moment in her life."

Bless Millie and the strength of her convictions. "I'll bear that in mind."

"You should invite Logan to dinner. You're a wonderful cook and I'm sure it's been ages since he's had a home-cooked meal. Logan always liked good food."

The way to a man's heart is through his stomach? How pathetic and desperate would she have to be to use that old ploy? "Okay, I'll extend an invitation," she promised. *Sometime. Like for Thanksgiving or Christmas. Next year.*

"This week would be fine, Catherine," Millie went on. "I'd love to see him again. He was always such a nice young man. And so good-looking, too. I had a serious girlfriends only rule, you know."

Serious rule? Or serious girlfriend? Big difference there. "No, I didn't."

Millie sat up a bit straighter. "I did indeed. And made no apologies for it, either. They could bring their girlfriends over for a team dinner only if they were thinking of marrying them. Nothing can ruin a genteel gathering more quickly or easily than an overreaching puck… rabbit. Not that some of them didn't marry such girls, you understand. And most of them quickly regretted it. Of course, to be fair, there were a few of the girls who reformed and made themselves into decent wives and mothers. But they were most definitely the exception."

Puck rabbits, huh? Kyle called them hoochies. In her day they'd been called groupies. Amazing how the terms changed to describe timeless behavior. But all of that aside… "Why are you telling me this?"

Millie frowned for a few seconds and then shrugged. "I'm sure there was a reason, but it escapes me now. The mind, Catherine," she added as she smiled and rose from her chair, "is a terrible thing to have wander away. I think I'll take what's left of mine back to bed now."

"Good night. Sweet dreams."

"Good night, Catherine." As she headed toward the hallway, she added, "Give Logan a little kiss for me when you see him."

Not on a bet.

"Oh, now I remember," Millie said, turning back, her smile broad. "I thought you should know that Logan never brought a young lady to the house. Just lovely bottles of Merlot. Have I mentioned that he was very polite?"

"Yes, you have."

"So few men understand the concept of a hostess gift," Millie observed, again walking away. "Good night, Catherine."

Well, it had been about as subtle as Millie ever got. And the message was clear: Logan Dupree was a prize, and if she had a brain in her head, she'd go for him. Cat laughed softly. Her brain was going to be too otherwise engaged for the next few months to even think about adding a husband hunt to her schedule. Mom, sister-in-law-slash-caretaker, team owner and now head fund-raiser. Yep, the plate was full. There was no room for Logan. Too bad. So sad.

Cat checked the time and then turned off the television. The world was on its own for the time being. It would have to muddle through without her. She had a fund-raising strategy to develop, a team to let into the rink, a kid to get up, fed and off to school, a coach to bring on board with the grand plan, a—

Damn. Carl was going to be in this morning to clean out his desk. Okay, she could handle that bit of certain ugliness. She was woman, she could roar with the best of them.

After that… Oh, yeah, and a housekeeper to hire. That was on the agenda, too. The agency was sending possibles over today. The first was supposed to come into the office for an interview at nine. If there was a God, the first one would be perfect. And if God were really nice, it would never occur to Millie that most live-in housekeepers didn't have degrees in gerontology.

Success went to those who had coffee running in their veins, Cat assured herself as she got up and headed for the kitchen. Sleep was for wimps. And Logan was for… Man, she could make a mint auctioning him off.

Other than that, though, Logan Dupree was for anyone but her. She couldn't fit him into her life if she used a shoehorn. Millie would just have to get over it.

Chapter Five

Cat lined up the stacks of paper on her desk, took a deep breath, slowly let it out and then picked up her clipboard and a pen. "Lakisha," she said as she moved through the outer office, "I'm heading over to the ice. If the housekeeper prospect shows up early, hand her a cup of coffee and put her somewhere. If Carl waltzes in, don't let him out of your sight and call me on my cell."

"What if the president calls?"

"Tell him he's on his own."

It was a beautiful morning, the air crisp and cool, the skies clear and a lovely, clean shade of blue. The wind was swirling leaves around in the almost empty parking lot. She smiled and tipped her face up to the sun as she went down the walk and toward the back of the building. Autumn in the air. A definite change in season was one of the nicest things about having moved north. And fall had always been her favorite. Pumpkins and frost and bare-limbed trees made her happy.

It was as though the world was giving everyone permission to slow down for a while.

And slowing down was something she so desperately needed to do. Maybe this weekend she and Kyle could rake leaves. And if it was cool enough, have hot cider. Light a fire in the fireplace and have homemade stew for dinner. God, Millie made the very best stew. It was good that dementia didn't take old memories. Millie would remember the recipe. All she needed was a little supervision so that she didn't wander off halfway through making it. And if Millie wanted to invite Logan over for dinner, stew was probably a good choice. Hearty and simple and all that. A real manly man kind of meal. And once he'd eaten and burped, Millie would be happy. Just as importantly, the social obligations would be done.

Cat pulled open the glass door and slipped inside. Through the viewing windows on her left she could see the team, dressed in what looked like ragbag rejects, gathered together in a semicircle in the middle of the ice. Logan—in a spiffy red wind suit—stood in front of them, talking, a stick in his hands and his back to the dressing room side of the rink. The boys were nodding. In a weak, exhausted sort of way, she decided as she let herself into the rink proper.

A blast of frigid air hit her. So did the smell. It was awful. Part of it was the gear, she knew. Kyle's could make the whole car reek and have her eyes watering by the time they got home. Airing out in the garage helped, but not nearly enough. The other part of the hideous odor was simply male sweat. Thankfully Kyle hadn't reached that point in his development yet. If there was a God, he'd be old enough to drive himself to and from the rink by the time he did.

She stepped into the nearest box and gave Matt Hyerstrom a little wave when he looked over at her. He looked genuinely glad to see her. Logan, on the other hand, didn't.

He glared at her over his shoulder for a second, turned back to the players for another and then whirled around and skated toward her. Fast. Really fast. She held her breath, wondering if he intended to stop or come through the boards and mow her down. At the last moment, he turned sideways and leaned hard toward the ice. A shower of frost shot up. Some of it fell back onto the ice. Some of it landed on the dasher board in front of her. Some of it fell on the tops of her shoes and instantly melted. Cat stamped her feet to get rid of it and then looked up into hard, dark eyes. Really up. On any day he was a good head taller than she was. On skates, he towered over her.

"Eh," he said.

Not hello. Not how are you. Just the shortest possible acknowledgment of a person's presence. Not exactly rude, but darn close to it. She clutched the clipboard to her chest and gave him a smile. "Sorry about tossing the keys at you this morning and taking off. Mom duties were calling. How has practice gone?"

"No one's died."

"Well, that's good to hear," she said, cheerful despite his obvious bad mood. "Did Matt have everyone ready like you asked?"

"Those that wanted to be ready, were. And practice isn't over yet, so if we can make this quick… Whaddya need?"

Oh, to hell with trying to be pleasant. If he wanted to be grumpy, far be it for her to interfere. "I was reading the boys' contract this morning and there's a community service clause."

"There always has been."

"Good. I need to know what they're doing. You know, what organization they've signed on with, what they do and when they're there and all that. I've got a publicity idea and I thought that after they came off the ice, they could each visit with me about it."

He considered her, but didn't say anything. She showed him the clipboard. "I thought we could do it after practice. Either as they were heading into the showers or after they came out."

"I'll take care of it," he said, taking the clipboard from her.

"But—"

"No buts." He laid the board on the wet dasher and either didn't see her wince or ignored it. "You going to be in your office in the next hour?"

She blinked. "Yes, but—"

"I'll bring you your list."

And then he skated off, back to center ice and the team. She'd been dismissed. Summarily and coolly. Matt threw a quick look her way that brimmed with obvious pity. And then his gaze was riveted on Logan. Cat considered her options. She could stay just to defy him. But it smelled awful and it was cold and she had other things to do. All in all… She stood where she was for just a few seconds, though. Just so her leaving would look more like an escape from boredom than the retreat it was.

"Men," she informed Lakisha as she passed the secretary's desk, "think the universe revolves around them."

"Until they want something," the other woman called after her. "And then they're all lovey-dovey and kissy face."

"Well," Cat declared, dropping down in her chair, "he can just be as charming as he wants. He's not getting any stew."

Lakisha appeared in the doorway and flung her braids back over her shoulder. "I'm not following that, but I probably don't want to."

God, she was getting the rabbit look again. "What's the problem now? Did the housekeeper cancel?"

"The Coliseum called. Something about damages in the locker room. They want you to call them back."

"What they want is for me to write a fricking check," she

groused as she snatched up the phone. "Don't they have insurance for this kind of stuff?"

Lakisha, who obviously recognized a rhetorical question when she heard one, shrugged and left her to deal with it on her own. Cat closed her eyes while she waited for someone to answer. The longer she owned the team, the more she wondered why Tom had gone through this day after day. Dreams were nice, but the Warriors really qualified as more of a never-ending nightmare.

Logan stood in the doorway and looked around the locker room with decidedly mixed feelings. It was good that they were too damned tired to move; it meant that they'd put something into practice. But the fact that it had worn them out told him that it had been a long, long time since anyone had pushed them. Which meant that the road ahead was going to be killer.

"Same time tomorrow, gentlemen," he announced. He lifted Cat's clipboard and added, "Spend this afternoon getting your volunteer commitments set. You won't have time tomorrow. You'll be working in the weight room."

They groaned in response. Logan smiled and left them to their misery, knowing that as soon as the door swung closed they'd start calling him every name in the book. He'd been in their place before. More than once. And although he'd die before he admitted it to them, he was more than a little sore from the workout himself. And it wasn't entirely from wearing borrowed skates. Self-pity and too much money weren't good for a man. The boys weren't the only ones who were going to find the next few weeks a challenge. He really needed to call his stockbroker and make sure he had some money in BenGay stock. And aspirin futures, he added as he pulled open the Warriors office door and his shoulder twinged.

It was a strange office. More like a ghost town than a business. Lots of empty desks. Only the one front and center was in use. And by a woman who looked like she'd just fallen out of the pages of *Ebony* magazine. The party time edition.

"Hi," he said as she gave him the once over. "I'm Logan Dupree, the new coach."

"Lakisha Leonard," she replied, sticking out a hand that glittered at the tips and jangled at the wrist. "The only secretary. I don't cook. I don't dust or wash windows. Anything else, we can negotiate."

He grinned, said, "Nice to meet you, Lakisha," and gave her hand a sincere shake.

She motioned with her head toward the back of the office, then picked up a manila folder and handed it to him. "The boss is waiting for you. Be a dream and take this file to her while you're going, will ya?"

It really wasn't a request. But as orders went, it was put nicely enough. He took the folder, gave her a salute with it and then headed to Tom's old office certain of two things: Lakisha was a power to be reckoned with, and that between the hair beads and the bracelets, she wasn't ever going to sneak up on him.

Cat was a different matter, Logan decided as he stopped in the doorway. She was sitting in Tom's chair, the phone to her ear and looking just as he'd imagined she would—small and innocent and really out of place. And yet there was also something about her that had a way of catching him off balance. Every time he met up with her, his breath caught for a second. He couldn't even begin to guess why.

He'd just leaned his shoulder against the doorjamb and decided that it probably wasn't her hair when she hung up the phone. Her eyes were definitely a possibility, though. They were so blue. And such an open window on what she was thinking. At the moment, she was feeling pretty beat-up and hoping like hell that he wasn't expecting her to go a round with him.

"Your list and the file from Lakisha," he said, handing her the stuff across the desk. He didn't wait for an invitation to stay or to sit. He parked himself in the chair and settled in even as she was thanking him.

"There's nothing on it," she said, flipping through the blank forms on the clipboard.

"That's because they're young and their idea of a charitable cause is supporting the dancers at the local strip club. You didn't push them to do anything when they first came to town, so they blew it off. They've been served notice and have until Monday to come up with something for you."

She gave him a smile that seemed on the tired side. "Thank you."

"You're welcome. And now that we've finished that bit of business, we have some things we need to get square."

"Such as?"

Okay, maybe he'd been wrong about her not wanting to tangle with him. There had been a definite edge in that short little question. "First, practices are closed. To everyone, including you." Her lips parted and he could see a shadow of hurt in those eyes. "You're a first-class distraction," he clarified. "Every single one of them watched you come through the doors. Both sets of them. I need their heads on the ice, not over in the box, thinking about…other things. If there's something you want from me or them, leave a message on my cell and I'll make sure it's done." He pointed to the clipboard on her desk. "The number's on the top there."

She looked down and nodded. Then asked, "Would you like to have my number?"

"Sure. Why not." As she wrote on a pink sticky note, he mentally kicked himself. *Sure. Why not?* Geez. Talk about blow-offs. He needed to get his brain to wake up and work.

"Are we square now?" she asked as she handed him the note.

God, if only they could be. The longer he talked the greater the odds that he'd stick his whole leg in his mouth. "Not quite. Did you notice anyone missing during your visit?"

"No," she drawled. Cautiously.

"Then your assistant coach must not make much of an impression even when he does show up. Got his number handy?"

Her back stiffened. She glanced at the Rolodex on her desk, but didn't reach for it. "Just exactly what are you planning to say to him?"

"Get your butt in here in the next thirty minutes or you're fired."

"It's so unlike Jimmy to miss and not call. Maybe one of the kids is sick."

"And his wife can't handle it?" Logan countered.

She winced and shook her head. "The story is that his wife took off last fall with one of the players Tom traded to Amarillo. She left Jimmy the kids. All four of them. The oldest is only eight. He needs this job, Logan."

Oh, man. Four kids and a long-gone wife. Poor bastard. "How does he handle the traveling?"

"He gets babysitters. Usually it's Lakisha and her sisters and cousins. There's a total of about twelve of them and they just pass the kids around and take shifts."

It was like being back in Des Moines! Everyone was connected. One person moved, everyone did. Amazing. He'd thought that sort of life had fallen by the wayside. He sure hadn't seen it anywhere he'd been lately. Wichita, middle of nowhere and caught in time. Logan thought back, trying to remember how things had been done when he was a kid. "I'll listen to his story," he offered, "but it had better be a good one."

"He's a really nice guy."

"Nice isn't what counts, Cat," he said as gently as he could.

"I need an assistant on the ice. I assume he's a defensive coach?"

She shrugged and gave him a smile that said she had no idea what Jimmy did. Then she picked up the folder Lakisha had sent in and asked, "Is that it for now?"

"I wish it were," he admitted. "There's going to be some personnel changes in the next few weeks. As we get closer, I'll let you know who's going to be released and what I need to bring in. In the meantime, I need Tom's scouting reports so I can figure out which teams are open to trades and what Triple A teams have players who might be ready for a shot."

"I'll have to look for them. I don't know where—"

"I do," he assured her. He got up and went to the credenza, pulled open the file drawer and pulled out the thick, hanging file labeled *Wishes*. "Tom was a creature of habit," he explained as he sat back down, the folder in his lap.

She put her own folder back on the desk. "Who are you thinking about letting go?"

She was trying to sound businesslike, but he could hear the Mother Hen under it. "Look, Cat, this is a business, not the Waltons. You want to make money, then you have to win. And to win, you need the right combination of skills and talents. Right now, you've got some glaring deficits. The players either step up and fill them or they have to go. They know it. You have to accept it, too."

"They have feelings, you know."

Ah, geez. "Yep. And I'm not going to crush them in the process. I've been traded. I know how it feels to be told you're not Mr. Perfect. But when the time comes for the reality talk, I'm going to handle it and you're not going to be anywhere around. Understood?"

"It's my team."

Why couldn't Tom have had a brother? He didn't have any choice except to lay down the law. Nicely, of course. But firmly and clearly. "Granted. But you have your responsibilities and I have mine. There are clear lines between them, Cat. I handle the players on and off the ice. You handle the office and the paperwork and all the PR stuff. If you need anything from the boys, you go through me to get it. They need anything from you, they go through me for it."

She looked at him for a long moment and her eyes turned a kind of steely color. "Am I allowed to attend the games? Or am I supposed to just read about them in the paper?"

God, he didn't want her pissed, just out of his way. "I didn't suggest any such thing," he countered. "If I ruffled your feathers, I didn't mean to. Of course you should go to the games. And the boys would really miss your parking lot cheerleading if you gave it up. All I'm saying is that the day-to-day stuff with them is my responsibility and that I'd appreciate it if you'd trust me do it."

She closed her eyes and expelled a long breath. "Sorry if I got snarky," she offered. "It's the lack of sleep and the mountain of problems."

He breathed his own sigh, but his was one of pure, unadulterated relief. "I know the feeling," he confessed. And, since they had a truce of sorts, he added, "Are any of the problems things I can help you with?"

Cat opened her eyes. Handsome, hunky, and—apparently with just a little effort—capable of being not only apologetic, but accommodating. She'd take it and run with it as far as she could. "Yeah, I'm going to hand you a couple of them here in a minute. First things first, though. I talked to Liz Smith this morning. Rink managers blow through here like the wind, but Liz is local and rooted. Officially, she runs the pro shop. Unofficially, she's the one who makes this place work. She says there's no problem with the extra ice time. And she thinks paying for it can ride until Canada sends us another manager *du jour.*"

"Okay."

"Make the time count, please," she asked. "At seven hundred and fifty a practice session, every minute is golden."

"Two hundred and fifty dollars an hour?"

Gee, he actually looked a little pale. Good. She got queasy whenever she thought about it. "When you're the only ice in town, you can charge whatever you want."

"That's robbery."

"That's reality. Which is why I've come up with some fund-raising ideas."

He cocked a brow. His smile looked a little nervous. "You're not going to ask them to sell magazine subscriptions door-to-door, are you?"

"No, of course not," she assured him brightly. "The big money's in candy bars." His jaw dropped and she couldn't help it—she laughed out loud. "You should see your face."

His wonderfully chiseled cheeks flushed with color. His eyes twinkled. Obviously struggling to contain a grin, he asked, "Enjoying yourself?"

"Immensely."

"You need a life."

"Oh, tell me something I don't already know." She sagged back in her chair, swiped her fingertips over the corners of her eyes, and filed The Candy Bar Look in her memory bank for future amusement. After a calming breath, she began again. "Seriously, I'm planning a gala-type auction. Millie was telling me about it last night. Well, actually, it was early, early this morning, but that doesn't matter. We'll have a fancy dinner at the Petroleum Club and—"

"High bidder gets a date with a player," Logan finished in a voice that reminded her of Eeyore.

There was a story to be told. A good one. "You were here the last time Tom did it?"

"Oh, yeah."

"Was it a negative experience?"

He cleared his throat. "Not completely. The food was good."

"And your date with the winning bidder? How was it?"

The color flooded back into his cheeks. The twinkle came back to his eyes in the same instant that his smile went wide. "It was a notch above strolling South Broadway. But just barely."

She so wanted to ask him if there had been a No Tell Motel involved, but restrained herself. "We'll impose some strict rules and make sure it's classy this time. I don't want any of the players arrested for prostitution." While he snorted, she again picked up the folder he'd brought from Lakisha. "Which brings me to the next item on the agenda. Miscellaneous expenses. Or, more to the point, controlling them."

Settling back in his chair, he asked, "What kind of expenses are we talking about?"

"Well, let's see," she drawled as she sifted through the bills and made a selection. "Here's a good one. Two weeks ago, Tiny was in the emergency room in Tulsa. It seems that he has a tendency to spread and crack his toes and it drives his roommates nuts when they're on the road. So, while he was sleeping, they superglued them together."

He burst out laughing, then apparently thought better of it and scrubbed his hand over his lower face until he could get himself under control. "Sorry," he finally offered with a grin, "but that's good. That's really good. So creative."

She hadn't thought so at the time, but now… "It cost three hundred sixty-five dollars to have them separated," she pointed out, determined to hold the high ground. She selected another one from the pile. "Here's a bill from a local crane company for five hundred and twenty-three. Apparently that's the going rate for getting a Mini Cooper off the roof of a Hooters."

He lost the battle again. "Someone must have really frosted their flakes."

His laughter was so infectious. Under other circumstances, she could actually enjoy it. But not now. Not really. Someone had to be the grown-up. "I'm not amused, Logan. I'm broke. I need this sort of stuff to stop. I can't afford it."

Sobering, he nodded. "I'll see what I can do."

"And while you're at it, I want the fighting to stop, too."

The smile left his face in an instant. "Who's been brawling in bars?"

"No one that I've heard about." She closed and tossed the folder aside. "I mean out on the ice. I hate it. And it's embarrassing to have people think of your team as nothing but a bunch of thugs. I'd much prefer that the team have a reputation for playing a good game of hockey."

"Fighting's a part of the game, Cat."

"As I've been led to understand. But it's not the whole game, is it? It's not the major reason they go out there."

He hesitated and then, with obvious reluctance, replied, "No, it's not."

"It makes it really difficult to get community support. Businesses and organizations don't want to be associated with gratuitous violence. I went to the Boy Scout office last week to see if they wanted to do a group thing and you should have seen their faces. They were appalled. And they didn't mince any words about how Warrior hockey isn't in line with the goals of an organization dedicated to instilling high moral values and good civic conduct."

"Ouch."

"Yeah, ouch. The Girl Scouts and the Junior League aren't even in the realm of possibility. I need to fill the seats, Logan. I can't do that unless I have a wholesome entertainment package to offer the general, non-ambulance chasing public. The fighting *has* to stop."

He sighed and shook his head. "They can't be patsies."

And she couldn't afford to let them go on as they had been. "I want a higher standard. All the way around. On ice and off. They're supposed to be professionals, and it's time they acted like it. I don't think it's too much to ask. Do you?"

He was just opening his mouth to reply when Lakisha stepped through the doorway, announced, "Crisis has arrived and he's eyeing my stapler. If you don't get in here, I'm gonna hurt him," and then took off.

Great. Just what she needed. The roller coaster of her life was off and running again. Cat grabbed the edge of her desk with both hands and pried herself to her feet. "I'm afraid that visiting hours are over."

Man, she looked like there might be a firing squad out there. Logan stood, too. "Who's the crisis?"

"Carl Spady," she answered as she came around the desk. "And I'd really appreciate it if you'd do a disappearing act. He thinks I dumped him because I have the hots for you and I don't have the energy to deal with another round of that right now."

The hots? God, he hadn't heard that expression in *years*. "Don't you? Have the hots for me?"

She stopped dead in her tracks. If she'd been on blades, he'd be covered with ice shavings. "No!"

Big eyes. Red cheeks. A chain just begging to be pulled. "Liar, liar, pants on fire."

She blinked, gasped. Then took off for the outer office, saying as she sailed past him, "In case you haven't noticed, I'm *not* a puck rabbit."

A puck rabbit? Oh, Lord. Sometimes she was just too damn adorably cute for her own good. He trailed after her, trying not to choke on his laughter. Puck rabbit.

As Cat headed toward the office on the other side of the main room, Logan stopped halfway and settled down on the corner of Lakisha's desk. She moved a pile of papers over to make more room for him. Carl Spady was standing behind his desk, yanking open drawers.

"Good morning, Carl," Cat said pleasantly from the doorway. "I've had Lakisha make a copy of your contract and draw up your payroll check. I've also had her get together the paperwork you'll need if you want to continue your health and insurance policies. You'll find it all there on your desk blotter."

"She's smooth," Logan said softly.

"Yeah," Lakisha countered, "but Carl's mind lives in the gutter. It's going to get ugly."

And as if Carl Spady was determined to prove her right, he snarled, "Your brother is rolling over in his grave."

"As you may recall, Tom was cremated." She pointed to somewhere in the man's office. "Those boxes are for your use. Please feel free."

"I brought my own."

"Then I'll thank you for the good years you've put into the team, wish you all the best in the future and leave you to your packing."

She'd barely started to turn away when Carl said, "I see pretty boy over there. You didn't waste any time, did you? Can he skate or have you even gotten around to asking him yet?"

"Walk away, Cat," Logan whispered. "Walk away."

"Five bucks says she doesn't."

And sure enough, Lakisha was right. Cat squared up. For a woman who didn't like fighting, she apparently knew how to do it. "He can skate with the best of them, Carl. And, in fact, has. Now, if you'll excuse me, I think—"

"Hey, pretty boy!"

Logan met the blazing gaze of the other man and silently swore. There was going to be no getting around this.

Cat took another shot at refereeing, though. "Carl, you're making an already difficult situation grossly and needlessly unpleasant. Could we please maintain just a shred of dignity and decorum?"

Carl ignored her. "Is it possible for cold-hearted bitches to be hot in bed?"

Cat actually staggered back a bit. Logan came off the desk slowly, just so Carl Spady—if he had half a brain in his head—knew that he was very deliberately making the choice to beat the hell out of him. "I'll take it from here, Catherine," he said as he moved toward her.

She turned, her face ashen. "Please don't make this any worse than it already is."

"It's not up to me," he said as he stopped in the doorway. He met Carl's gaze squarely. "My name's not Pretty Boy. It's Logan Dupree. And you've stepped across the line, Mr. Spady. The lady has gone out of her way to be pleasant about all this, and you've done nothing but insult her. Now, you can either offer her a sincere apology, or you can be pitched out into the parking lot. Your choice."

"You're just looking for an excuse to flex your muscles and make her ooh and aaah while upright. Have a little performance problem last night?"

So much for the Carl Spady and the half a brain possibility. "Three seconds. I suggest you use them to pull your head out."

He'd gotten to a silent *two* when Cat poked her head between his side and the door frame. "Carl, just leave. Please. I'll have a courier service bring all the stuff to your house later today."

Carl's response was to offer the universal sign of instruction. Cat gasped and Logan left her where she was. "Okay, time's up and so is my tolerance," he declared, striding into the office. "You're out of here."

"Logan, don't!"

He looked back over his left shoulder to make sure she was still outside the office. And all hell broke loose. He heard it first, on his right, on his blind side, and—like a dumb shit—whirled that way instead of going around from his left. In the split second longer that it took, Carl Spady was out from behind the desk, past him and to the doorway. Logan was facing the right way just in time to see Carl's hand impact Cat's shoulder and knock her off her feet. She went back and down, her arms flailing. Her butt hit the carpeted cement floor and her upper body snapped back from the waist, stopping abruptly when the back of her head hit the side of a metal desk.

Logan was already moving toward her, keenly aware of sounds. Over the pop of the metal, he could hear Lakisha cursing and the main door straining on its hinges. And then there was only silence. A silence in which Cat struggled to sitting and reached for the back of her head.

Logan went to one knee beside her. "Are you all right?" he asked, even as he lifted her chin so he could see her eyes.

"I hit my head."

Lakisha called, "You check her for a concussion and I'll go get some ice," and then she was gone.

No concussion; he could see that plainly. Her eyes were clear except for the angry tears welling along her lower lashes. "I'm sorry, Cat. I had no idea that the fat, old geezer could move that fast."

"He surprised me, too." She moved her chin from his grasp and swiped her palms over her eyes as she took a deep sniffle. Then she looked back up at him and smiled. "They say fear's a great motivator. Guess we know now that it's true."

Fear wasn't anywhere near the motivator big blues were. He couldn't run, so he did the next best thing—he pretended to be a doctor. "Is your vision blurry at all?" he asked as he checked the back of her head. "Even just the least little bit?"

"It's fine. Well, except for the little sparks around the edges every time my heart beats. Which is kinda fast at the moment. Is there blood?"

He knew all about accelerated heart rates. And his had nothing to do with dealing with Carl Spady. "Nope, just a little goose egg," he assured her. "I've seen lots worse. Some ice and a couple of aspirin and you'll be as good as new. Well, in a day or two. Knots don't go down instantly."

"Thanks for being a Sir Galahad."

"Yeah, it went so well."

"Seriously, Logan," she said, reaching up for the edge of the desk. He stood and extended his hands. As she allowed him to pull her to her feet, she added, "I really appreciate the effort. I can't tell you the last time—" She swayed and blinked. "Whoa."

"I got you," he said, tightening his grip on her hands and stepping closer. She looked up at him and his mouth went dry. Sahara desert, no-oasis-in-sight dry. He cleared his throat, called himself an idiot, and then said anyway, "Anyone ever tell you that you have the most gorgeous blue eyes?"

She licked her lower lip. She swallowed. "I'm not a puck rabbit."

Something inside him melted. It was a nice feeling. Really nice. He grinned. "It's puck *bunny,* sweetie. And no, you're not."

"Really, it's bunny?"

"Really. I wouldn't lie to you."

Kissing her would be stupid. Crossing the professional line was always a bad idea. Business and personal should never mix. The combination never led to anything except an ugly explosion. He knew all of that. He'd learned it the hard way. He also knew that she would taste wonderful. Soft and luscious and sighing. God, he couldn't remember the last time he'd wanted something so over the line, something he was so willing to get burned for.

"I *knew* it! It's a blonde."

Logan looked over his shoulder, hoping it wasn't. But it was, and—after firmly and repeatedly denying there was any cookie—he'd been caught with his hand on the lid of the cookie jar. There was a tickle of embarrassment for it, but the sensation barely registered. The snarling sound of offended good judgment was louder and way deeper.

His insides went cold as his heart slid into the iron pit of his stomach. He put on a polite smile, let go of Cat's hands and stepped back. Then deliberately turned away from the stupidity of temptation.

Chapter Six

In certain respects, things were getting better. Tiny, their Gentle Goliath, had really come through. The piece on his after school reading program that had run in last Sunday's paper seemed to have had an effect. The "We Love You, Tiny" signs were the tip-off. That and there were just a lot of kids in the arena for the game tonight. Way more than usual. And since they were too young to drive themselves, there were more adults in the seats, too. From the looks of things, they all were keeping the concession stands hopping. A slice of that pie was going to be nice. When added to ticket sales, she'd be able to not only make payroll next week, but the team wouldn't have to sleep on the bus when they played in Albuquerque on Friday.

In other respects, though... Cat took off the headphones and switched off the radio. She didn't need to hear the commentators' running analysis to know that things weren't quite gelling down on the ice.

Yeah, they were better. Before, there'd been so many pen-
alties that the box officials had had to practically use a shoehorn to get players in and out. Now, it was usually a
one-at-a-time thing. At the moment, Matt was serving the last
thirty seconds of a two-minute slashing call. A bogus call,
she knew. She'd been watching. The Eagles player was a
good actor and the ref obviously hated Matt. She didn't know
why. Matt was a really good kid.

In the larger scheme of things, the Warriors were actually
winning a game every now and then. Which was something
they hadn't been doing at the start of the season. Of course
it seemed like it happened more by luck than skill, but she'd
take them however they could get them. Oddly, though,
whether they won or lost didn't have anything to do with at-
tendance numbers. No, ticket sales had started to pick up
when the boys had been forced out into the community to do
volunteer work. She could tell by the way the people cheered
that they weren't so much fans of hockey as they were fans
of the players.

Cat couldn't help but think that was a good thing. Sooner
or later their hockey playing days would end; to have community connections then would make finding and starting another career easier. Not to mention a whole lot less personally
painful for them. Apparently Tiny was a darn good teacher.
She grinned. It was a sure bet that no one was ever going to
throw a spit wad at him.

Okay, so maybe things weren't just better. They were, over-
all, much better. Logan had accomplished a lot in the past
month. She looked down into the bench area. Logan stood at
one end, controlling the comings and goings of the forwards.
Jimmy James stood in the middle with his clipboard and pen.
Dominic Parisi stood at the other, working with the defensemen.

What an odd pair Logan and Nic were. They were both in

suits and ties, but that was about it for similarities. Logan was cool and composed, sending a player out by simply touching his shoulder, calling them in by a silent jerk of his head. He paced back and forth almost constantly, his arms crossed over his chest and his attention always on the ice.

Nic on the other hand… Geez Louise, half the time she thought he was going to jump over the boards and into the game. He waved his arms and yelled. He climbed up on the side walls, clung to the glass and yelled. At the top of his lungs. At everyone. The Warriors, the other team, the refs.

Off the ice, Nic was more civilized. Well, sorta, in a big city East Coast way. She'd been studying him for a month. He'd brought Logan's things and stayed. First out of curiosity about the weird world in which Logan had been snared, and then to help his deluded friend coach. It was Nic who functioned as the intermediary between her and the team, Nic that she spoke with almost every day, Nic who had taken over Carl's old office.

Logan had become someone she waved to across the parking lot. Which was probably for the best. Being around him… Well, she became the village idiot when she was anywhere near him. The last time—on basically the second day she'd known him—she'd been ready and willing to throw decency to the wind and herself into his arms. Lord love a duck.

Yeah, keeping a safe distance from Logan Dupree was definitely the smart thing to do. The farther the better. It was just too easy to fall under his spell and forget to think. She had enough to worry about without adding the consequences of impulsive actions. Maybe some other time, some other—

She started at the buzzer and looked at the scoreboard. Game over? Already? She sighed and shook her head. Another one in the loss column. But only by two goals. That wasn't bad at all. Tomorrow night they could win. They were pretty evenly matched with Tulsa. Three days after that was

Albuquerque. That one was likely to be a tougher fight than tonight had been. The Scorpions were good *and* liked to scrap.

But winning against the Scorps wasn't her problem, she reminded herself. It was Logan's. She snagged her purse and headed out of the box and down the stairs. Her major problem at the moment was meeting Kyle and Millie at the car and then being appalled at how much money Millie had spent in buying the kid souvenirs.

When it came to her nephew, Millie never even thought about uttering the word *no*. Indulging Kyle was Millie's greatest joy in life. And Millie had flat out said she expected Cat to indulge *her* on the matter. No one, Cat silently groused as she entered the underground tunnels and headed for the parking lot, ever seemed to think that she needed indulging every now and then. She chuckled and had to admit that she had no idea of what she'd ask for even if they did. A Rolls-Royce was just a bit flashy for Wichita. With her kind of luck, any pristine desert island would be wiped off the map by a hurricane. A long bubble bath was already in the realm of possible. So was dinner out at a linen tablecloth restaurant.

"Simple wants for simple lives," she muttered as she headed out into the private parking lot. Or was it more a case of simple minds? she wondered as she opened her purse and searched for her car keys.

"Catherine!"

She looked up. Her smile died, instantly but not at all painlessly. Millie and Kyle were standing by the Jeep. With Logan.

Glide, her mind instructed. *Be cool. Be smooth. This isn't high school.* "Hi, guys," she said, her smile firmly back in place as she joined their circle. She looked at her son. "Did you clean out the vendors as usual?"

"Got some cool posters, Mom. Logan said he'd get them signed for me."

Even as he handed them over, Cat shook her head. "It's Mr. Dupree, Kyle, until permission is given otherwise."

"We've already covered that ground," Logan countered, tapping the rolled tubes against his leg. "Permission has been granted."

She believed in picking her battles and this one wasn't worth a fight. Which left her with the need to make small talk. "The team's looking good."

"It depends on who you're comparing them to, you know?"

"Well, I'm very pleased with what I'm seeing. I think you've accomplished a lot in a very short period of time. I wish I could reward you with a raise, but…" She shrugged.

He did, too. "It's not necessary. But we do need to have a personnel talk. It's time to do some trading."

Oh, God. "Who?"

His gaze went to the back door of the arena, to the bus, and then back to her. "Let's have the talk somewhere else, okay?"

"The house," Millie volunteered. "Why don't you come by the house? We're on our way home now. You can follow us."

He blinked, shifted his stance, and said, "Umm."

Cat added, "Uh," to the awkward moment.

Millie beamed. "I'm sure it won't take long at all for you and Catherine to make your decisions once you have some peace and quiet. And besides, there are some pictures of Tom and you that I'd like for you to have. I know you've been too busy to get by for dinner, and I do understand how invitations can be overwhelming when you have so much to do, but surely you can take just a few minutes to come by tonight."

He cocked a brow and shot a quick, dark look at Cat. He

smiled. "Sure, Millie. No problem. My car's at the rink, though. I'll ride back with the team and come over to the house from there. You haven't moved, have you?"

"Of course not." She opened the front passenger door of her Town Car and slid in, saying, "See you at the house."

Her door closed just as Kyle opened the rear one and disappeared into the backseat.

"Just so I can get my ducks in a row," Logan drawled. "What invitations for dinner?"

It sounded as though he was accusing her of being a coward. She had a news flash for him. "Between my schedule and the team's schedule," she explained calmly, "there hasn't been an evening open for anyone to come to dinner. I've explained that to Millie a hundred times. How that's all filtered through the dementia, I don't know. I just go with the flow and do the best I can." She didn't add that she'd considered the scheduling conflicts to be a minor blessing. That wasn't relevant. She'd have bitten the bullet if she'd had to.

Logan nodded and then backed toward the bus, saluting her with the posters and saying, "Okay. Thanks. See you there."

That had gone well. Exceedingly well, Cat thought as she slid behind the wheel and started the car. Her brain had kept working. And her insides hadn't gone all squishy, either. The last time had to have been because of the blow she'd taken to the head just before it. It was soooo nice to know that there wasn't a puck bunny deep inside her, yearning to be free.

"I like Logan. He's pimp."

She looked at her son's reflection in the rearview mirror. "Excuse me?"

"*Pimp.*"

Like that helped, she groused silently as she joined the line of cars streaming out of the lot. "I heard you clearly the first time. What do you think pimp means?"

"Pimp means cool."

Apparently *rad* and *da bomb* were now passé. She could hear Martha Stewart saying, *And that's a good thing.* "Cool's the better choice of the two," Cat observed. "I'd prefer you to use it instead."

"Why?"

She briefly met Kyle's gaze in the mirror. "Because pimp comes with a set of very negative connotations."

"Conno whats?"

"Con-no-ta-tions," she said. "Meanings that are implied. Actually, it's more like value judgments." The sheriff's officer waved her out onto the main road and she joined the dash for the interstate. She waited until she was up the ramp and merged in before she added, "I'm sure there are some pimps in the world who are basically nice men forced into their business by deprived childhoods and the lack of legitimate adult employment opportunities, but the rest of us view them as being leeches and abusers and generally unsavory people. To call someone a pimp is an insult."

"How do you know so much about them?"

It wasn't going to help her argument to admit that the only real world contact she'd had with the type was driving past them on the fringes of seedy neighborhoods. She took the discussion to the ridiculous instead. "After you go to bed at night, I read encyclopedias."

"That is *so* lame, Mom."

"Lame is my middle name. I thought you knew."

"That's not what pimp means anymore."

"As you've already explained. It doesn't make any difference. Please don't use it."

"Aunt Millie…" Kyle whined.

Her hands folded in her lap, Millie smiled and continued to look out the windshield. "I'm afraid that I must agree with your mother on this one, Kyle. In my day, one didn't say the word aloud."

"So what did you call them?"

"Well-raised young men and women didn't talk about such subjects. I don't recall even knowing there were such people in the world until your Uncle Tom took me to New Orleans in August of 1973 and I happened to admire one's hat and inquired as to where he'd purchased it. Tom, when he could finally manage to get a word out, was horrified that I'd struck up a conversation with the man. Since I didn't have the slightest idea of why he was so upset over it all, he was forced to broaden my horizons. It was all very shocking, to say the least."

"Did he tell you? The hat guy? Where he got it?"

"He was most helpful. No doubt he was one of the nice but desperate young men your mother was talking about."

"Did you end up getting the hat?"

Millie laughed. "I did. Despite your Uncle Tom's sputtering and muttering the entire time. It's in a box up in the attic. We'll have to get it down someday so you can see it."

"When we get home?" Kyle asked as Cat eased onto the off-ramp at Maize Road.

"You're going straight to bed when we get home," she announced, turning the corner and heading north. "It's way past bedtime. We'll haul it down tomorrow night."

"But I want to visit with Logan."

"We're going to be talking business. And it's a school night. You're going to bed."

A heavy sigh. "I never get to have any fun."

Says the kid who's been taken to the hockey game tonight, been bought posters and is having them personally autographed. But since reason tended to be confrontational when applied to twelve-year-olds, Cat again opted for the ridiculous. "I know. It's my job as a parent to make sure that you're as miserable as possible."

"Ha ha."

"I'm going for a spot in the Ogre Mom Hall of Fame." She

turned in to the drive and hit a button on the visor to open the garage door. "Things are looking pretty good so far. I figure by the time you're eighteen, I should be a shoo-in. I hear they do bronze busts of the inductees."

"You're wearing it out, Mom."

"I'm enjoying myself," she countered as she shifted into Park and the car doors were flung open. "Roll with it, kid, and cut me some slack. It's been a long day and there's miles of road left to go."

"I'm sorry, Catherine," her sister-in-law offered as they trooped up the steps and into the kitchen. "I didn't think before I invited Logan by the house. I should have considered the day you've put in already and not added to it."

Cat hit the wall button to close the garage door. "There's no need to apologize," she assured Millie as Kyle turned on the lights in the family room. "I'm fine. And you're right. It won't take long for Logan and I to get decisions made."

Kyle turned on the television. Knowing that the next step in the process was to throw his body onto the sofa in front of it, she called out, "Shower and bed, buddy. Get moving."

He huffed and made a major production of heading for the rear of the house, but he went.

"Catherine?"

She plopped her purse down on the end of the serving bar. "Yes?"

"I've forgotten why Logan's coming by the house."

Not unexpectedly. The later in the day it got, the wiffier Millie's memory became. That she'd held it together this far had been unusual. "So you can give him the pictures of Tom and him. And so he and I can talk about trading some players."

"Oh, yes. I'll go find them."

Millie started off and Cat headed toward the sink, saying, "I'll put on a pot of coffee."

"He's still a very handsome young man, isn't he?"

Ah, the pictures had been forgotten again. Millie was sitting on one of the bar stools. "I don't know that I'd call him young anymore," Cat observed, "but yes, he's most definitely still handsome."

"He's never been married. And he hasn't had a steady girlfriend in over three years."

Uh-oh. She suspected she knew the answer, but it was always better to be sure. "And how do we know this?"

"I asked him and he told me. While we were waiting for you to join us in the parking lot." ·

All right. If she looked at it calmly, it was all a positive. Logan knew Millie was trying to put them together. As long as *she* made it clear that it was only Millie interested in the possibility, everything would be cool. No cause for mortification. No reason to feel even the least bit awkward around him.

"You were going to find the pictures for Logan."

"Oh, yes. I'll be right back. I know exactly where they are."

Cat smiled weakly. Millie knowing where to find them was one thing, not being distracted along the way to and from was entirely another. They'd been really lucky so far. Millie hadn't started the oven or the stove and then spaced out. And she hadn't noticed that all the candles in the house had disappeared. But they were on borrowed time and Cat knew it. Yeah, she'd suspected that finding a live-in elder care specialist wasn't going to be easy, but geez, she hadn't expected to have to add "non-Nazi personality" to the selection criteria. The storm trooper orthopedic shoes had been the warning sign on the first candidate for the job. The second one had looked like American Gothic on steroids. Cat shuddered at the memories.

And then suddenly straightened. Age! Age was the factor! Both of the candidates the agency had sent over were older women, closer to being Millie's age than her own. She needed someone younger, someone less interested in imposing control and more inclined to be a caring, sympathetic friend.

And the place to find such wonders were the universities! There were three in town. Surely Wichita State, being the biggest and the public one, had a social work or a nursing or a gerontology degree program. She'd check. And she'd check out Kansas Newman, the Catholic university, too. And Friends, the Quaker college. Surely Quakers didn't tolerate Nazi behaviors and attitudes. The placement offices were where she needed to go. The people who ran the jobs centers often found part-time work for students. If anyone knew a nice little coed who would jump at the chance of free room and board and a weekly paycheck, it would be the placement people.

"Where has my brain been?" she asked as she grabbed the phone book. She flipped to the back of the yellow pages. Her jaw dropped. Good God, apparently every college and university in the state had a satellite campus in Wichita. "Who'd a thunk?" she whispered, grinning. "Oh, Lakisha, honey, do I have a job for you tomorrow morning."

The coffeepot sputtered and hissed the last of the water into the filter basket. Cat closed the phone book and got a cup from the cupboard. She had just started to pour when the doorbell rang.

The frantic thud of feet served as a warning to stand clear and as permission to take her time answering it. Cup in hand, she went to the corner where the kitchen met both the family room and the hallway that led past the formal living and dining rooms to the front foyer. From there she could see the glass storm door opening and Logan stepping fast to keep from being swept off the front porch.

Logan teetered on the brick edge of the porch, balanced on the balls of his feet, aware that if the kid got any more en-

thusiastic, he was going to end up in the front bushes. He took
the door in hand, both to steady himself and take control of
it.

"Hi, Logan! C'mon in!"

"Hi, yourself," he said, crossing the threshold. He handed
Kyle the roll of posters in his hand. "It's a school night. Why
aren't you in bed already?"

From down the hall, Cat laughed. "Thank you. Say good-
night, Kyle, and get going. Have you brushed your teeth?"

"Yes," the boy answered as he unrolled the posters and
studied the signatures on the lower corners.

"I'll check the toothbrush, you know."

Kyle looked up at him and muttered, "Mothers."

"Would you rather she didn't care? Consider yourself really lucky that she does and go brush your teeth."

The posters snapped back into a tube shape. "You're a disappointment to men everywhere."

"Oh, well," Logan laughed. "Good night."

"Night." He headed down the hall, paused to kiss Cat's
cheek, said "Night, Mom," and then turned off to the right
and disappeared.

"Sweet dreams," his mother called after him. "And don't
forget to tell Aunt Millie good-night on your way past." Cat
turned her attention back to him and lifted her cup. "Can I
get you a cup of coffee?"

"Thanks. Black, please."

And then she was gone, too. He stood there a second, smiling, and wondering how long it would take her to come back
and invite him past the foyer. Probably forever, he decided.
The last month had proven that Cat was every bit as stubborn
as he was. For the sake of the team, one of them had to give
ground. And since there was coffee on hers…

Logan wandered into the kitchen. "He seems like a really good kid."

"He's a typical twelve-year-old," she replied, setting a steaming cup of coffee on the counter. "Lately we've been pushing the boundaries. Mostly, I think, just to see how firm they are. But, bottom line, he's a joy to have around."

Logan sat on the bar stool and picked up the cup. It was hot, and the brew was good. "Speaking of bottom lines…" he began.

She arched a brow and took a sip before she said, "How's the team's financial one and what can we afford to buy in the player department?"

"Yep."

Standing on the other side of the bar, she leaned down, put her elbows on the counter, and cradled the cup between her hands. "Your best hope is either someone desperate and hungry or consumed with a burning, lifelong desire to live in Wichita."

He forced his mind off the desire to touch the breasts under her nicely fitted knit top. He stared down into his cup to make it easier. "That good, huh?"

"Hey, it's a whole lot better than it was two months ago. Even one month ago. The bank balance may be low, but at least the ink is black for a change."

"Have you put my paychecks back in? And Nic's?"

"No."

"Didn't Nic tell you to do that?"

"Yes, he did. I refuse to do so. You're working, you get paid. I think there's probably a law about that somewhere. I'm not taking any chances."

Damn that stubborn streak of hers. He looked up again, being real careful to bring his attention straight up to her eyes. "Call what we do volunteering, then. We don't need the money. You do."

She took another sip. "Let's agree to disagree on that for the moment, okay? What's important is who you want to trade and how much his replacement is going to cost. Who do you have in mind to let go? And please tell me it's Wheatley."

Whoa, he hadn't expected that turn. "Why?"

"He's the only who's blown off his volunteering. Yeah, he signed up. At Rainbows to work with handicapped kids. But he's yet to darken their doors."

Yeah, well, that was no surprise. Wheatley wasn't a team player. But Cat's thinking on the matter was kinda interesting. Enough that he was willing to play devil's advocate just to see more of it. "He's the leading scorer. He put up two of the four goals tonight."

"Big woo."

"Winning matters, Cat. And you have to put the puck in the net to do it."

"If you have a decent defense, you can get by with fewer goals."

What a difference a month made. He grinned. "You've been reading your *Hockey for Dummies* again, haven't you?"

"I've been reading a lot of books," she countered, her smile dazzling. "Am I right or wrong on the importance of a good defense?"

"You're right. To a certain extent. There's the fan factor to consider, though. They tend to like goals."

"Maybe other places, but not here," she shot back. "Wichita is different. You've got too many things on your mind at the games to watch the crowds, Logan. I don't, so I have been. And they come to watch their friends, the boys, play. For the new fans, winning doesn't matter all that much. They just want to be able to talk about it all the next time they see them. At the school, the Y, the hospital. They buy tickets and sit in the stands because they have a personal connection.

"And Wheatley is the only one who hasn't brought a single solitary new fan into the Coliseum. I don't know what he's like to coach, or how the other boys get along with him, but to me his refusal to haul his own freight in the sales department makes him my vote for *adios, vaya con* Wayne Gretzky."

"That was a pretty impassioned little speech. Have you been practicing it long?"

"Right off the cuff," she said, laughing. "And I'm not even warmed up yet. Tell me you want to trade Tiny or Matt and we're going to go to Fist City."

Oh, shit. The fun part was over. "Well…"

Her smile disappeared. "Which one?" she demanded. "Why?"

"Both," he admitted. "*And* Tyler Vanderossen. Tiny because he's too slow, Hyerstrom because he's not big enough, and Vanderossen because he just can't keep his focus. I think it's his marriage. He spends more time looking up in the stands for his wife than he spends looking down the ice."

She paced back and forth alongside the bar, her hands shoved in her hip pockets. He tried not to think about the nice curves—both front and rear—and couldn't.

"No one's going to want to trade us faster and bigger and laser-focused for slow and small and distracted."

He knew all about distracted. He stared back down at his coffee. "Probably not."

"So what you're basically saying is that you're going to tell them it's time to pack up and go home."

How women could manage to sound both mad and on the verge of tears at the same time… *Eyes. Keep it on the eyes.* He took a deep breath and looked up again. "I'll do it with compassion," he assured her. "I'm not a heartless monster. Hell, if anyone knows what it is like to be asked to turn in your sweater, it's me."

She stopped and grabbed the edge of the counter with both hands. "Can't you get Tiny to go faster? Isn't there some way for Matt to compensate for his size? I'll have a 'come to Jesus' talk with Tyler's wife. I've met her before. She's a twit. I can scare her."

She couldn't scare a mouse. "I've tried on the first two, Cat. I've honestly tried. And if you want a winning team, they're the deficits that have to be fixed. I'm sorry."

"While Wheatley goes blithely on his merry little way."

At least the tears weren't there anymore. Now she was just mad. "I'll give you that Wheatley's a major pain in the ass. He's no coach's dream. If I can find someone with his skills and a better attitude, I'd gladly send him on down the road."

"The rest of the players don't like him very much, do they?"

Uh-oh. He knew the sound of a setup when he heard one. "There's some friction there."

"I have a proposition."

Oh, God. Here it was. "I'm listening."

"Trade Wheatley and see if the others improve with the new guy on board. It may be a simple matter of chemistry. I'll still have the talk with Sherry Vanderossen."

Aw, shit. It wasn't going to make any difference. He knew that. But she didn't and wasn't about to take his word on it. He could kick himself now or later. Right now, he didn't feel like dealing with the wrath of Attila the Hen. "How long are you willing to wait for this miracle?"

"You'll do it?"

God save him from perky and big blue eyes. "How long?"

"Two weeks," she offered, practically dancing. "If Tiny and Matt and Tyler can't get it together in two weeks, I won't say another word and you can do whatever you think needs to be done."

Oh, yeah, like he'd lay money down on that one. He scrubbed his hands over his face and through his hair. Two weeks wasn't long enough, but then two years wouldn't be either. There weren't going to be any miracles where Tiny,

Matt and Vanderossen were concerned. Ever. The sooner the
two weeks started ticking, the better. "What are your plans
for this Friday night?"

She got the coffeepot and topped off their cups as she answered, "Popcorn and a DVD from Wally World. It's Kyle's
pick this week. Which means it'll be short on plot, lousy on
dialogue and long on loud, fiery explosions. Why?"

"If you think changing the chemistry is the answer, then
you get to pick Wheatley's replacement. That way I don't get
blamed when it doesn't work."

"That sounds fair enough." She slid the pot back on the
warming pad. "What does that have to do with Friday night?"

"Nic says the Scorps have made some noises about being
open to trades. Their center isn't bad. You need to take a look
at him, see if he's what you have in mind to be Mr. Magic."

She tuned and leaned back against the counter by the sink,
her arms crossed over her midriff. Her nice, trim midriff. "I
can't leave Millie and Kyle here alone."

"Then bring them along." *They can chaperone,* he silently
added. She stared at the refrigerator door and didn't say anything. "Getting cold feet?"

"No," she answered slowly, "doing the math on what another motel room will do to the expense sheet."

What an innocent. "You guys are welcome to crash with
Nic and me."

She laughed and came off the counter. "Thanks, but no
thanks," she said, grinning as she picked up her mug again.
"We'll get our own room."

Yeah, Nic was right. She was a babe in the woods. Nic always put an accent on *babe,* though. But Logan would behave himself, even if it killed him. It would be just too easy
to sweep Cat off her sweet little feet. Logan cleared his throat
and changed the subject. "Speaking of Millie, where is she?"

"In the study, I think. She went after the pictures of you

and Tom and probably got distracted by something else. I'll go check on her. Be right back." She came around the bar and headed out of the kitchen, adding over her shoulder, "If you want a cookie, help yourself. There are fudge covered grahams in the jar."

A cookie would be nice. But the kind in a jar wasn't what he had in mind. He closed his eyes and shook his head. Needing and wanting were two different things. He didn't need a cookie. Of either kind. The one out of the jar would put him back on the fat sloth track. And the one wearing jeans and the knit shirt would complicate the hell out of his life. Aside from being the owner of the team and his employer, she wasn't the sort of woman who did one-night stands. And he sure didn't want anything more than that.

"She's gone to bed," Cat said from behind him. "I looked for the pictures, but didn't see them anywhere. I hope you don't mind not getting them tonight."

He watched her come around the breakfast bar. Nope, wants got a man into trouble more often than not. The deeper the want, the deeper the regret. "Some other time. Maybe Millie can bring them along to Albuquerque."

"Good idea. I'll make sure they get packed."

He absently twisted his cup on the counter and asked, "Is she forgetting this kind of stuff often?"

"It sort of depends on how much has been crammed into the day. If there's been a lot of information to keep track of, or a lot of tasks involving complex steps, she's more likely to drift away."

"Can she handle traveling anymore?"

Cat shrugged one slim shoulder. "I have no idea. Guess we'll find out this weekend, huh?"

She didn't look all that optimistic about the possibilities. "If you ever need any help with her, all you have to do is ask, okay? Whatever, whenever. Call me."

She looked at him like he'd just morphed into a lost puppy. "Thank you. I really appreciate that."

His stomach quivered. His blood went hot and straight to his groin. And his brain said, *reach for her or run.* "Well, I should be going," he said, climbing off the bar stool. "It's getting late."

"Yeah, tomorrow is a workday," she agreed, coming around the end, apparently intending to walk him to the door. "At least I don't have to be at the rink by five."

He didn't exactly run down the hallway, but he didn't waste any time, either. As retreats went, it probably would have gone into the "cool but desperate" column. "I've moved practices to six if we play the night before," he supplied to cover it. "My days of operating well on four or five hours of sleep are long gone."

She said something about understanding how that went, but her comment didn't require a reply, so he didn't offer one and kept going. He was out on the porch, breathing cool air and with his car and escape in sight when she said, "Hey, Logan?"

He stopped, took a deep breath, and turned back.

"Thanks for being willing to compromise."

He shrugged and waved goodbye without saying another word. He'd already said way too many of them tonight. And made deals he shouldn't have. He'd even invited her out on the road with the team. He was already sorry he'd done that and they weren't even to the motel in Albuquerque yet. Thank God Millie and Kyle were going to be there. Little old ladies and young boys were great buffers.

Chapter Seven

Cat rolled her suitcase down the sidewalk thinking how wonderful it was that sometimes, usually when you least expected it, life served up a reward or two. A weekend away. Alone. Well, not exactly alone, but close enough to have her practically hyperventilating in anticipation. Bless Lakisha's aunt Florence. Bless the exterminator who said the older woman had to vacate her house for a few days. It had been a sign from the gods of bubble baths and romance novels. To ignore it would have invited a lightning bolt.

Florence Jackson was delightful and grateful that she didn't have to go to a motel. Millie and she had taken to each other in an instant and discovered a mutual love of cribbage within the next five. Kyle had been bummed to discover that he wasn't going to get out of a science and a math test after all, but was relieved to know that he wasn't going to have to miss his Saturday morning hockey game. Add in *two* new DVDs, *two* older women who considered him an absolutely darling boy who deserved to be spoiled rotten… On balance, he was happy enough with the way things had worked out that he was even willing to learn to play cribbage.

She stopped beside the underneath storage compartment of the bus and undid the bungee cords that held the cardboard box on top of her suitcase

"Where are Millie and Kyle?"

She smiled up at Logan as he stopped beside her. He was tall and just too handsome to be real. And Lord help her, she couldn't remember ever seeing a man who looked as sexy in a suit and tie. She cleared her throat quietly. "Home," she supplied, handing him the box. "Lakisha's aunt is staying with them this weekend. Millie didn't come right out and say so, but I think she was incredibly relieved to get out of going. She and Florence—that's Lakisha's aunt—have a very busy weekend planned. Music Theater is doing *Chicago* and the library is having a used book sale." She punched down the handle on her suitcase and handed the whole thing over to the bus driver for stowing.

"Kyle's thinking he's fallen into the honeypot," she went on as they ambled toward Nic, who stood beside the bus's open door. "He had his hockey catalogs out this morning, looking for things he can't possibly live without. I begged Millie not to dial any one-eight hundred numbers while I'm gone, but I think she had her fingers crossed when she said she wouldn't."

"So it's just you going along."

It was a good summation. A little lacking in enthusiasm, but accurate. "Me, my freesia bubble bath and a couple of romance novels that have been on my TBR pile forever."

"TBR?"

"To be read. I can't wait to curl up and get lost in a romance. Do you have any idea how long it's been since I've had three whole days of not being a mom-type person? It's going to be bliss, pure bliss."

"They must be big books," Nic said, eyeing the box Logan held.

"Oh, the books are in my carry-on bag." She patted the black nylon courier pouch hanging at her left side. "They're just regular paperback size. The box is full of trip munchies. I baked brownies and made a big batch of cereal mix. There's some granola bars, too. And a four pound package of string cheese—individually wrapped portions, of course—and two boxes of those little buttery elf crackers."

Nic slid a wide-eyed sort of look at Logan. Logan's smile looked slightly pained. He cleared his throat. "We're going to stop along the way to eat."

"You never know when traveling," she countered, wondering if he had a wedgie or something. "It's always best to be prepared. Especially when the bus is as old as this one is." She took the box from him. "Are there assigned seats?"

Nic answered. "I'd suggest you take one of the ones up front. That way you're not going to be bothered as much by everyone moving up and down the aisle."

"Sounds good to me."

She started around them, then stopped as Jace Dody bounded past her and onto the first step. He turned back, grinning. "Hey, Ms. Talbott. Are you going with us this time out?"

"I am." Since she wasn't going any farther than the front row of seats, she held out the box, saying, "And if you'd be so kind, Jace, as to put this box of goodies somewhere on the bus where everyone can get into it, I'd be really appreciative."

"You're awesome, Ms. T."

She followed him up and into the bus, glad that someone appreciated her procurement and late-night cooking efforts. Too bad Nic and Logan didn't know how to have a good time on a bus. It was their loss, though, and she wasn't going to waste one minute of reading pleasure over it. Cat dropped into the first seat, scooted until her back was against the side, then turned and put her feet up. She was into chapter two by the time the doors closed and the bus lumbered out of the parking lot.

Cat opened her eyes and looked around. God, the last thing she remembered was seeing the sign for the World's Deepest Hand Dug Well and thinking that it might be something they should stop and see on the way home. The sun had been drifting slightly toward the west then and they'd been in Greensburg. Kansas, still, but definitely with a desert edge. Now… She studied the town and land outside the window as the boys filed past her and out the door. The land was not just past the edge of desert, it was well into the middle of it. The buildings were adobe—white and pink and tan, their windows lit with neon signs. One of them claimed that the Tucumcari Café had good eats.

She scrubbed her hands over her face and swung her feet to the floor. Her book tumbled to the seat beside her and she quickly found the last passage she remembered reading, then laid it facedown so she could come back to it when they started rolling again.

Her knees creaked as she stood and a twinge shot through her lower back when she straightened. Thinking that being able to stand under the overhead storage compartment was the one good thing about being short, she looked back to see if there was a break in the manly parade that she could slide into. Nic, the very last man in the line, grinned and made one for her, inviting her to step into it with a sweep of his hand.

Cat smiled her thanks and forced her stiffened joints to move. She managed to be fairly smooth until she started down the steps. It was there that her knees and ankles had to really coordinate. They didn't. And Logan was there to see the less than graceful effort.

His grin went from ear to ear as he stepped up and held out

both hands for her. Under normal circumstances she'd have hesitated to take them. But having all the elegance of a drunken sailor made a difference; accepting help was a whole lot less embarrassing than falling off the bus. She grabbed his hands, held on for dear life, and let him guide her down the steps.

A series of realizations stuck her as she reached the ground and looked up at him. He smelled really, really good. Spicy and woodsy. His hands were huge, but gentle. And she liked the way hers felt wrapped up in them. She liked standing in front of him even more. She felt warm and wonderfully sheltered. God, he'd be heaven to kiss. And, judging by how his smile softened, he knew just what she was thinking.

She mentally kicked herself and pulled her hands free. To salvage her dignity, she stepped to the front of the bus and looked around Tucumcari. The boys were spreading out, heading in twos and threes toward various fast-food places. Will Rivera was the only one alone and he was walking slowly, his head down, toward a Laundromat.

She looked over her shoulder at Logan and Nic. "Where's Will going?"

Neither one of them moved to where they could see him. Nic shrugged. "Who knows. He's a goalie."

She thought about it and then frowned. "If that's supposed to be an explanation, I'm not getting it."

"Goalies are different," Nic explained. "They go around in their own world. It's a zone thing. It's kinda like they can never quite come all the way out of it and be regular."

She must have looked as confused as she still was because Logan added, "It takes incredible focus to be a goalie. They hone in and the stuff on the edges just floats out there, not important or worth reacting to until it comes into the center. It's a playing skill that they have a hard time shutting off sometimes."

At the moment, Will Rivera looked honed in on a bank of Maytags. "He won't wander off into the street, will he?"

"If a car comes into the zone, he'll knock it out of the way," Logan assured her as he stepped to her side. He slipped his hand around her upper arm and gently turned her away from the street. "Let's go see if the eats really are good."

Whether she was walking any more smoothly than before, Cat couldn't say. Physically, all she was aware of was the warmth and strength of Logan's hand. Beyond that, in a vague sort of way, loomed the Tucumcari Café.

She blinked, found her brain and made it focus. Oh, God. She could tell just by looking at the place that everything on the menu was breaded, fried and served up on a bun. A chef salad was her only hope and, if they even had one, it would be nothing more than a few chunks of iceberg lettuce, a handful of processed ham cubes and some shavings of American cheese.

And the food options aside… Judging by the number of pickup trucks in the parking lot—and the ropes and rifles in the rear window racks inside them—the café was a local hangout. It most definitely wasn't the kind of place she would have gone into without a cool mountain on one side of her and an Italian fireplug on the other. Nic and Logan were going to be seriously overdressed.

And she was right. All conversation stopped as they came through the door. Heads turned. Eyebrows went up and the brims of Resistols were pushed back. Her instincts said to turn and walk out. Logan's and Nic's apparently said otherwise because they kept right on going. The hum of conversation was just starting back up as they reached the only empty booth in the place. Four older Hispanic-looking men occupied the booth behind the seat Nic and Logan slid into. Two women—the younger of them looking like she'd been in a car wreck that morning—were in the one behind Cat.

Oh, yeah, just a great place, she silently groused as she tried to find a comfortable place to sit on the vinyl-covered bench. The center springs were totally shot. If she sat there, her chin was only inches off the table. But shot was better than having the springs poke her in the butt like they did on either side of the hole.

She was resigning herself to Midgetville when the waitress brought over three plastic glasses of water and three plastic-covered menus. They all ordered coffee and Mavis— she'd pointed to the name embroidered on her pink uniform—left them to go get cups and the coffeepot. Cat studied the menu as Logan and Nic did the same. The dinner choices were laid out simply enough: beef, pork, mutton. No salads except those that came with the dinner specials. You could get potatoes fixed six different ways, though. Or opt for three warmed tortillas instead.

Mavis came back, filled the cups and then set the coffeepot on the table so she could get her order pad and pen out of her pocket.

Nic ordered the KC strip, cooked Philly black-and-blue style. Mavis gave him a long look and he changed it to very rare. Logan ordered the strip as well, but went for medium. Mavis didn't have a problem with that. Both of them picked the Freedom Fry option and passed on the hominy side vegetable. Cat handed her menu over to the woman and took a chance on a medium rib eye. Mavis thought that a steak all alone on a plate was weird, but she eventually shrugged and walked off.

Cat was taking the first sip of what was an amazingly good cup of coffee when Logan reached into his jacket pocket and brought out a folded square of paper. He handed it to her, saying. "I brought the stat and personal sheets in so you could take a look at them. Crockett is the Scorp's center."

She unfolded it, read and winced. "Poor kid."

Logan leaned back and cocked a brow. "Why do you say that?"

"His first name is David. How cruel can a parent be?"

Nic frowned. "Huh?"

"Davy Crockett?"

He shook his head. "Still not getting it."

Unbelievable. Cat started reading again. "You had some lousy teachers along the way."

"I thought they did real well, considering."

She looked back up at him. "Considering what?"

"They were fitting it all in around practices and traveling."

"You're telling me that you went to a school where hockey came before education?"

He shrugged. "I played Junior Triple A. We didn't go to a regular school. It was more like tutors came to us. Logan came out of pretty much the same deal."

Logan shrugged one shoulder and nodded. "Good God," Cat whispered, stunned. Not that she should be, she reminded herself. When she'd lived in Texas, she'd often thought that football was more important to people than academics.

"We always finished in the top five in the nation," Nic added. "Had pro scouts watching us from the time we were fifteen or so."

Cat sighed. "It's too depressing for words."

A hint of a smile lifted the corners of Logan's mouth. "Just read the scouting report on Crockett. It doesn't matter whether or not he knows his multiplication tables."

He was right, not that that didn't depress her even more. She was halfway through the personal bio stuff when she heard the woman behind her say, "So he roughs you up every now and then."

Cat sat back, stunned, and turned her ear toward the conversation. Across the table Logan said, "Ignore it, Cat. It's none of our business."

"If you stopped going to get stitches, honey, you two would get along better. The cops showing up at the house just pisses him off all over again."

Cat's mouth fell open. She started to turn. Logan reached across the table and grabbed her by the wrists. "We are in Tucumcari, New Mexico," he growled. "These people have the means to kill us."

"Honey, he wouldn't beat you if he didn't love you."

"That's it!" Cat declared, wrenching her hands from Logan's loose grasp.

"Catherine, don't!"

"Aw, shit," Nic whimpered.

At the edge of her vision, she could see Logan with his head buried in his hands. Nic's eyes were huge. She turned her back on them and stepped up to the next table. She planted her hands on it and leaned forward, looking squarely at the young woman with blonde hair, black eyes and a stitched lip.

"Look, honey," Cat began. "I couldn't help but hear the advice to the lovelorn that you've been getting from whoever this person is here. And no, you don't know me. But—as one stranger to another—as one woman to another—let me tell you that no one—*no one!*—has a free pass to beat up on you. And anyone who takes a swing at you sure as hell doesn't love you. And anyone who tells you otherwise has taken one too many blows to their own head. They don't care about you any more than whoever's beating you does. All they want is someone in the same miserable boat they are.

"If you don't like getting beat up, get out! If you need help escaping…" Cat straightened and pointed to the parking lot. "That bus is going to Albuquerque. You want a ride, we'll be glad to give you one. We'll see that you get to a women's shelter. That you're safe. If you've got kids, I'll go with you to get them. He *luvs* you, my sweet Aunt Fanny. He loves having someone weaker to bully and beat. And that's all."

The girl looked across the table and squeaked, "Mom?"

Mom? Mom was the one telling her to take the beatings? Oh, this was beyond believable! Cat took a deep breath and launched back in. "Okay, take a look at this situation. A good look. Your mother obviously is a victim of abuse if she thinks a black eye and a split lip are signs of undying love and devotion. But the fact that she's having to talk you into being a passive victim just like her tells me you're not nearly as happy about it as she is. Is this the kind of life you want for your daughters when they grow up?"

"Don't have no—"

Whatever else she'd been about to say died on her gasp as a wiry, ball-cap-wearing dirt ball stepped up beside Cat and announced, "Danae, it's time for you to come home." Danae's good eye filled with tears. Cat looked the man up and down. He did the same to her. His lip curled. "Who the hell are you? Some state social worker?"

She was squaring up to give him a load of verbal buckshot when Logan's hands came down on her shoulders. Not hard, but hard enough to momentarily knock the words off her tongue. "Her name's Pollyanna," Logan said, turning her around, "and she's going back to her booth now."

She was glaring up at him and he was pushing her into the seat when the beater said, "Get up and get out to the car, Danae."

Logan leaned close. Fire blazed in his eyes. *"Let…it…go."*

"You gave it a shot," Nic chimed in. "It's her choice."

Cat clenched her teeth and tried not to look over her shoulder at the sound of the girl sliding off the vinyl seat. Logan held her gaze and slowly straightened. Danae suddenly stumbled past him, her upper body way ahead of her scrambling feet. Cat held her breath and sighed in relief when an arm shot out two booths up and caught her.

"What you do in your home is your business. When you do it in front of me, it's mine."

Logan! Her attention snapped back to him. That scary cold fire in his eyes, he stood squarely in the other man's path.

The bastard who had apparently shoved Danae toward the door did a bit of upper body bobbing that Cat supposed was to be a demonstration of confidence. "She's my wife."

"That's not the point," Logan countered, clearly neither impressed nor deterred. "You don't lay a mean hand on a woman. Any woman. Anytime. Anywhere."

A curled lip. Disdain. He'd used that one on her. "Says you?"

Logan didn't waver, didn't so much as blink. "If I don't know about it, I can't stop you from doing it. But if I do, I will."

"Nice tie, dude."

Nic sucked a breath. Cat stopped breathing altogether.

"Touch it and I'll flatten your nose."

It was an invitation, a warning. And Danae's husband reached out, and with the tip of his finger, plumbed the depths of macho stupidity. Just one punch. Lightning-fast, straight on, accurate and hard. Moron Man went airborne, the soles of his cowboy boots slightly higher than his head. The downward arc of his flight put him flat on his back in the middle of a table. The two cowboys sitting there had seen him coming and had vaulted to their feet, their dinner plates in hand, a half second before impact.

And what an impact it was. Cat's jaw dropped. It was better than in the movies. Wood splintered and chunks of it flew in all directions. China coffee cups shattered. Plastic water glasses went spinning through the air. Catsup and mustard bottles, the little creamer tubs, packets of sugar, the basket of dinner rolls… It was a mess. A glorious mess with Danae's abusive husband lying right in the middle of it, wailing in pain and hold his hands over his mouth and nose. Talk about perfect poetic justice!

"I'm calling the cops!" Mavis shouted.

"Thank you," Logan said calmly as he stood there watching the man kick and thrash in the debris. "That would be nice."

Nic grinned and slid out to stand beside him. "Gotta wonder how many brain cells the guy's missing, don't ya?"

Mavis came storming over. "Someone's paying for that broken table and china!"

Cat snagged her purse and pulled out her wallet. "I'll write you a check."

"I want cash."

"And I want world peace," Cat shot back, writing. "You'll take a check or nothing at all. One hundred and fifty should buy you top-of-the-line replacements."

"It'll cost at least three hundred."

"Get real." Cat snorted and tore the check off the pad. She held it out toward the sputtering Mavis. "It's one-fifty or your lawyer can talk to mine. What's it going to be?"

Mavis glared and put her hands on her hips.

"All right, folks," someone boomed from the front door. Mavis snatched the check and stomped off as the speaker asked, "What's going on? Danae's out front bawlin' her eyes out and sayin' someone's in here tryin' to kill Billy."

"She should be so damn lucky," Cat declared—loudly—as she slid out to join Logan and Nic. *Billy, huh? Billy Butthead.*

The patch on the boomer's shoulder said he was with the Tucumcari police department. His name tag said Alvarez. The size of his belly said he spent a lot of time at Mavis's counter. "Ma'am," he drawled, meeting her gaze, "you and your friends want to step outside with me a moment?" He didn't wait for her to say yes or no; he just turned and headed back to the door, adding, "Mavis, get Billy a towel with some ice in it."

As Logan motioned for her to lead the way, Nic tossed two twenties on their table and said, "And when you get done with that, Mavis, we'll take our dinners in a to-go box, please."

"Are you happy?" Logan asked as they crossed the parking lot toward the squad car.

"Actually, yes I am," she admitted. Several of the boys were standing beside the bus, spectating. And probably speculating, too. Oh, well. "I stood up for what's right. In defense of the weak and powerless. And when push came to shove, you did too." She took him by the arm and made him stop. "You're a good man, Logan Dupree." She stretched up on her toes and kissed him on the cheek.

He kinda checked a wince and rolled his eyes instead. And then he looked past her at their oohing and laughing team. "Knock it off and get on the bus!"

No one scrambled to obey, but they did inch toward the open door. "Hey, Stover!" Nic called as he joined the two of them. "Take Vanderossen to watch your back and go inside and get our to-go boxes, will ya?"

Officer Alvarez cleared his throat and jerked his head in a silent command to close the distance a bit more. When they reached the side of his car, he looked between the three of them and asked, "Wanna tell me what happened in there?"

"I'd be more than glad to," Cat volunteered. She started at the top, introducing each of them, and then told him the whole thing. Three-part harmony and pantomimes thrown in at no extra charge. Halfway through, Nic started singing the "uh-huh, that's right" chorus. Logan apparently didn't think she needed any more help than that. He leaned back against the squad car with his arms crossed and stared up at the streetlights.

When she got to the part where Alvarez had made his entrance, the officer held up his hand. "Tell you what," he said. "I'd rather not spend the next hour and a half writin' all this down in a report. So if you folks would be willin' to just mosey on down the road, I'd be willin' to forget it ever happened."

"That seems quite reasonable," Cat offered.

"And the next time you all are through here on your way to or from Albuquerque and thinkin' about eatin' dinner, stop in somebody else's town."

"We can do that," Logan announced as he came off the car. "Have a good day, Officer."

Cat trotted up beside him. The look he shot her was borderline disgusted. "What?" she demanded. "We're not in any trouble."

He stopped on a dime. "For someone who says they hate fighting, you're damn good at squaring up to them."

"Well, there's a huge difference between fighting for the sake of fighting and fighting for a principle or in self-defense or the defense of others who can't."

"She's got ya there," Nic said as he walked past. Logan glared after him.

"Oh, c'mon," Cat pleaded. "What else could I have done and lived with myself, Logan? Tell me."

The steam slowly went out of him. With a sigh, he raked his fingers through his hair. "You have to pick your fights," he said gently. "The ones you can't win, aren't worth wading into. That one wasn't worth it, Cat."

"But you know that only in hindsight. What if all she's been waiting for is someone to tell her she doesn't have to be a punching bag and offer her a ride out of town?"

"People do not grow backbones at the sight of a bus."

"No, it takes time and encouragement. If she thinks about what I said and it helps her along the road to escaping, then it was worth it. If she thinks about how you stepped in to protect her, maybe she'll decide she's worth more than her mother and her husband say she is. If that moves her off the dime, then the cost of buying Mavis new furniture is worth it."

"You are—without a doubt—the most idealistic, optimistic person I've ever known."

God, when he was being nice, he was beyond yummy. "Is that good or bad?"

He grinned. "It means you're a walking, talking threat to public peace and safety."

"That's better than boring any day."

"Boring you are not."

Stover and Vanderossen walked up and handed her a stack of three square foam containers. "Thanks, guys. Did you happen to snag us some silverware?"

"Sporks were all they had." Stover handed them to Logan, said, "Nice job in there, Coach," and then, chuckling, climbed aboard the bus.

Logan took the meals from her and motioned with his head toward the steps. "After you, Ms. Quixote."

Quixote, huh? That was enlightening. She stepped into her seat area and waited for Logan so they could sort out which container was whose. As he held them and she inspected the contents, she said, "Your education wasn't limited. You know who Davy Crockett was, don't you? You were just yanking my chain."

His grin was an admission. "Nic's wasn't limited, either. He just hates to read. He doesn't read at all now and I suspect he didn't do one lick more of it than he had to back then."

"What are you reading now?"

"I'm just about done with a Ludlum. Read it years ago and remembered that I liked it. Still do."

With the rib eye found, she took a spork from him and sat down. "Well, if you get done, and need something else to read, I'll share my stock."

His gaze went to the book on the seat beside her. "I wouldn't be caught dead reading that stuff."

He was one of *those*. "You have no idea what's between the covers."

"Don't want to know, either."

"You're missing something good."

"Yeah, right," he said with a snort as he headed toward the back of the bus.

Cat shook her head, opened the lid of the box, and considered the slab of meat and then the plastic combination spoon and fork utensil. She'd about decided to try to stab the steak and just gnaw around the edges when Logan reappeared. He handed her a wood-handled steak knife.

"Compliments of Nic's sticky fingers," he explained. She was laughing when he turned to the driver. "Harold, let's get this thing rolling before Mavis counts the silverware and all hell breaks loose."

"I'll mail them back when we get to Albuquerque," she promised Logan as the bus moved forward and he lurched past her.

"Polly!"

Not really. A real Pollyanna Goody Two-shoes would get up and take the knives back right then and there. She cut a bite of the steak and popped it into her mouth. And she wouldn't be wishing that Nic had managed to steal a bottle of steak sauce while he was at it.

It was a sure bet that no true-blue Polly would spend so much as a single solitary second wondering what would happen if she ever had a chance to prove she had just a touch of puck bunny in her soul.

Chapter Eight

How the woman could walk, read and pull a suitcase at the same time... Okay, so she wasn't walking fast. But she was moving in a deliberate direction, and she wasn't in danger of knocking anyone over or smacking into a wall. All in all, it was a pretty good trick. Logan waved the boys onto the elevator and let them go ahead without him. Judging by Cat's pace, the car would be up to the third floor and back by the time she reached the button to call it. *If* she came up out of her book long enough to think about pushing any buttons. He'd be a gentleman and wait for her, make sure she got to where she was supposed to go.

What an interesting woman she was. Man, he'd never seen anyone do righteously indignant better than she had in the Tucumcari Café. She deserved either an Oscar or a pulpit for that performance. And the parking lot reenactment for Officer Alvarez... That one had been worth a second Oscar. How a woman two seconds away from being slapped in cuffs for creating a public disturbance could be so damn oblivious to that fact and bubbly and cute… Not that he hadn't been grateful for it. His butt had ended up on the bus instead of in jail on an assault charge because Alvarez had been just as damn dazzled as he was. And the way she'd handled Mavis after the table had been busted… Logan grinned. *And I want world peace.*

God. And he'd once thought she didn't have the grit and the growl to be an owner. Well, she'd impressed him on every count so far. She'd gotten them more ice time, put the boys out to do volunteer work and dragged more people in to see the games. If she could pull off a good trade with the Scorps, he'd admit that he'd been totally wrong about her. A woman who could execute a strong building plan, scrap with the best of them *and* make a kick-ass brownie. So what if half the sprinkles were pink? In the big scheme of things, that didn't matter.

And she could hold a book and turn a page with just one hand. The walking part of the act slowed to almost nothing while she did it, but given the look on her face, it probably had more to do with what was going on in the story than anything else. She could give Rivera lessons on focus.

She came to a stop beside him. Apparently completely unaware that she wasn't the only one waiting for the elevator. He looked up at the numbers, saw the car was on its way back down, and then reached out to lightly tap the top edge of her book.

Her gaze snapped up instantly. She stiffened for the second or two it took for her to blink a couple of times and recognize him.

"In your zone?" he asked, grinning as she relaxed.

"I guess so." She glanced down at the page number, then closed the book and shoved it into her courier bag.

"Well, I'm afraid you're going to have to come out of it

for a while tonight," Logan said as she punched the already lit call button. "We're meeting Ralph Van Ecks for dinner and drinks in the restaurant at nine."

The bell dinged and the door opened. They stepped into the empty car with Cat pushing the button for the second floor—his floor, too—and slowly saying, "Van Ecks… Van Ecks…" He could practically see a lightbulb over her head go on. "I met him at Tom's funeral. He's the one with the thing for cleavage." Another lightbulb went on. She checked her watch. "An hour and a half. No problem."

The bell dinged and the door opened. "I'll stop by the room for you a few minutes before," Logan offered as they rolled their suitcases into the hall. "What's your number?"

She took the little white key holder from the side of her purse. "Two fifteen."

"Nic and I are in two thirty-four if you need anything."

She nodded in a vague sort of way and they both turned to read the sign that told them their rooms were on opposite sides of the elevator shaft, at opposite ends of the motel.

Logan watched her walk away, her floral fabric suitcase in tow. Oh, yeah, she and Rivera had a lot in common. Except that the goalie's inattention didn't bother him the way Cat's did. Women, as a rule, didn't ignore him. That Cat apparently could… He tilted his head and smiled as she rounded the corner and disappeared from sight. Yeah, well, let her try to zone him out when he showed up at her door later. If there was such a thing as asbestos panty hose, she better have a pair.

Holding the wineglasses between the fingers of one hand, he knocked on the door of two fifteen with the other. It opened in two seconds flat and without Cat having even bothered to look through the peephole to see who it was.

"Hi," he managed to get out as his brain took in the shimmery black hose, the black spike heels and the deep pink silk robe. Just-above-the-knee deep pink robe. Technically, she was covered, perfectly decent. And it had zero effect on the direction of his thoughts. He swallowed and held out one of the wineglasses. "I brought you something."

"Thanks. I love Zin."

Yeah, he'd guessed that; it was pink. He hadn't guessed how damn well it'd go with her robe, though. She looked like she'd just fallen out of an ad, one of those drink-our-wine-and-you'll-get-blow-your-mind-lucky ads. Jesus. He should probably rethink this whole get-her-attention thing. He hadn't planned on it being a two-way street.

"Where's Nic?" she asked as she closed the door behind him. "Isn't he going to dinner with us?"

Nic? Oh, yeah, Nic. "Someone has to ride herd on the team. Since he's the assistant coach, it's his job tonight."

She sipped, smiled and stepped into the bathroom. "I'm almost ready. Give me two minutes."

And then, in an act of pure mercy, she closed the door. Logan took a big gulp of wine, shook his head hard and headed for the desk on the far side of the room. He threw himself into the chair and swiveled around, looking for the remote to turn on the television. It wasn't on the desk. But her purse was. Not the brown leather thing she'd had on the bus. This one was little and black and spangly. If she was planning to wear a dress that went with it…

The remote was on the foot of the bed. He snatched it up and hit the power button and then the code for ESPN. What sport, what teams, didn't matter. His brain needed a distraction. Soccer was on one channel. Talk shows on two of the others. He went back to the soccer.

The bathroom door opened and Cat stepped out, wineglass in hand. He took one look at her and turned off the TV. It was too late for distraction, too late to rethink his plan. He was in trouble. Deep, deep trouble. He'd had no idea. None. If he could get through the evening without making a serious move on her, it would be a fricking miracle.

"Is something wrong?" she asked. She turned her hip and looked back over her bare shoulder. "Is my hem coming down? Is there a stain?"

They needed to be someplace public and quick. He took another gulp of wine and stood. "You look just fine."

"Then why do you look like a cat choking on a hair ball? If something's wrong, for God's sake tell me what it is."

There was honest and then there was too honest. He took a deep breath and hoped for the best. "That neckline's pretty daring."

Her mouth fell open and she turned to look at herself in the mirror over the bureau. "Oh, please!" she said, facing him again. "It's very conservative for evening wear these days." She grinned. "And besides, I told you Van Ecks has a thing for cleavage. This is meant to totally distract him from the negotiations."

Distract? "He's a geezer. It's likely to kill him."

She laughed. "I doubt that. If he keels over, it'll be because he's hoping I'll straddle him to do CPR."

Oh, God. He could have done without that mental image. Logan picked up her purse and took it to her. "Are you ready to go?"

"Absolutely."

She put her glass on the bureau and headed for the door. Logan drained his before setting it down and following. "Just out of curiosity," he said as they waited for the elevator. "Do you always travel with that dress in the suitcase?"

"Sure do. It doesn't take up much room and it's always better to be prepared for the unexpected cocktail invitation than not. Having to shop for a dress at the last minute in a town you don't know is a major frustration."

He could write a book on frustration right about now. And he suspected that it was only going to get worse as the evening went on. The call light blinked out and the doors opened. Jace, Georgie, and Tiny were inside the car, obviously headed for the motel pool.

"Miss-usss T.," Jace said as they stepped in to join them for the ride down.

Tiny swallowed a couple of times, but managed to whisper, "Wow."

"Wow?" Georgie countered, grinning. "Nuh-uh. That's hot damn, honey, I'm in three twenty."

A pretty pink color washed over Cat's cheeks. "Thank you, I think," she offered as the doors opened and she led everyone out.

Logan motioned for his players to go ahead. They stopped dead just outside in the hall and watched Cat walk toward the lobby. None of them were actually drooling. But it was only a matter of time.

"Aren't you all on your way to somewhere?" Logan asked dryly. All three of them started. With stupid, knowing grins they wished him a fun evening and headed off toward the pool, elbowing each other into the walls.

Fun. Yeah, right. Business meetings were never fun. Either they were so boring he could barely stay awake, or they were verbal chess games where it was against the rules to say anything in plain English. Adding in a sexy blonde in an off-the-shoulder dress with a neckline that screamed no bra and a hem that was going to slide to mid-thigh the instant she sat down…. Well, he wasn't likely to fall asleep, that was for sure. But God help them both if Cat was counting on any help from him in the negotiating department. His brain had slipped below his belt and it wasn't the least bit interested in rising to any occasion that had to do with hockey.

* * *

Logan shook Ralph's hand, thanked him for being reasonable, and then left him to wait for his driver at the motel's front door. Cat stood at the elevators, her smile wide and her eyes twinkling bright enough that he could see her excitement from across the lobby. She'd been incredible. The minute she'd walked into the restaurant, Ralph's jaw had dropped and he'd never fully recovered. She hadn't taken advantage of him, though. She'd been fair and honest. Both teams were getting a good deal. And Ralph could go to the next owners' meeting with bragging rights to what were probably the only trade negotiations in the history of the game to have been sealed with a hug and kiss on the cheek.

Yeah, it had all gone down beautifully. And he hadn't been the lump he'd imagined going in, either. It was hard to believe that being blind in one eye could be a positive, but having Cat sit on that side had really helped. Not exactly out of sight, out of mind. He'd have to be in a coma not to know she was there. She smelled like island flowers of some sort and her laugh made him warm from head to toe. But not being able to see her unless he deliberately turned his head had worked for keeping his hands to himself and his brain in the conversation.

Now all he had to do was get up to the second floor and through the good-nights without doing something stupid. It was a short distance. It wouldn't take long. It was possible. Probably a little more possible for a man who hadn't had six ounces of booze in a ninety-minute stretch, but he was willing to give it his best shot. On the polluted scale, he wasn't exactly a superfund site.

The elevator opened. Cat stepped in and held the door. He trotted the last of the distance and punched the button for the second floor as he went past the panel. Cat stood on his good side and beamed up at him as the doors slid closed.

"That went exceedingly well, don't you think?"

"It went great. You're a natural."

"And it was fun, too. I didn't expect that. Who else has players they might want to trade?"

Ding, lurch, slide and they were at the crossroads. A stone-cold sober blind man would have said they'd just have to check it out later, congratulated her again and wished her a good night. "Do you want to see the folder?"

"Yes, please."

His conscience staggered and burped something about giving her a fair chance. "It's in the room. Do you want to come get it now or have me give it to you the next time we're on the bus?"

"Oh, now. I'm on a roll."

More like thin ice on a warm day, he thought as they headed down the hall. His mom had always said things happened for a reason. Maybe this was one of those things. Cat wasn't a ditz and she hadn't just fallen off the turnip truck. She had to know that going to a man's motel room had some potential for one thing leading to another. Maybe she wanted it to. He'd just take his cues from her.

Jesus. There wouldn't be any cues to take if Nic was in the room. Nic could have found a twinkie somewhere and invited her up to check out his scars. Or just be sprawled out alone, watching a game in his underwear.

Logan put the key card it the slot and opened the door just enough to poke his head in and check the mirror over the bureau. The beds were empty. With a sigh of relief, he pushed the door all the way open, then stepped back and held it to let Cat go first.

Logan stood there a second with the door in his hand, wondering what he should do with it. Close it and say to hell with appearances. Throw the bolt bar so it didn't actually close, and look like a good guy.

He threw the bar just as Cat said, "What's this?"

She was standing at the foot of his bed, a *gotcha* grin going from ear to adorable little ear. "A book," he answered, knowing he was in for a grilling.

"What kind of book?" All sweetness and light and faked innocence. She glanced at the back cover. She looked up at him and batted her lashes. "Well, I'll be. It's a romance. Wasn't it just this afternoon that you were telling me that you weren't interested in this sort of reading material?"

He leaned his shoulder against the wall and crossed his arms. "I finished the Ludlum and the bookstore downstairs didn't have anything on the rack except that kind of stuff. My choice was between picking one or doing without, so I decided to see what they're all about."

"And what do you think so far?"

Well, she'd asked. "Any book that has the heroine boinking the hero—in great detail, I might add—on page fifteen is okay by me."

Her mouth fell open in that delicious way it always did when she was surprised. "No way." She flipped it over and looked at the cover. "It's an historical."

"Check it out yourself. Page fifteen. I marked it."

"Ohmigod," she whispered as she sank down onto the bed. She went to the first page, then back to the fifteenth, and then shook the book at him. "No self-respecting Victorian woman would do such a thing!"

Gorgeously indignant again. Logan grinned. "Obviously she's not all that self-respecting."

"Then she's not a heroine. There are standards." She tossed the book down on the bed. "That's just awful."

"I was thinking that was the redeeming part of it. The hero is kinda…" He shrugged.

"He's kinda what? A first-class jerk?"

"Well, more like a wimp. He doesn't think like a man." Cat's brow went up and Logan gave it another try. "He spends a lot of time wondering what the heroine's thinking and feel-ing. Real men don't do that."

"They don't?"

She'd read way too many of those books. "Have you seen those redneck comedy guys? One of them says that men think only about beer and seeing something naked. He's right."

She laughed. "I don't believe it. They think about hockey. I know that for a fact."

He came off the wall and turned to adjust the thermostat. "Playing hockey's how you earn beer money and pick up chicks."

She was laughing again and he was rolling the temp down another five degrees when the door flew open and Nic blew past, making a beeline for the honor bar.

"Eh," Nic said as he turned the key and pulled open the door. "Don't let me interrupt or anything."

"What are you doing?" Cat asked.

He took four bottles of beer out. "They cut us off in the bar."

"There's a good call," Logan observed as Nic kicked the bar door shut. "Where are you going with those?"

Nic didn't pause. "The pool," he answered on his way out. "There's a girl down there wearing a thong and a top the size of a couple of Band-Aids."

The door banged against the bolt bar. Logan looked over at Cat and gestured toward it in a silent combination of *ta-dah!* and *I rest my case.*

She laughed, her eyes sparkling. "You paid him to come through here and say that."

He shook his head and held up his hand, palm out. "Hon-est to God."

"Have you spent all evening thinking about…" She started and blushed.

Just too adorable. "Beer never once crossed my mind. But the something naked part? Oh, yeah."

"It's really not a low neckline."

And she really wasn't offended by his interest. "It's low enough for me. I can imagine the rest."

She thought about that for a second and then took a deep breath and stood. "I better be going."

As statements of intent went, it lacked a little on the conviction side. Nothing ventured, nothing gained. "It's either that or bolt the door so Nic can't get in for more beer."

She gave that some thought, too. Her smile was definitely halfhearted. "I should go. May I have the folder?"

She wasn't out the door yet. And she was a thinker. The longer he gave her to do it, the more likely she'd be to keep on talking, to stay. He nodded and took his time getting to the desk. He had the folder in hand when she said, "Logan? May I be real up front with you?"

Oh, man, she was so predictable. He managed to keep himself from laughing out loud, but there was nothing he could do about the smiling part.

"Okay, bad choice in words," she said, pressing her hands to her bare chest. Her blush deepened as his smile went wider. "But aside from that…" She sobered. Then went straight to apologetic. "Look, I'd be lying if I said I didn't find you attractive, Logan."

Aw, damn. This wasn't what he wanted to hear.

"I'd also be lying if I said that I wasn't flattered and tempted by your interest. But I know that getting involved with you is a bad idea. I'm the owner. You're the coach. I'm a long-term woman and you're a short-term man."

"You can save the you're a country girl and I'm big city guy part."

"You see my point, don't you?"

"Yeah. I see it." He was the one who'd given her the time

to think. It was his own damn fault she'd remembered that there was a line. He handed her the folder and gestured toward the door. "Doesn't mean I'm not disappointed, though."

"Me, too. But I know that resisting temptation, just walking away, is the smart thing to do."

She was right. He knew it. He reached past her and pulled open the door for her. She stopped short of the threshold and looked up at him.

"I have a confession to make." She touched her lower lip with her tongue and took a shaky breath. "I didn't wear this dress just to distract Ralph. I also wanted to knock your socks off."

Whoa. If she could be that honest, so could he. "You succeeded. My toes are kinda curled, too."

"I also wanted you to know that I'm not a Pollyanna."

The jury was still out on that one, but he knew what he was supposed to say. "I got the message. Loud and clear."

Her smile was faint. She didn't move. God, he'd only thought her laugh had made him warm. The *kiss me* look was smokin'. It was also an invitation and he decided to take it. "Wondering," he asked softly, "just how much further you can go and still be safe?"

She blinked. And checked a backward step. "What makes you think that?"

"It's what I'm wondering." He reached out and slowly tucked a strand of hair behind her ear.

"Reach any conclusions?"

Hours ago. He slipped his hand through her hair and drew her against him. "Only that sometimes smart and safe are way overrated," he murmured as he bent his head.

Trouble had never tasted or felt so damn good. And a kiss had never gone from *May I?* to *God, yes!* as fast. The door hit him in the back when he let go of it to wrap his arm around her. The folder spilled on the floor, the sound muffled by her moan as he kissed her hard and deep, cradling her head with one hand and skimming the other down over her backside.

The sound of the elevator ding floated in the back of his mind. Nic's laughter exploded in the front. He jerked his head back and took Cat firmly by the shoulders, saying, "They've thrown them out of the pool."

She blinked and then jumped out of his grasp. "Oh, God." In the next second she was squatting at his feet and gathering up the spilled papers. He'd dropped down beside her to help when Nic stopped in the hall.

"Eh."

Logan didn't look up. "Eh, yourself." He neatened the papers he'd collected and handed them to Cat as they stood up. Her gaze met his and he gave her a quick wink and an *it's cool* smile. "Good night, Cat. If you have any questions about the reports, call. I'll be up for a while."

She took the cue without missing a beat. "Thanks, Logan. I'll have this back to you in the morning," she said as she walked away. Over her shoulder she called, "Night, Nic."

"See ya!"

Nic walked past him and into their room. "I wouldn't have thought so, but you look pretty good in red."

Logan frowned, confused. He was wearing a charcoal-gray suit, a white shirt and a royal blue, Warriors team logo tie. There wasn't so much as a speck of red anywhere on him.

"Apparently the Feminist Avenger doesn't wear that kiss-proof lipstick."

Shit! He flipped on the bathroom light and checked himself in the mirror. A slash of red cut across his lips from right to left. The memory flashed and his chest ached from a new rush of adrenaline. He grabbed a tissue and scrubbed it away.

Nic filled the doorway and met his gaze in the mirror. "You don't need to tell me the story," he said with a smile. "I can guess. You just accidentally brushed your face against hers while you were helping her scoop up the papers she dropped, right?"

That he hadn't been as smooth at protecting Cat's reputation as he'd hoped was bad enough. He was *not* going to provide a play-by-play.

"Oooh, the Billy Bad Ass look. Feeling guilty?"

"It's pissed. Your sense of timing sucks." He threw the tissue in the toilet and faced his friend. *Get out of my way,* he silently ordered.

Nic had the good sense to do so. "If you want," he offered as he headed for the remote, "I can go do the room checks and then hang out in the lobby for a while."

Logan tore his tie loose and pushed open the closet door. "Thanks, but the moment's gone." Not that the effects were. Not by a long, long shot. His heart was still pounding and his senses were still on high alert. If Cat walked back through that door, he could pick up where they'd left off in a heartbeat. He tossed his tie around a hanger and stripped off his jacket. Bending over to remove his shoes, he realized that Nic hadn't turned on the television. He tossed one shoe into the closet and glanced over to see Nic staring down at the carpet. What was the saying? A frown is a smile turned upside down?

"What now?" Logan asked as he got rid of the second shoe.

"She's pretty cute. And she's just frickin' gorgeous when she's all worked up."

She was also intelligent, articulate and the most decent person he'd ever met. But telling Nic all that was just too personal. He yanked out his shirttail. "So what?"

"So I can see why you're attracted to her."

Nic was heading somewhere. "I'm hearing a *but* waiting to happen. Would you just spit it to hell out?"

He had his shirt unbuttoned and halfway off before Nic answered, "I've spent way more time around her than you have. She's a nice woman, Logan. She's not the kind you boff for three weeks and then leave behind."

"I know that." He reached for the hanger.

"She's the kind of woman my mom is hoping I'll bring home."

He froze as his gut twisted. The hanger in one hand, the shirt in the other, he turned and looked his friend square in the eye. "You're interested in Cat?"

Nic shook his head. "You're not getting it, man. I'm saying that Cat's the kind of woman a man marries. Don't even get started with her if you're not seriously thinking about going down that road. She doesn't deserve to get hurt."

He knew that, too. He went back to hanging up his clothes. "Well, don't lose any sleep worrying about it, okay? We're both adults and we know where the line is. Neither one of us is going to cross it."

"You're an idiot," Nic said quietly as he walked past. "I'm going to go make the rounds."

An idiot *how*? Because he thought there was a line and there really wasn't? Or because there was a line, he didn't have a prayer of staying on the safe side of it and Cat was going to get hurt? Or was it something else? Something bigger. Was Nic interested in her? He hadn't really answered the question. Logan scrubbed his fingers through his hair. He was going to explode at any minute. God, he needed a beer.

The bar was unlocked. Okay, no beer. Nic had cleaned them out. A workout, then. He'd exercise until his body was too damn tired to want. And then he'd sit in the motel hot tub and think about the pluses of drowning himself.

Cat dropped her shoes and collapsed on the end of her bed. How long was it going to take her to lose the shakes? she wondered. Considering that they were for about a half dozen reasons, it might be next year. Lord, she'd thought that between Ben and the onset of perimenopause, these kinds of urges were long gone. It had been at least twenty years since she'd gotten even the least bit squirmy over a kiss. That one had taken hot and bothered to all new heights. Amazing. And just too damn good to be at all embarrassed about it. Now, having Nic almost catch her in the act…that she could be embarrassed about. Forever. At least it hadn't been Kyle or Millie. She'd have had to kill herself if they'd walked in.

But she hadn't been caught. Logan had saved them just in time and then pulled off a smooth as silk escape for them. Bless his hunky heart and experience at this sort of thing. God, he was good. Really, really good. He could give lessons.

Cat grinned. Lessons on all sorts of things. She'd sign up for them. They'd have to be private lessons, though. Very private. Boy, could he flip her switch. How long it would take for the novelty of that to wear off and for ho-hum to set in, she didn't know and couldn't guess. But it would be a ride to find out.

"Pollyanna," she said, sliding an arm out of her dress, "is dead. No services pending. A memorial has been established with the Lingerie of the Month club."

Was that…? Yes, the light on the phone was flashing. Her heart shot up to her throat. Had…? No, Florence had her cell number. If something had happened to Kyle or Millie she would have used it. A bit calmer, she picked up the handset and punched the message button.

There were two and neither of them was a crisis. Cat hung up the phone with a sigh of relief and the perfect plan for bringing herself the rest of the way back to earth. Lakisha had faxed her some information on the auction; stuff that needed a decision made the minute she got back to Wichita. The business center downstairs had called to say that they had it waiting for her and were open 24/7.

She'd just change, snag a split of Zin out of the honor bar

and go pick that puppy up and figure things out while decompressing in the hot tub. And when she'd turned herself into a prune, she'd come back upstairs and sleep like a baby.

Chapter Nine

The feet stopped just at the upper edge of her peripheral vision. Cat glanced from her file toward the door. Her heart skittered for a second. It might have gone to her throat if Logan Dupree hadn't looked like a man facing a suicide mission. But he most definitely did and so her heart just kinda sank to somewhere around the water jet that pounded her midriff.

For a second she thought he was going to turn and walk away. Hope died a quick and permanent death when he shrugged and reached for the hem of his sweat-soaked T-shirt. An entirely different kind of hope bloomed as he drew it over his head and tossed it on one of the plastic pool chairs. Well, maybe not hope, she admitted as he stripped off his sweatpants. More like appreciation. Oh, yeah. Deep appreciation. There hadn't been a more wonderfully sculpted set of pecs and abs since Michelangelo had whisked the cover off David. Talk about *voilà!* moments. And legs... Lean and long and… God, the muscles were the ideal stuff of late night TV ads. She'd never seen anything like them in real life.

Altogether, he was an incredible package of stunningly gorgeous male physique that even the boxer style swimming suit couldn't play down. If he could dance, Chippendales would hire him in a New York second. Hell, if he'd be willing to just walk out, turn and walk back, they'd sign him up. Which, all in all, was pretty damn intimidating. She considered tugging the edge of her bathing suit down over her butt, but quickly decided against the effort. One, because it wouldn't go anywhere near far enough to matter. Two, because the bubbling, swirling water was a fairly decent camouflage. And three, because it would be just too pathetically obvious that she was nervous.

He didn't seem to suffer from buzzards in his stomach, though. Nope, he sauntered over to the edge of the hot tub, down the steps and in like he did it every other day of his life. Which he probably did, she realized. For physical therapy. She had the bills from the rehab clinic to prove that hockey players spent a helluva lot of time in front of water jets.

Of the two of them, she was probably the only one who had even a niggling fantasy about making love in one. Given that he'd yet to look her in the eye or so much as grunt in greeting… She needed to put her overexcited libido on the shelf and get a grip. And she needed to do it now.

She snagged her split of Zin, polished it off and then turned to sit on the seat and face him. The water that had been only to her waist when he'd come in, went to just beneath her shoulders with the shift in position. Feeling a lot less exposed and a little braver, she smiled and managed a breezy, "Hello, again."

He leaned his head back against the surround, stretched out his legs and closed his eyes. "How goes the scouting reports?"

His indifference was a godsend. "I don't know. Haven't gotten to them yet. Lakisha faxed some auction information while we were at dinner and I got sidetracked in dealing with that."

"How goes the auction?"

"I think it's going to be a wonderful event."

"That's good."

Okay, obviously indifference was a double-edged sword. Now that her nerves had settled and she'd found a bit of Zin-induced confidence, it was kinda insulting. No one liked to be dismissed or ignored. And she was as human as the next person. "Would you mind being put up for auction?"

"Yes."

Amazing how empathic a single word could be. She grinned. "Aw, c'mon, Logan. Be a good sport."

He opened his eyes and met her gaze. "Oh, I'm one of the best sports you'll ever meet. The answer's still no."

Good God, he was smoldering! And it wasn't the flash kind of heat that came from thinking about being auctioned off to the richest woman in town, either. Oh, no. The hunger that had been in his eyes just before he'd kissed her was still there. Only deeper and harder. And a lot closer to being out of control than the last time she'd seen it.

He closed his eyes and went back to his silence. It didn't help her one bit. She knew what was percolating behind it. And there was no denying that her heart rate was going ninety miles an hour. And not out of fear. No, it was sheer delight and anticipation. Every nerve in her body tingled with it.

God, she was insane. Completely and totally insane. And, because she was, that certainty had absolutely no effect on her rational mind. Kyle had a poster in his room. A quote from The Great One. *You miss 100% of the shots you don't take.* She'd made sure that Kyle understood that Wayne had been talking about life in general, not just hockey. And if the lesson applied to the son, it also applied to the mother. Odds were she was going to regret the decision, but she'd rather that than always wonder if it might have turned out well if she'd taken the chance. She moistened her lips with her tongue and took a steadying breath. "Logan?"

"What?"

"I was wondering if—"

"No," he said firmly, his eyes still closed.

If she really wanted to be a coward, now was the time to go for it. He'd never know that she'd chickened out. Only she would. For the rest of her safe, boring, goody-goody miserable life. "May I please finish?"

"The answer's going to be no, but go ahead."

No? Let's see. "I was wondering if maybe it isn't time for me to try some different things. Life's gotten a little too predictable lately and I'm bored."

His jaw tensed a couple of times and he shifted slightly on his seat. But his eyes were still closed when he drawled, "Like what kind of things?"

Getting straight to the point would have been way too easy on him. "Oh, I don't know. Say, low-carb peppermint ice cream."

"Yuck."

"Bungee jumping."

"Get real."

Cat grinned and studied his jawline. Yep, the tension was out of it. The time was right. "Well, I've never had a brief affair."

Even the bubbling water couldn't hide the fact that he stopped breathing. And his jaw didn't turn to granite again. Nope, it went slack. She waited until he opened his eyes and looked at her before she added, "If I were willing to give that a shot, would you be willing to show me how it's supposed to be done?"

It took him a minute to clear his throat and sit up straight. "Like a personal coach," he said. His voice was calm and controlled, but she could clearly see the warning in his eyes. *Watch your step. Don't mess with me.*

Think I'm going to back down, Dupree? "Yeah. Although probably more like a personal trainer than a coach."

A faint smile tipped up the corners of his mouth. It was a done deal and they both knew it. "It depends on who you're thinking of having the affair with."

"Nic," she countered, grinning and easing off her seat.

"No way."

"Georgie?" she suggested as she floated across the tub.

He laughed. "You don't need a trainer, you need your head examined."

Goody suggested that she slide onto the seat beside him and pretend to be something of a lady. But the bunny had already had one panty-scorching kiss and wasn't interested in pretenses. She slid over him, planting a knee on either side of his hips and both hands on his shoulders. "How about with you?"

Looking like a kid trying to be cool in a candy store, he put his hands on her waist and kept her from coming any closer. "Define your idea of brief."

"A week. Maybe two. Definitely less than a month."

So much for the attempt at cool. He grinned. "And when is it that you'd like to start?"

An hour and a half ago. She twined her fingers through the hair on his nape. "I think now would be just perfect. How about you?"

His hands tightening around her waist, he checked her effort to lean into him. "Sweetie," he said, his voice just as tight as his grip on her, "my fuse has been lit all night. If we start something right here, right here is where it's going to end. In about ten seconds flat."

Talk about power. Knowing that she had it was beyond nice and way into *wow*. Part of her was tempted to push the limits of bad. Another part said ten seconds wasn't going to be nearly long enough. "It is a little public, I suppose. Would my room be better?"

He nodded and rose to his feet, carefully setting her on hers in the process. His hands stayed around her as she turned toward the stairs. He took them away at her first step. "I'll give you a five-minute head start," he said when she was out and reaching for her towel.

She nodded. Discretion was a good idea. Running into one of the boys on his way back to the room with a bucket of ice—while they were on their way to hers—wouldn't be fun. No explanation for being together would get them off the hook. The boys weren't toddlers.

Her towel wrapped around her waist, her sandals and cover-up on, she turned to retrieve her auction folder from the edge of the hot tub.

Logan, still in the water, handed it to her. "If you change your mind," he said, "just hang the Do Not Disturb sign out on the handle and we'll both pretend this moment never happened."

No way, Dupree. She smiled, winked, said, "See you in five," and left him to do whatever it was men did with five minutes to kill. Lord knew that five minutes was going to be cutting it really close for a woman about to get lucky for the first time in over two years.

Logan let himself into his room, ignored Nic's quick look, and went straight to the closet. Stripping out of his wet clothes, he pulled on a dry pair of khakis and a clean T-shirt, then scooped up the pile on the floor and carried it into the bathroom. Nudging the door closed with his shoulder to cut down the view Nic had of the mirror, he threw the damp mass in the tub and then made quick work of the reason he'd had to come back to the room. Two ought to be enough, he decided as he slipped the foil packets out of his shave kit and into his pocket. He couldn't spend very long with her. Much less the night. Nic would make his life a living hell if he did.

Logan considered his shoe options on the way to the bureau to get his wallet. Anything more than flip-flops would be a hassle. In getting them on, but mostly in getting them off. And he wasn't in the mood for taking any more time than he absolutely had to. He was slipping his feet into them when Nic asked, "What's up?"

"Nuthin'." *That I'm going to tell you about.*

"Where you going now?"

He headed for the door. "Down to the gift shop for something decent to read." If Nic said anything in response, Logan didn't hear it. Between his flip-flops and the pounding of his heart, the rest of the world could end and he'd never know it.

He'd have preferred to have this little rendezvous on the spur of the moment; by deliberate decision always took some of the thrill out of it. Not enough, he admitted, grinning, to pass on it, though. Yeah, it was probably a mistake. Something he was going to look back on and wish he hadn't done. But right this second, he was feeling luckier than he had since he couldn't remember when.

God. He'd once looked at Cat and thought of her as cute in a kid sister sort of way. Well, it hadn't been anyone's kid sister who had settled herself across his lap in the hot tub, that was for sure. Hot had taken on a whole new meaning with that little move. Not that he'd been surprised by her willingness to do it. Cat wasn't a wimp. And the Shirley Temple-Pollyanna thing was... Okay, it was real. She was a to-the-bone innocent in so many ways. So idealistic and optimistic. The combination of all that *and* a kick-ass body...

Jesus, when she'd leaned down to towel off her legs… The oversized shirt she used for a cover-up hadn't concealed even one awe-inspiring curve. She was just too damn sexy to turn down. Not tonight. If he needed to, he would kick himself for it later.

Cat slammed the hair dryer back into the wall receptacle and did a quick check of the time. Ten minutes. He was late, thank God. There were still a couple of things she wanted to do. No, she corrected as she left the bathroom, there was a difference between "need" and "want" and she really *needed* to soften the light in the room. Bright light was no friend to a forty-two-year-old body. Especially one that considered deliberate exercise a form of corporal punishment.

She turned off all the lights except for the pole lamp on the far corner, the one with the three-way bulb, then turned down the covers on the king-size bed and fluffed the pillows. And then she stood in the center of the room, hearing the sound of passing traffic, the pounding of her heart, and the niggle of doubts. Had she crossed the fine line between direct and slutty? It would be easy enough to do. She had absolutely no experience at this sort of thing. Had Logan sent her on to the room never intending to follow her? What if he didn't show up? She really didn't know if she had the *umph* to pretend she hadn't been turned down.

She had pressed her hands to her stomach to still the butterflies when there was a knock on the door. One quick, light rap. The sound of a man trying to arrive without attracting undue attention. Grinning, she bounded to the door and pulled it open.

"You really should check the peephole," he said, grinning back at her as he came across the threshold. "What if it had been Nic?"

"He'd have seen a look of utter disappointment, been

crushed, and then I'd have had to make up a story about room service or something to make him feel better."

"Change your mind while I was gone?"

Yeah, right. She was standing there with nothing on except a pink silk robe. "I was beginning to think that you'd changed *your* mind."

"I was trying to find a longer fuse." He reached for the hem of his T-shirt and pulled the thing off over his head.

"Did you have any luck?"

He dropped the shirt on the floor and reached for her, threading his fingers through her hair and saying. "I guess we'll see, huh?"

She couldn't help herself, such a rippled body just begged to be touched. "I should probably mention that I don't have a fuse at all," she admitted, slowly skimming her hands down his chest, across his abs, stopping at the waistband of his pants. His eyes twinkled.

Taking his reaction as permission, she went to work on evening them up in the clothing department. She had the button undone when he cocked a brow and let go of her with one hand. "Hold on," he said, reaching into his pocket. He brought out two foil packets and turned slightly to toss them on the end of the bed.

Condoms. Boy, there was a bummer. "We don't *have* to use them, you know."

"Oh, yeah?"

She nodded and undid his zipper. "My tubes are tied. And you have to have had a partner in recorded history to have any diseases."

"Very true."

Or at least that's what she thought he said. Her brain wasn't interested in conversation anymore. Logan had gone commando. No boxers, no tidy-whities. Just Logan. "In all his glory" was the understatement of all time. God, he was the stuff of legends. Touching was a must. An absolute must. If he wasn't ready for it, too bad. And if he thought she was being fast and slutty, too bad about that, too.

His breath caught somewhere in his upper chest. There was slight pain that went with it, but it was nothing compared to the sharp edge of delight. What she was doing to him with her hands… Logan grinned down at an upturned face and closed eyes. And deliciously parted lips. He undid the sash around her waist, let it fall to the floor and then tried to send the rest of the robe right after it. His success at that wasn't complete; it fell only as far as her forearms. But the effect of the silk draped around her hips was stunning. Her breasts were bare, high and firm, and he cupped them to scrape his thumbs over nipples already tight and hard.

A soft little sound came past her lips and a tiny little smile tipped up the corners of her mouth. Beautiful. Sexy beyond belief. And his for the taking. He bent his head and nipped at her lower lip with his teeth. She sighed and the friction of her hands intensified. His knees quaked at the pleasure. His breath shuddered out of his lungs. He wasn't going to last long if she kept—

Jesus! He had no idea what she'd done, but it was fricking magic. It was like a velvet bolt of lightning had shot up his shaft to singe both his brain and his toes. He'd barely put himself back on balance when she did it again. He rocked forward, pinning her against the wall in a desperate effort to keep himself from falling over backward.

"Sorry," he offered just before he captured her mouth with his. She wiggled beneath him, trying to keep the rhythm of her hand work going. He won the battle because he had to, because if he hadn't, he would have come in her hand. She didn't give up easily and her surrender came with a little growl of protest, a little nip of his tongue for revenge.

And he loved it. Loved how she felt against him, how her

curves molded so perfectly around his planes, how hot and smooth her satin skin was. But mostly he loved how she didn't back down, didn't passively accept. He wasn't the only one on fire, the only one starving.

This was going to go fast. And there was nothing he could do to stop it, or even slow it down. His nerves were too keen, the sensations too raw and intense to be shoved to the back of his mind. Her nipples burned holes in his chest. The tiny pillow of her abdomen cradled his erection. Her arms twined around his neck, she battled him for control of their kiss. She rose on her toes, the slow friction of her body branding his skin, stroking his shaft. He moaned, wanting more and wanting it *now*. She whimpered in reply and strained upward again, dragging her leg up the side of his and snapping the last strand of his restraint. She wanted to climb, he'd oblige.

Yes! Oh, yes! Cat choked on a cry of gratitude as Logan cupped her buttocks and lifted her up. She wrapped her legs around his hips and kissed him harder, desperate with need. For speed. For more. For him to understand.

And he did. She threw her head back and gasped for air, a new desperation consuming her. Wonder and heat and power and joy. She had to feel it all, as deeply as she could. She needed it, craved it. And Logan understood that, too. He drove into her, again and again, filling her, hard and fast. Her senses, reeled, staggered with the delight of pleasure and weight of promise.

Yes. Oh, Logan, yes! Don't stop! Please don't stop. More. I need— She dragged a ragged breath as deliverance began to unfurl deep in her core. She shifted—her legs, her arms, her hold—on the powerful body pressed against hers. She pressed, demanded. Begged.

And sobbed out his name in gratitude as he held her hard against his hips and sent her over the edge. Wave after glorious, body-racking, wondrous wave consumed her. Heat and light and thundering, splintering release.

.For a second there was nothing but the pleasure, raw and exquisite. And then it faded, leaving her to gently drift back to the world. Heaven, pure sweet, sweet heaven, her mind whispered in ragged awe. Like none she'd ever felt before. She was spent, her body totally exhausted by satisfaction. Her mind floated away, happily wasted in a sea of delight.

A new sensation. A gentle one. On her neck. It took real effort to call her brain back to work. And it didn't function much better than her body did when she pried open her eyes and tried to put her head back square on her shoulders.

Logan. God, he had the most delicious smile on his face. Relaxed and happy and full of life. Like he'd looked in the old days. Her heart melted and turned the rest of her body to soft butter. She sighed as she slid down his body, accepting that she was going to end up in puddle at his feet. She didn't care. Maybe he'd come with her. That would be nice.

Logan laughed softly and bent to catch her behind her crumpling knees. God, if he could have just enough strength left to get them to the bed. He grinned. Not that Cat would notice if he didn't. Jesus. For as long as he lived… She was absolutely incredible.

He collapsed onto the bed with her in his arms, grateful to have made it. She barely moved, turning only slightly to nuzzle her face into the curve of his neck. He closed his eyes and ran his hand slowly over the curve of her hip. "Are you okay, Cat?"

She sighed. "I'll let you know when I can feel something other than intensely satisfied." He grinned. She kissed his neck and added, "If it wasn't that good for you, please be nice and keep it to yourself. I'm enjoying my bubble."

He laughed and hugged her close. God All-fricking-mighty. If he could bottle what Catherine Talbott had, he could put the little blue pill people right out of business. "It was spectacular. Over way too quick, but spectacular."

She made a humming sound. He couldn't tell what she meant by it, and he wanted to make sure she understood that he wasn't just being nice. He rolled over and put her on her back, then, lying on his side, waited for her to open her eyes and look up at him.

It took a couple of seconds. The wait was worth it, though. No more beautiful woman had ever smiled at him. His nerves came back to life and heat flooded through his veins again. "Honest, Cat. On the Fujita Scale that was a ten."

She laughed. "It only goes to five."

"That's what they think."

"Thank you," she whispered, brushing the back of her hand over the hair on his chest.

Yeah, for as long as he lived, he was going to remember tonight. Being with her. He blinked as the sensation shot from his chest to his groin. He looked down as a second charged after the first. She flicked the tiny nub of his nipple again and grinned when he sucked a breath.

"You're gorgeous," he murmured, trailing a fingertip over her lower lip. "You know that?" He moved his hand lower, making a slow, deliberate path down over her chin and throat.

She settled her shoulders into the mattress and slightly arched her back to offer him a destination. "Yeah, well, what do you know. You're blind in one eye."

He drew a circle around a hard, rosy peak. "But there's nothing wrong with the one I have left."

"Please don't take this the wrong way," she countered as her hand slipped down his chest. "You have wonderful eyes, but they're not the part of you that blows me away."

He laughed as that part of him rose to the invitation. Leaning over, he took her nipple into his mouth and teased it with his tongue. Cat moaned and arched up and took him into her hands. His intentions lasted for maybe thirty seconds and then he gave up hope of a slower go the second time around.

Cat jolted awake. Both physically and mentally. Logan was up. Her cocoon was gone. There was no moving; her body was lead. Her mind wasn't in much better shape, but the sight of Logan snatching his pants up off the floor got her attention. No fire alarms were going off. She was going to have to ask. "What's wrong?"

"I fell asleep."

She managed to move her head to look over at the clock. Three-oh-seven. "And that's bad because…?"

"I have a roommate to keep tabs on me," he answered as he yanked his shirt over his head. "Do you have a book I can borrow for a day or two?"

She had no idea how one thing went with the other, but apparently, in his mind, they did. "In the courier bag in the corner chair." Pointing toward it occurred to her. She didn't have the energy to actually do it, though. All she could muster was to watch him dash over, take out the book and come back around the end of the bed.

"Thanks," he offered, heading toward the door.

"Good night, Logan. Sweet dreams."

He stopped and came back, climbing up on the bed to plant a hand on either side of her head. "There's a couple of Triple A kids I want to take a look at up in Des Moines. I was thinking about flying up next Friday night and coming back Saturday. We don't play until Sunday. Any chance you can get another weekend away?"

She'd move heaven to let him move her earth. "I'll see what I can do."

He kissed her, quick and hard, and then took off again, saying, "I wish I could stay, but it would just be inviting grief we don't need."

"I understand," she said. The door opened and closed. "Okay, not really," she admitted, staring up at the dark ceiling. "It's after three. Nic's gonna guess where you've been." But if Logan thought he could pull off a good story, then, hey, she'd let him. Next weekend it wouldn't be a concern.

She frowned. She'd never looked forward to a weekend of sex with Ben. Probably because it had never been this good with him. Good God. She'd settled. That's what she'd done. Of course, in her defense, she hadn't known that sex could be any better. Hadn't had so much as a clue.

But, boy, she knew better now. There was a whole new, wide world out there. And she was going to enjoy the hell out of it. Bless Logan. She'd have to think of some way to convey the depth of her gratitude. She grinned at the possibilities.

Chapter Ten

Cat hung up the phone and pulled her planner front and center. Hotel and rental car reservations made. "Lakisha, days ago," she murmured, putting a check mark beside it. Flight departure time confirmed. Check. Two o'clock appointment with the PC banquet staff confirmed. Check. Bank balance still black? Check, check. Call Friends placement office. She drew a line through that one and put a check mark beside "Florence on board." She'd been by the ATM on her way into the office hours ago. Her suitcase was packed and sitting by the door. Her happy pills were in her purse. Check, check, check. She was ready to go.

Clicking sound. Lakisha. Cat looked up. Her secretary stood in the doorway, her hands behind her back and a strange sort of smile on her face. A little bit guilty, a lot more amused.

"Yes?"

"I was opening the mail and not really paying attention to

the address labels and... Well..." She stepped forward and laid a slightly lumpy, plain brown envelope on the desk. "Here."

"Oh." Cat picked it up and reached inside. Yep, spaghetti strap. She knew what it was. Bless the Internet and next day shipping. She laid it aside.

"Oh, *mama* is more like it. That's..." Lakisha touched her finger to her tongue, pressed it to her hip and made a sizzling sound. "You trying to kill the man?"

Oh, damn. How to handle this one? There was no point in lying. The peignoir was out of the bag. "He has a very strong heart."

Lakisha arched a brow and grinned. "Apparently that ain't all he's got going for him in the Iron Man department."

Oh, God. She was blushing. Even worse, her grin was every bit as big and wicked as Lakisha's.

"Just between us girls... Is he as hot as he looks?"

Aw, man. She'd been busting to share her excitement with someone all week. With Lakisha standing there, already knowing... The pressure was too much. "Hotter."

Lakisha made a squeaking sound and did a little hip rolling dance. Her beads clicked. Her bracelets jangled. "Oh, you ride him, cowgirl!"

"Trust me, I am. For as long as it lasts."

The dance stopped. The bracelets went wild as Lakisha put one hand on her hip and struck her other arm straight out and waved her hand. "Whoa! Whoa right there! Nuh-uh. Whaddya mean for as long as it lasts?"

"This is a fling. Intense, but temporary."

She snorted and put both hands on her hips. "Says who?"

"You'll just have to take my word on it. I'm not going to give you a videotape and let you give us a score."

"No. No, no," Lakisha shot back, waving her hands again. "Who says this is temporary?"

"We agreed to that before we started."

"Did you sign papers?"

"Of course not. Don't be ridiculous."

A dismissive wave. A jangle. "Well, then it's an open-ended deal. You can change the terms if you want. Nothing says there's a clock running on this thing."

"I can't change the terms all by myself," Cat pointed out, leaning back in her chair. "I'm not having an affair with a vibrator, you know. He sorta has a say in it, too. And he's more than a little used to being unattached."

She snorted again, adding an eye roll this time. "If he appreciates a fine woman and expensive black lace, he's gonna be waving a white flag. Right before he whips out a huge-ass diamond ring."

Cat laughed. "Have you been sniffing the correction fluid?"

"They changed the formula. No fun in it anymore. I'm telling you, he's going down."

It was an erotic image. Completely unexpected and incredibly detailed. "Oh, I hope so."

"Not that kinda down!" Lakisha paused, smiled and said softly, "Although, I gotta say…" She shook herself and rallied back. "Never mind. I mean him going down in flames. Holding his heart and begging you to have mercy kind of flames."

"Oh, yeah. That's gonna happen."

"Seriously." She wagged her finger at Cat. "And when he does, don't you dare stand back and say, but it's only *tempor-ar-y.* You grab him while he's weak and you drag him down the aisle, girl. Don't you let him get away."

"Okay."

Hands back to hips. "You're just saying that to shut me up."

"Yep."

She leaned her shoulder against the doorjamb and crossed her arms. "Does he fart in his sleep or something?"

Cat's mouth fell open. Never in all of her life had anyone ever asked her—

"Then fan the blankets?"

Oh, God. Shut this down. "I really wouldn't know."

"Haven't you gotten around to the sleeping part yet?"

Give her an answer and get this done. "It's been more like going comatose, okay? I wasn't aware of any bodily functions. His or mine. Now, if we could—"

"Is he into kinky?"

"Lakisha!"

"Well, I'm trying to figure out why you'd be willing to let him go. Help me here, girl. Is he into ropes and whips or something?"

"No!"

"Does he—"

"No. He's a perfectly normal and considerate lover. And we're done with this conversation." She sat forward and reached for her planner.

"Is it you? You know, once burned, twice shy and all that?"

Okay. Enough. "Yes. Yes, it's me. I'm a nymphomaniac. Ben set me free. I'll never be able to settle down. There are too many men out there, just waiting for me to make their every fantasy come true. I'm going to change my name to Pinky Zinfandel and dedicate my life to wrecking homes all across America. I'm just warming up with Logan Dupree."

Lakisha sagged and stared. "Logan? *Logan?* I thought it was Nic."

Cat clamped her hands over her mouth in case the scream escaped. She leaned to the side to look past her secretary and into the office across the main room. It was empty. She could breathe. Someday. "Nic? What have I done that makes you think I'm interested in Nic?"

"Nothing," Lakisha answered, her tone somewhere between awed and flabbergasted. "I just thought you were really smooth."

Nic. Nic Parisi. The man who wore patent leather loafers. "Ohmigod."

"Oh, you got a problem, girl. A big problem."

Oh, jeez. Lakisha was right. "You think Nic's interested in me?"

"Well, he's the one I see watching you." The bracelets jangled as she pointed back over her shoulder. "Always has this big silly grin all over his face like he knows the best joke in the world and can't tell anyone. He's the one who had me order—" She looked off toward the window and puckered her lips. "Oops," she finished quietly.

"Order what?"

Lakisha met her gaze for a half second and then went back to staring out the window. "Ah…"

Cat came to her feet. "Order what, Lakisha?"

"Logan, huh?" She considered her nails. She glanced up. "It's not you and Nic going to Des Moines this afternoon?"

"No. It's Logan. What did Nic have you order?"

"So why is he grinning all the time and looking so damn happy?" she asked her nails. "What's he got to be happy about? He ain't got the girl."

"I don't know. What—"

"Logan Dupree." She shook her head and turned to go back to her desk. "Lord have mercy."

Okay, begging might work. "Lakisha, please. I hate surprises."

Lakisha turned back and wagged her finger. "Well, don't you worry. Next time Dominic Parisi brings that fine Italian butt of his through here, I'll just pin him to the wall and ask him. And he's not getting loose until he spills it. His *mama* won't have any secrets left by the time I'm done with him."

She walked off, calling back, "You have fun this weekend, you hear? Bring him to his knees and make him beg."

"Order what?" she whimpered, dropping back into her chair. "I'll kill him if he screws this up for us." She dropped her chin into her hands and sighed, feeling slightly queasy. Her gaze fell on the planner. Four o'clock flight. She was meeting Logan in the airport bar.

She glanced at her watch. Just over two hours. She blinked and looked back down at the planner. The meeting with the banquet people! She vaulted to her feet, grabbed the package and snagged her purse off the credenza on her way out the door.

"See you Monday!" she said as she zipped past Lakisha. She managed to open the door and extend the handle on her suitcase in one smooth motion. And then she was running for the car, too late to give Nic another thought.

Logan absently circled his glass around in the puddle of condensate on the table and watched Cat cross the drive with her suitcase in tow. Why the woman always wore clothes too big for her... A man would never know looking at her that there was a killer body under the baggy jeans, the draping henley and the hanging leather jacket. Maybe that's what she had in mind. He was glad she'd let him past the camouflage, though. Damn glad. He couldn't remember the last time he'd spent a week counting the days to a business trip.

Of course if she got around to thinking about the actual business part of this little jaunt they were taking, some of the fun was going to go out of it. Well, for a few seconds, anyway. Logan smiled. She had awesome buttons and he knew just how to push them. He could make her forget all about team rosters. He stood as she came through the revolving door, smiled back at her as she made a beeline toward the entrance to the bar.

"Hi," she said, walking into his arms. Her kiss was sweet and open and so good he practically whimpered when she drew back. "Congrats on the win in Tulsa last night," she said, her arms still around his waist. "I thought it was a good game. Crockett seems to fit well."

The new kid wasn't working the miracle she hoped he would. But Logan wasn't going to open a can of worms by telling her that. "He's doing his job." He kissed the end of her nose and pulled his arms back saying, "You cut it kinda close. We taxi in thirty."

"This is Wichita, not LAX or LaGuardia," she countered as he pulled up the handle of his bag. "It doesn't take long to screen ten white bread people. Finish your drink."

"Nah, it's watered down."

She reached past him and snagged the glass. "Good, I'm thirsty." She tipped it up and downed the contents in three huge gulps. Logan blinked, mentally calculating just how little of the double he'd actually consumed. She shuddered, wrinkled her nose and put the empty glass down. "Eeeuw, scotch. Only thing worse is gin."

He chuckled and took her hand. "You'll never be an alcoholic," he observed as they headed out of the bar and toward the ticket counter.

"Who would want to be?"

Interesting question. If he'd been forced to answer it, he'd have to admit that he'd spent the past ten years flirting around the edges of it. The last year, he'd definitely been giving it a serious try. But in the past couple of months, since he'd come to Wichita, he'd barely thought about tipping one back. Yeah, every now and then he'd had one. But it was more for something to do with his time, with his hands, than trying to get oblivious.

He provided his driver's license, answered the ticket girl's standard questions and handed over his bag while wondering why the whole drinking thing had changed for him. Being a coach was more time-consuming than being a player had been. He didn't have as much time to drink. And then there were the effects of boozing, too. Being wasted on the ice wasn't nearly as noticeable as it was behind the bench. Instinct took over once sharpened steel hit frozen water. Off ice, he was learning by doing and it was way too easy to screw up if his brain was even the least bit fuzzy or distracted.

He stopped abruptly, brought up short. Stopped dead in her tracks, Cat was staring down at the boarding passes in her hand.

"Is there a problem?"

She looked up at him. "We're in first-class."

"That's not a problem, Cat. It's a blessing." He drew her along, past the gift shop and up the ramp toward security.

"Did you upgrade the seats?"

"You booked us coach?"

"Well, yes. I've never flown first-class in my life. I don't have this kind of money."

"If it's a mistake," he said, dumping the contents of his pockets into the tray, "I'm damn glad for it. If they catch it and ask you to pay the difference, I'll take care of it." He passed through the security gate without setting it off and went to pick up his belongings at the end of the belt. Cat was a single step behind him.

"You're not going to argue with me over that?" he asked.

She slung her purse over her shoulder. "Over what?"

"Never mind. What's worrying you now?"

"I'll bet it was Nic. He knows about…" She motioned between the two of them.

Chuckling, he slipped his arm around her shoulder, drew her close and then turned them toward the gate. Her arm went easily around his waist. "Yeah," he said as they ambled along, "when I put on my shirt that night, I put it on wrong side out. When I got back to the room, I just fell into bed, dead. He noticed first thing the next morning."

"I knew when you left that he was going to figure it out."

"So he knows, Cat. It's no big deal. We're both of legal age and neither one of us is cheating on anyone. I'm not going to feel guilty about enjoying ourselves. And you shouldn't, either. Okay?"

"Okay," she said easily as she slipped away from his side and toward a water fountain. He stopped and watched her fish a pill bottle out of her purse, shake something out and then throw it into her mouth. It went down her throat with a drink of water while she tucked the vial away.

"Headache?" he asked as she came back to his side.

"Nope," she said. "Twenty milligrams of chemical courage."

In other words, a honking sedative. "You're a white knuckle flyer?"

"Oh, the worst," she admitted, laughing. "Without drugs, I'm one air pocket away from being a national news story."

"Why didn't you say something? We could have driven up."

She grinned up at him. "Because with one little pill and twenty minutes, it won't make any difference. I guarantee you that I'll be the only one on board smiling as we spiral toward the earth."

The flight attendant keyed the mic and called for all first-class passengers, unattended children and those needing assistance to board. Logan checked the flight numbers posted behind the woman to make sure it was theirs and then motioned Cat toward the ramp door. "After you, Ms. Earhart."

"She was a Kansan, you know."

"No, I didn't."

Cat handed the attendant their boarding passes and they each produced their driver's licenses. As they moved on, she looked back over her shoulder at him and said, "I'm a cornucopia of trivia. Did you know that the black box on a plane really isn't black? It's orange. So they can find it easier in the wreckage."

"Then why do they call it a black box?"

"I don't know. Maybe we could ask the pilot. I bet he could tell us."

More like call security and have them hauled down to the local FBI office. "Or maybe we can keep ourselves out of trouble and let it be one of life's little unsolved mysteries."

They passed the flight crew and stepped into the first-class section. Cat checked their passes and dropped into their assigned seats. "You're right," she said softly while belting herself in. "Asking about black boxes is probably right up there with saying the word... You know." With her hands, she made a small pantomime. He couldn't read lips well enough to tell whether it was "boom" or "bomb," but he got the general idea. He also got the distinct impression that she had zero tolerance for drugs.

He sat down beside her. "Have you had anything to eat today?"

"A low-carb bar for breakfast. I haven't had time for anything else. Came here straight from a meeting with the people at the Petroleum Club to go over the menu for the auction night."

So what she'd had was no food to speak of in twenty-four hours, a good shot and a half of scotch and a sedative. She was skipping her way toward Toasted Lane.

"Do you like bone shows, Logan?"

"What shows?"

"Bone shows. Forensics, scientific crime solving, that sort of stuff. That's where I learned about the...*it*...really being orange. Did you know that the tail section of a plane has the greatest structural integrity? If the lavatory had passenger restraints, it'd be the safest seat in a crash situation."

"You need to stop watching those bone shows."

She smiled up at him. A relaxed, I'm-loaded-and-feeling-no-pain smile. "Really? Why?"

"You just scare yourself."

She leaned forward and took the plastic coated safety card out of the magazine pouch. "I'm not scared. I'm well informed."

And, Lord love her, she dug right into adding to the storehouse of her knowledge. Logan smiled, propped his elbow on the armrest, his chin in his hand, and watched her as the other passengers filed past. She checked to make sure the exit door was where the picture said it was. She studied the panel over their heads out of which the oxygen masks would drop if the cabin lost pressure. She felt the edges of the seat cushion on either side of her hips. He could see her mentally going through the motions of pulling it out and getting her arms through the straps like they showed in the drawings. He considered mentioning that going down into either the Missouri River or a farm pond would be a total fluke, but decided that it was probably information she was better off without.

The door to the ramp was pulled closed. Beside him Cat took a deep breath. Ahead of him, the chief stewardess began her final walk-through before they taxied back from the gate. He saw her gaze skim over Cat, saw her take note of the safety card clutched in her hand. The woman looked at him and arched a brow in silent question. He nodded and smiled and mouthed "I got her."

Satisfied, the woman moved out of first class. Logan reached over, took the card out of Cat's hands and returned it to the pocket. She wasn't comfortable about letting go of it, but the scotch and the sedative had dulled her just enough that she didn't fight him. He laced his fingers through hers. She looked up at him and smiled. On the surface she was calm and accepting, the easy, done-it-a-thousand-times traveler. But deep down in her eyes, he could see the edgy, desperate current of fear. How could he make that go away?

Her attention darted away from him and came back just as quickly. "You need to pay attention, Logan. They're getting ready to do the safety thing."

"I've seen it before."

"Well, so have I, but you need to make sure they haven't changed anything since the last time. Your life and the lives of others depend on knowing what to do in an emergency."

God, so damn earnest. So committed to jumping through the hoops. Like if she didn't, he realized, she'd be jinxing herself. He settled back in his seat and made a real effort at doing his part to avoid disaster. Anything to help her get through this. They'd rent a car and drive back, he decided as the stewies strapped themselves in and the plane turned onto the runway.

She tightened her grip on his hand. "I hate this part," she said as the engines went full-bore and they picked up speed. "Did you know that, percentage-wise, most crashes occur during take—"

She melted the instant his lips touched hers. The plane bumped and lumbered down the concrete and he compensated for the motion, slipping his hands through her hair and drawing her closer so he could deepen their kiss. So he could make her forget about everything in the world except him. He went slowly, to make it last for all kinds of reasons that had nothing to do with landing gears and flaps and banking out. She was so delicious. Ripe and lush and so incredibly thrilling. Better than any buzz that he'd ever gotten out of a bottle.

And way more addicting, too. He eased away, slowly ending their kiss. Thoughts about the Mile High Club flickered through his mind again as she smiled and sighed in a contented, dreamy way. He slipped his arm around her shoulders and drew her close.

"You are so good," she whispered, nuzzling her cheek into his shoulder.

He chuckled and wrapped his other arm around her. "And you are so stoned."

"I feel wonderful. And it has nothing to do with pharmaceuticals."

Yeah, right. And he had two good eyes. "How long is it going to take to wear off?"

"A week. Maybe two. Definitely less than a month."

His smile faded. Being with Cat wasn't like any other affair he'd ever had. There was a wholeness to it. Everything ran deeper. It was more than just going through the motions to get laid. He swallowed hard and faced the truth squarely. Yeah, they both knew this was for fun, not forever. But, a week into it, he already knew what Cat apparently hadn't figured out yet—that it was going to take longer than a month for this affair to wind down. Actually, it could be the end of the season before it went the way all the others had, before the new wore off and the boredom set in. His smiled again, deciding that it could turn out to be the most satisfying season he'd ever had off the ice. He wasn't about to walk away from that. Not *too* soon, anyway.

Cat sighed happily and let Logan lead her down the concourse toward baggage claim. If she could travel with Logan all the time, she'd fly to the moon and back twice a month. It was nice cuddling in big wide seats. It was really nice to get a kiss whenever it occurred to you to ask for one. And it was an incredible relief not to have to worry about navigating through airports with your brain fogged. Changing planes in Denver had been an absolute breeze. Logan had taken care of everything, of her. The only time he'd left her was to buy a couple of little pizzas and bring them back to her. And dear heart that he was, he'd brought her a fork, too, so she wouldn't have to pick the toppings off with her fingers.

Yes, she'd go with him anywhere he wanted to go. As often as the bug to travel bit him. The effects of her happy pill were wearing off, but the usual post-plane feeling of having escaped a horrible destiny wasn't creeping up on her. No, she was wonderfully relaxed. Like she'd spent the last four hours napping in a shaded hammock. Not a care in the world.

The world. She kinda needed to check to make sure it was still there. She glanced out the terminal doors. There wasn't much of Des Moines to see. Not that she really looked. The man in the navy blue suit, holding the neatly lettered sign demanded attention. Talbott-Dupree, huh? Cool. Just like in the movies.

"Look, Logan. There's a chauffeur waiting for us."

He chuckled and shook his head. "Nic strikes again."

"Why's he being so nice?"

"He's setting us up. That way the joke's all the better when it comes down."

"Is being nice for the sake of being nice out of the question?" The first pieces of luggage tumbled onto the belt.

"Hey, I know Nic. I know better than to trust him." Her hand in his, he drew her toward the door, saying, "But while we wait for the zing... Ever ridden in a limo before?"

"Like you have to ask. What about our suitcases?"

"People who ride in limos don't fetch and carry."

Apparently not, she decided as Logan handed over their claim checks and they climbed into the back seat of a luxury sedan. Vivaldi, leather, wood grain, a DVD player, a handsome man in the seat beside her... Oh, yeah, a girl could definitely get used to this kind of living.

The driver returned, put their bags in the trunk, climbed behind the wheel and slipped smoothly into traffic. Relaxed, contented, Cat sat back in the curve of Logan's arm and watched the world go by as they zipped down city streets.

"You know," she said after a bit, "Des Moines looks just like Wichita. Except with hills."

"They are a lot alike. Same kind of down-to-earth, hard-working, no-nonsense people. Same kinds of expectations for their kids, each other, life."

Cat chuckled, remembering her father's constant refrain. "Do what's right and don't disgrace the family name."

"Take the name from nothing to something," he countered tightly. "Make the world sit up and take notice."

The pressure to succeed. She knew that song, too. "What did your dad do for a living?"

"Worked on a production line. Putting little parts together to make a bigger part to send to the next person down the belt."

"What did he think about you making the big leagues?"

He snorted and shifted in the seat. "He never let me forget where I came from."

Not a happy father-son relationship. "And your mom?" she asked, hoping he had better memories on that front.

"She…" He cleared his throat and expelled a hard breath before he came at it again. "My dad worked second shift because the pay was twenty-five cents an hour more. Weekends were his time to unwind with the guys. He was into bowling and hunting and fishing. My mom was the one who did the rink time with me."

His mother had raised him. "She sounds like a good mom."

"Yeah. The only thing she asked me for when I hit the majors was the money to hire a lawyer so she could divorce my dad."

And he'd given it to her. And seen that she'd wanted for nothing. "She turned out a very good man, Logan. If I can do only half as well with Kyle, I'll be happy."

"You'll do fine," he assured her with a hug. "What did your dad do for bucks?"

"He was a plumber. He owned his own company and retired rich by Wichita standards."

"Did your mom spend her life hauling you around?"

Only in my dreams. "She was the trophy wife. She was one of the ladies that lunch. She played tennis on Mondays. Did Junior League on Tuesdays. Bridge on Wednesdays. Thursday was for committee work. Friday was the day for private lessons on whatever she was into that month."

"What kind of lessons?"

"Let's see…. There was fencing. French cooking. Flower arranging. Art appreciation. And Robert."

"Robert, huh? The tennis pro at the country club?"

Well, Logan got points for being quick on the uptake. "He gave her flying lessons."

"I'll just bet he did."

Yeah, everyone had. "He gave her one big lesson on crashing a plane and that was that."

"Aw, geez, Cat. No wonder you hate to fly."

"Actually," she admitted as the car pulled under the portico of an obviously upscale hotel, "I don't think it had much of an…" She grinned up at him. "Pardon the pun…impact that way. There's huge difference between a jumbo jet and a single engine. And to be real honest with you, I'd rather fly than eat French food. She was a better pilot than she was a cook. Dad always said that she was trying to kill us."

Logan shook his head in amazement and opened the car door before the driver had to come around. *She crashed and that was that.* Just gone without leaving an apparent ripple in her daughter's life. Helping Cat out, he asked, "How old were you when she passed?"

"Twelve. Dad lived another twelve after that. He didn't go the trophy wife route again."

Since it didn't seem to bother her to talk about it… "Did you miss her?"

"You can't miss something, Logan, that was never really there to begin with."

The bellhop came for their bags and Cat followed the man inside. Logan took care of the driver's tip and then followed after her. He'd had a game to play in Denver the day of his dad's funeral. He'd scored his first pro hat trick that night. Everyone thought he'd been playing through the grief. Of all the people in the world, he never would have guessed it would be Catherine Talbott who'd know the truth.

"Ah, Mr. Dupree," the desk clerk said, calling him back to the moment. "We've been expecting you. Welcome back to Des Moines, sir." He laid a packet on the counter. "Your suite is ready. Room service has your order and will serve promptly at nine-fifteen as requested."

"Thank you." He took the folder, tipped the bellhop and waved him off.

"Suite?" Cat whispered as they walked into the elevator.

Logan checked for the room number. Twenty-second floor. Top of the world in Des Moines. He pushed the button. "Room service, too. He's really outdone himself."

"I'm getting nervous."

Logan grinned. "I'll be gentle. I promise."

She laughed outright and nudged him with her shoulder. "That's not what I mean. I'm waiting for the other shoe to drop. What do you think it'll be?"

"I don't even want to imagine." He had other things he'd much rather spend the creative energy on.

"What's he done to you in the past?"

"The last one was saying he'd meet me for drinks. Only he didn't show. The opposing team's left winger's wife did. Wearing nothing but a fur coat."

"So what happened?"

That she had to ask… "You don't want to know."

"Logan! You didn't!"

Pollyanna was alive and well and visiting Des Moines. "Hey, I'm single and she was easy. It's the way it goes, sweetie. All the time."

"Did her husband ever find out?"

"If he hadn't, Nic would have been a good guy in the whole deal."

"And you consider him a friend?"

He shrugged. "We're even up."

"What did you do to him?"

Looking back, it wasn't something he'd do again. Telling Cat wasn't something he was going to do even once. Not in detail. "I pretty much put the same shoe on his foot."

The car stopped with barely a lurch. The door opened with a soft chime and they stepped out into the hallway. He was sliding the card into the room lock when Cat quietly asked, "Are there any solid, traditional marriages in the big leagues?"

"Sure, lots." He pushed open the door and held it for her. "And a lot that aren't. Same as everywhere."

Whether she heard him or not, he couldn't say. And didn't really care. She was dazzled by the room. The size, the architecture, the draperies, the baby grand piano, the whole nine yards. All of it paled beside the brightness of her smile, the wonder in her big blue eyes. He wandered in her wake, watching her, enjoying her delight.

She looked back over her shoulder at him, her grin huge. "It doesn't look like the kind of place that would have a mirror over the bed."

"That's your biggest fear?"

"No, a mirror *and* a trapeze is. I'm going to go check."

He laughed as she bounded across the living room, through the open French doors of the bedroom and disappeared. Now that he wasn't totally distracted… He looked around. A huge vase of pink roses sat in the center of the coffee table. The florist's card was propped against the base. Ah, there was the zinger. The gotcha. Probably his credit card number. Just to let him know that this whole high-end ride was going on his tab. "Don't care, Nic," he said as he picked it up and pulled it out of the envelope.

Take the shot. He turned it over and looked at the back. Nothing. He read it again. And again. Definitely Nic. Even though it wasn't signed. *Take the shot? What shot?*

"Good news, Logan!" He put the card in his pocket just as Cat leaned around the doorjamb and grinned at him. "No mirror, no trapeze. And you gotta come see this bathroom."

God only knew what Nic was trying to tell him; he'd figure it out later. Right now, all he really cared about was getting Cat out of her clothes and into the king-size bed. In the next five minutes. Two would make him even happier.

"You could have a party in this shower," she said, shaking her head as she swung the glass door open and closed. "With six of your closest friends."

"I'm not sharing you," he said softly, kissing her cheek and taking the door in hand. He reached inside the marble stall and turned on the controls. He backed out as the first clouds billowed. One look at her at face… Never in his life had he so enjoyed simply being with a woman.

"It's a steam shower," he explained. "I gather that it's in the same league as first-class seats and limos?"

"Yeah."

He took off his watch and checked the time as he laid it on the bathroom counter. Forty-five minutes before dinner arrived. "Wanna try it out with me?"

He was a cynic at heart, she knew. He didn't believe in relationships that went beyond right here, right now. Players were traded to other teams. Wives were traded to other players. Nothing was worth holding on to. But as long as she knew that, as long as she understood that he'd pass through her life like he had all the others… She pulled her shirttail out and then the whole thing over her head. God, she loved how his eyes lit up, how deeply his cheek dimpled when he grinned.

He pulled his shirt off, tossed it into the bedroom, then pushed the door closed. The mirror instantly began to cloud. Heated mist rolled over the glass walls of the shower enclosure and billowed around them. Her skin damp, her heart thumping in anticipation, Cat grinned, propped her foot up on the commode, and leaned down to undo the zipper on her boot.

She sucked a slow breath and froze as Logan skimmed his hands up the center of her back. She murmured in approval as he unhooked her bra and smoothed the straps down her arms. Straightening, she let it fall away and leaned back into him as his hands came around to pluck her nipples. In the hazed mirror, were two vague shapes, one tall and dark and angular, one fair and short and curved and feeling lusciously hot.

She pried off her loosened boot, nuzzled the back of her head against his chest and undid the zipper on her jeans. He cupped her breasts, bent down and kissed her shoulder, sending a wild current flaring into her core. Oh, yeah the clothes had to go.

With a quick kiss in apology, she turned in the circle of his arms and put her other foot on the commode, bent over and reached for the zipper tab. And froze again as he stepped up against her backside and leaned forward to nibble at her earlobe.

"Logan," she moaned, fitting herself closer to his body. "If you don't stop…" She moaned again as he lightly pinched her nipples.

"What," he murmured against her ear, "are you gonna do?"

"Die right here."

"There's an idea."

He shifted and for a half second she thought he might show her some mercy. She pulled down the boot zipper. And then threw her hands out, desperate for support as her knees went weak with delight, as he kissed his way down the center of her back and his hands skimmed down her sides, caught the waistbands of her jeans and panties and smoothed them over her hips. His mouth lingered at her waist, but only for as long as it took for him to get her clothes to her ankles. And then his mouth moved lower, onto the curve of her backside.

She kicked free of one pant leg, and then tried to shift her other to the floor. His hands tightened around her hips, lifting her slightly so she could. The instant it was accomplished, he took the task from her, scraping her pants and remaining boot away with one hand, holding her hips in place with the other as he blazed a trail of fire downward. Didn't he know she wasn't going to try to get away? She wasn't going anywhere but paradise. She leaned forward, her hands pressed hard against the wall, gasping in pleasure, hoping he hurried, hoping he took his sweet time.

"Logan," she moaned as his fingers slipped into her heat. "Oh, Lo—"

That she was way too easy flickered through her mind. And then it was gone, crushed by pure pleasure. He pressed and she shifted obediently, willing to do anything he wanted in exchange for more. And he obliged, taking her breath away and sending her senses reeling. A quiver of delight shot through her. Then another, slower and deeper, turned want into sudden need. She whimpered, too desperate to put it into words.

And she didn't have to. The bolt of sensation came again and didn't stop. It built and built and then exploded in body-quaking, breath-tearing deliverance. Panting, still trembling, she was putty as Logan slipped his arms around her and slowly drew her upright and back against him. She tucked her hands under his arms, let her head fall back against his chest, and hoped he didn't expect her to say anything coherent any time soon. Awareness niggled past her satisfaction and she smiled. She could feel Logan's erection pressed against her. Just when he'd managed to shed his clothes, she didn't know. But she most definitely approved of the effort and the result.

He nuzzled his lips against her ear again. "In case I didn't say so. I really liked the bra."

Cat laughed softly, delighted. For a strip of spandex, a couple of barely there straps and two patches of see-through lace, it had cost a fortune. But she'd paid it, hoping it would drop his jaw. "Yeah, but did you even notice the matching panties?"

"There isn't enough there for them to be called panties." He kissed her ear. "You'll have to model it all for me after our shower. I promise to control myself next time."

"Then no deal," she countered.

He chuckled and eased his hold on her to lead her toward the shower. She went, surprised by how steady her legs were and thinking that she really owed him a sexual favor. Not, she admitted, grinning, that she was keeping score. Not that she felt any huge sense of obligation. No, she decided as she pulled the door closed behind them, the truth was she was going to get just as much pleasure out of it as he was.

Logan closed his eyes and tilted his face up into the streaming water and shook his head, trying not to think about the delicious body pressed against his. He really needed to slow this down. He'd lectured himself all damn week about not racing to the finish line, about demonstrating a little more finesse and polish than he'd had in high school.

His breath caught in realization and he jerked his head out of the streaming water. "Not a smart idea," he said, trying to keep her from sliding any lower.

"Why?" she asked, neatly twisting her shoulders out of his grasp and easing down onto her knees.

She ran her hands up the backs of his legs and then onto his rear. He'd only thought he'd been hard before. "I don't have enough fuse left to take it, that's why."

She looked up at him and gave him the most wickedly confident smile he'd ever seen in his life. "Good."

Oh, man. She didn't really intend— He gasped as she took him into her mouth. The intensity of the pleasure rocked him back on his heels. He shot his hands out to the sides of the shower to brace himself. Against a too quickly building tide he looked back down at her and growled, "If you don't want—" She took more of him and he groaned, struggling to hold himself in check. "Cat. Aw, jeez, Cat. That feels too damn good. You gotta stop."

She smiled and hummed. She drew back and then rocked forward again. The sight, the feeling… His brain shut down and his body took over. He threaded his fingers in her hair and let her shred his best intentions, let her thoroughly and completely rock his world and blow his mind.

Chapter Eleven

It was the coolest, most incredible ceiling she'd ever seen. Cat knew she was gawking, that she was an island that people were having to go around, but... All that wood. The height, the sheer open expanse. She had no idea when the rink had been built, but she did know that they didn't make public buildings like this anymore. It was magical in a way. She could feel the ghosts of a thousand hockey games, hear the clash of steel and wood and bodies on the ice, the roar of the crowd swelling upward. She could feel the tension of hope and fear.

"My sisters used to play with their dolls over there. Mom would spread out a comforter for them." Cat brought her gaze down from wonder and focused it on Logan. His smile went a little crooked as he turned and pointed to the end of the concrete bleachers. "And that's where Roger Tanner punched me in the nose as I came out from the locker room after a game."

"Why?"

"I don't know. The next day his family moved to Cleveland."

"A lovely parting gift. Not quite as good as a year's supply of macaroni and cheese, but, probably more heartfelt."

His cheek dimpled and his eyes twinkled. "You're twisted."

"I know."

"Logan? Logan Dupree?"

Cat looked past him. A short, middle-aged man with a receding hairline and a noticeable gut stood there, staring at Logan, a hockey bag over his shoulder and two sticks in his hand.

Logan turned. "Max!" he exclaimed a half second later, sticking out his hand. "Man, you don't look any different than you did in the third grade. How are you doing?"

He'd been bald and paunchy in the third grade? More likely it was the goofy ears that hadn't changed. "Great," Max supplied, pumping Logan's hand, his smile going from ear to ear. It was a genuine, honest smile that somehow made the big ears seem just right. "Took over Dad's construction company when he retired. Have a wife and three kids. Two boys and a girl. You?"

"I'm coaching the pro team down in Wichita these days." He let loose of Max's hand and turned toward her. Drawing her up front and center, he said, "Cat, this is Max Hemmelmeir. We grew up together. Catherine's the owner of the Wichita Warriors. We're up scouting this weekend."

She took her turn at handshaking and got her own welcoming smile. "Pleased to meet you, ma'am. You working at settling this wild man down?"

"I don't think that's possible, Max. His ways were set long before I met him."

Beside her, Logan shifted his stance. "I see you're still playing."

Max laughed and patted his belly with his free hand. "Hey, gotta keep in shape, you know. The Blues could call any day." Logan was laughing, too, when Max reached out and gave him a thump on his washboard belly. "Hey, why don't you come on out with us? It's just a drop-in session. We'll take it easy on you."

He glanced toward the ice and then winced ever so slightly before he looked back to Max. "I don't have my gear."

"We can scrounge up enough for you. No checking since we're all geezers and no one wants to risk a hip. The rental skates are new this season. C'mon, Logan. For old time's sake. It'll be fun."

Logan's gaze slid to hers. "Oh, go ahead. You know you want to," she said. "You play and I'll just sit up in the stands and wonder why I didn't hire Max instead of you."

Logan's grin went slightly wicked. Max laughed and took off, saying, "Locker room two, man. See you there."

"You really don't mind?"

"Not at all. I've never actually seen you play. I'd like to."

He looked around, gave her a hug and a quick kiss on the cheek, said, "I owe you one, Cat," and then literally trotted off.

"And I am going to collect," she promised watching him go and wondering if he'd be willing to stay in town for a second night. Their team didn't play until tomorrow evening. As long as they were back by midafternoon… Of course he'd be willing. She didn't even have to ask. He'd had a really good time in that shower.

All the sticks went into a pile at center ice. Cat watched, fascinated, as Logan slid up to it and began throwing the sticks in alternate directions. One right, one left. One right, one left until they were all divided.

It was so easy to tell him from the others. He was taller,

leaner, more broadly shouldered than anyone else out there.
And an obvious cut above. Two or three cuts, actually. There
was an absentminded ease to the way he played. An effortless elegance to the way he skated past the others, moved
them out of his way, took the puck and slipped it to others
for the shot. Pure poetry in motion.

Cat grinned and shook her head. There was nothing poetic about Logan Dupree. The man was direct, open, right
there. There was no wondering about what he thought, what
he meant, what he wanted. Which, now that she thought
about it, probably explained why making love with him was
so mind-blowingly good. With Logan there was no playing
hard to get, no pretenses or games like Ben used to pull on
her. No "you owe me." No "you really expect something out
of this, too?" No need to think and worry about meeting
some top-secret performance expectation.

With Logan… God, check the brain at the door. No thinking required. No worrying about whether or not you were
good enough, knew enough, did the right things. Everything
was right. And easy. So, so easy. Being with Logan—in bed
and out—was a lot like how he skated. Smooth, effortless,
absolutely to-the-bone instinctive. It felt good. All the way
around. Like they'd been custom-made for each other.

She blinked and then swallowed, trying to control the
clench in her stomach. Yeah, she liked being with him. Liked
it a lot. He was good at conversation. He was considerate and
kind. And yeah, sex was beyond terrific with him. So? It
wasn't like she had a hundred other partners to measure him
against. Ben wasn't a tough standard to beat. There could be
lots of other men out there who could trip her trigger just as
well as Logan did. There might even be some who could do
it even better. Okay, that was probably a stretch, but, still…

This was an affair. They'd agreed to that right up front. It
was supposed to be a physical deal and nothing more. Think-

ing about being custom-made for each was over the line, a clear violation of the ground rules. It was about two steps away from an *I love you, Logan.*

Her stomach clenched again, harder, and then rolled. No. No, she wasn't that reckless, that blind. It was infatuation. A really good dose of that, true, but that's as deep as it went. And there was a good measure of lust, as well. Two years was a lot of pent-up hormonal action. And it was partly just wanting—for once in her life—to be a bad girl. To think only about herself for a while. Yeah, it was selfish, but it was also human and honest. It wasn't a crime. Logan Dupree was sexy and wonderful, yes, but mostly he was convenient and willing. That's all it was.

But her insides weren't listening to her brain. Oh, God. It was like flying. Only worse because there was nothing to turn her back on, nothing she could walk away from. It was all inside her. She was on the edge of disaster, just asking, just waiting to spiral out of control and into oblivion. It was irrational, groundless, she knew it, and it didn't make any difference to the swelling sense of panic.

Pill. Take a pill so you can get a grip.

The cap went rolling, but she ignored it for the moment, her priorities clear. She dragged a single pill up the inside of the plastic tube and flung it into her mouth. It stuck toward the back. Her heart was hammering too hard, too frantically for her to get it swallowed. *Water.* She scooped up the cap. With it in one hand, the pill bottle in the other, she bolted.

It took twenty-five minutes and a walk around the block, but the edge of panic finally began to wear off. She was okay now, she told herself when she went back inside. She had no idea why she'd gone off the deep end for a little bit, but she had it under control now. She wasn't going to make a fool of herself or torch their relationship.

She wasn't going to suggest that they stay another night,

either. That just wouldn't be smart. No, she needed some time and distance between them. The airport and plane thing was doable. It was pretty public. Then they'd land, shake hands and not see each other again for a few days. Logan was out of town most of next week. By the time he got back, she'd have all the fairy-tale cobwebs cleared away for good.

He was taking his turn on the bench when she sat back down in the bleachers. He smiled and waved at her. She smiled and waved back, wishing that he wasn't so damned handsome, so nice, so awesome in bed. Walking away from him was going to be a sacrifice. Cat chuckled, wondering how many women over the years had given him up for Lent.

She cocked her head, a familiar sound catching her attention. Just exactly what it was, though…. It took a minute and the bolt of recognition came in slow motion. So did the skipped beat of her heart. She reached into her purse and pulled out her cell phone.

"Hello."

"Hello, Catherine. This is Florence."

"What's happened?"

"Now, you just take a couple of deep breaths and calm yourself down. The EMTs say that it's likely a minor injury."

EMTs! She was going to throw up. "Florence, what's happened?"

"Kyle was knocked unconscious during practice. Just for a second or two. But the rink people said they had to call 911 no matter what. They're going to take Kyle to the hospital and we're following the ambulance over."

They were still at the rink? Weren't EMTs supposed to be in a hurry? What about the golden hour?

Florence went on, saying, "There's always so much paperwork to be filled out when you get there, you know. And they'll want insurance information. The sheet you left us with all the information is still on the refrigerator door. Do you happen to know your policy number so we don't have to go by the house and get it?"

Insurance… "Yes. Yes, I do. Hang on one second." She reached back into her purse and found her clutch. Damn the happy pills, nothing was moving at the right sped. Her fingers felt like they belonged to someone else. She found the insurance card and read the number to Florence.

"Got it. And thank you. It will be fine, Catherine. Please don't worry."

"Don't worry? How the—"

"They just wheeled Kyle past," the older woman interrupted. "He's asked me to tell you that being carted out is not pimp and he wants you to sue the rink for extreme mental and emotional damage."

Deep down inside her there was a flicker of relief. If Kyle's sense of outrage was intact, his brain probably was, too. But she wasn't there to see and hear it for herself, to know whether he'd said it through clenched teeth or not. No, she was in Des Moines, having an affair. "I'll be home on the next flight out of here."

"Catherine, dear, there's no need for you to do that."

Oh, yes there was. "Call me the minute they get Kyle into an examining room, okay? I'm on my way."

"You being here four or five hours early isn't going to change one thing," Florence said. "My boys had their bells rung I don't know how many times playing football. I know the routine by heart. Millie and I are perfectly capable of taking care of him. So you just come on home like you planned and don't worry about him."

No. "I'll talk to you again in a little bit. Thanks for calling, Florence. For being there."

She didn't wait for Florence to give it another shot. Cat ended the call and flipped the cover closed. Tossing her clutch back into her purse, she took one deep breath and stood.

Logan watched her make her way down the steps to the glass that separated the bench from the bleachers. He met her there, looking up and knowing that something was way wrong. He made an educated guess. "So who's having the crisis at home?"

"How'd you know?"

"You're wearing the universal worried mom look. Sorta," he added, recognizing the slightly fuzzy look in her eyes.

"Florence just called. Kyle was knocked unconscious for a couple of seconds during practice. They're taking him to the E.R."

All the bits of information whirred through his mind. Most of them connected neatly together. "And you're feeling guilty for being here and not there."

She nodded and pressed her hand to her stomach. "I'm going to have the limo take me to the airport and head out."

She was thinking of flying alone? "If you'll slow down for two seconds, I'll go with you."

"No, you have appointments scheduled," she countered, a desperate edge to her voice. "It's bad form to walk out on them. You stay and I'll see you later."

Something wasn't right. He could feel it. "No problem."

"Thank you for not trying to talk me out of it."

He shrugged. "It would be a wasted effort."

With a tight smile she turned and walked away. His hands resting on top of his stick, he watched her pull her cell phone out as she went down the stairs and headed for the main door. He went back through the conversation, slowly, looking to see how the stray observations fit into the larger picture. She'd been zoned. She'd said Florence had *just* called. Odds were she hadn't taken her pill and waited for it to kick in before she came down to talk to him. That meant she'd taken it before the phone call. Why? Their original flight was a good six hours off. It couldn't be anxiety on that front. She'd waited until she was actually at the airport on the flight out of Wichita. Whatever it was that had spooked her enough to take a pill, had been sufficient for her to back away from his company, too.

A possibility occurred to him and he glanced at the women sitting in the bleachers. If he'd run into Max, there might be some others around who remembered him from the old days. There were a few who wouldn't have anything even remotely nice to say about him. He didn't see any familiar—or glaring—faces. And besides, Cat was smart. She knew better than to believe jilted teenage girlfriends.

Deciding he'd shovel to the bottom of whatever it was when he got home, he headed for the locker room. Taking his pants down off the peg, he sat on the bench and fished his cell phone out of the pocket. It rang twice before Nic said, "Eh."

"It's Logan."

"Hey, having fun?"

"Yeah. Thanks for the nice touches. Look, I need a big favor. Cat's boy got beaned at practice this morning and she's hightailing it back home. I'm staying here to meet with the two kids and I need you to do two things for me. First, go check on Kyle at the E.R. The rink should be able to tell you which one they hauled him to. Second, meet Cat's flight. She's taken a sedative already, and if she takes another along the way, they're going to pour her off that plane. She needs someone there at the end of the ramp to collect her."

"You got it, man. Wait a sec." Logan heard a faint, distant voice. "Lakisha's just talked to Cat," Nic explained. "Kish is on her way to check with Liz in the pro shop to get the deets for us."

"Call me when you've checked on the kid. And thanks, Nic."

"What friends do, man."

He was about to close the phone when a thought suddenly

came to him. "Nic!" he shouted even as he brought it back to his ear.

"Yeah?"

Logan sagged back against the wall and studied the toe of his rental skate. "Two more things."

Nic snorted and laughed. "Always is. What now?"

"What did you mean by take the shot?"

"If I have to explain it to you…"

"Okay, so I've got the IQ of a brick," Logan admitted. "What did you mean?"

"That you're pathetic. What's the second thing?"

"When you pick up Cat at the airport, see if you can get her to tell you why she bolted."

There was a long second of silence on the other end of the line. "Her kid's hurt. Where the hell is your head, man?"

"No, it's more than that. Find out for me so I don't walk into it blind, okay?"

"Anything else, Romeo?"

He ignored Nic's obvious sarcasm. "Nah, that's it. I've got a pickup game going, but I'll take the phone out to the bench. Call me as soon as you know something."

He flicked the cover shut and then instantly opened it again and held it to his ear. The line was dead. He scowled and stood, his teeth clenched. He wasn't a fricking moron. What did Nic know about anything? Especially women? Nic's win-loss record wasn't any better than his.

"Take the shot," he muttered as he headed back to the ice. "I did, pal. And scored big every time. All night long."

She was running on empty and knew it. Cat shifted the purse strap on her shoulder and headed for baggage return. One foot in front of the other, she told herself. Haul out the cell phone and touch base, see if anything had changed while she'd been courting death high above the plains.

She had it in hand and was flipping up the cover when a familiar figure came out of the revolving door and headed straight for her. "Nic. What are you doing here?"

"You look fricking messed up."

"I'm a little drugged, a little wound up, but I'll be all right once I see Kyle."

"Your boy's okay," he promised her as they stepped to the conveyor belt and waited. "I checked him myself. When I left him to come here, he was shooting rolls of tape at the wall."

She blinked up at him. "He's home already?"

"He might be by now," he supplied with a shrug. "But thirty minutes ago, he was still in the E.R. waiting for them to get around to doing a CAT scan. Waste of time and money, but hey, you can't tell doctors a damn thing. They know it all. You can look at 'em and tell that not a one of them's ever had his chimes rung."

"Better to be safe than sorry."

"They're just covering their asses and running up the bill. The kid got dinged. He's fine. When they're all done playing with their machines, they're going to tell you the same thing they could just as well tell you now. Watch his eyes to make sure they react to light and bring him back in if he goes wiffy on you."

"Still."

"Still, nothing," Nic countered, shaking his head. "You didn't have to come back early. Logan's only going to be a few hours behind you."

"Yeah, I did."

The first pieces of luggage came through the strips and rolled toward them. She watched them, hoping hers wasn't going to be the last one off the damn plane. With no sleep to speak of last night, with the stresses of the day... God, her brain was so mushy she'd be lucky if she recognized her suitcase when it came around.

"So…what?" Nic said softly. "Kyle was like an excuse?"

She was really too tired, too wasted to do this. She sighed. "More like a sign from the gods of good sense."

"How's that? You weren't having fun?"

Cat turned square to him and smiled. "I had a wonderful time, Nic. Thank you for all the lovely touches. The room was gorgeous and supper was delicious."

"So why'd you bolt at the first chance?"

She rubbed her hands across her face and her fingers through her hair. God, she just didn't have the energy to deny it or make up a good story. "I've discovered that this affair thing is a little more difficult to manage than I expected. I needed to step away and get my head back on my shoulders."

Nic nodded and stuffed his hands in his pockets. Cat went back to watching suitcases. Floral. Hers was a green floral, soft-sided deal. With a multicolored neon shoelace tied around the handle so she could tell it from all the other green floral soft-sided deals in the world.

"So what you're saying is that you're falling in love with him and that wasn't part of the plan."

Oh, God, she really wanted to cry. Just lie down on the floor right there, roll into a ball and cry. Her suitcase saved her. Escape was only moments away. She kept her eyes on it as it made its way toward her. "Let's just say that when things are too easy, too good, it's usually not good for you. Okay? The smart person sees the train coming and gets off the tracks."

"What if he's falling in love with you, too?"

"When it snows in Haiti." She caught the handle and dragged her bag off the belt. "Which hospital is Kyle in?"

"No way are you driving yourself," Nic decreed as he took the suitcase in one hand and her arm in the other. "You're too fried."

Yeah, he was right. She had no business being behind the

wheel. She'd collect her car later. She let Nic lead her out the door and onto the walkway. "Where are you parked?"

"Lakisha's got my car. She'll circle back around here in a minute."

Lakisha, huh? That was an interesting bit of information. Did Lakisha drive Nic's car often? Apparently so, she decided as her secretary zipped the sports car to the curb, yanked the parking break, then scrambled over the stick shift and into the passenger seat. "Aunt Florence called just as Nic went in to meet you," she said, flinging open the door. She leaned forward and flipped the seat so Cat could climb into the back, adding, "They're on their way back to the house. And there's nothing major wrong with Kyle."

"Told ya so," Nic said, leaning close. "Not the only damn thing I'm right about, either."

Yeah? Cat silently growled as she climbed into the backseat. *What do you know? Just what is it that makes you think I'm any more damn special to him than the thousand other women who have gone before me? Huh? What makes you think I'm going to hand him my heart just so I can hear him say, 'Uh, it's really sweet of you, but no thank you'? Not on a bet, Parisi. Not on a fricking bet.*

Logan snapped the phone shut again and considered Millie's front door. There wasn't a doubt in his mind that Nic had turned off his phone deliberately, that his buddy, his ol' pal, was hanging him out to dry. Nic had called to let him know that Kyle probably wasn't injured at all, but hadn't called him back after Cat's plane had landed. What had sent her packing was still a mystery. And he hated walking into things without a clue. Part of him was tempted to get back in the car and go home, to let it ride until Cat brought it up herself. Another part of him said that if he'd done or said something stupid, the sooner he apologized for it, the sooner they could pick things back up.

He walked up the steps and rang the bell. Cat opened the door as he was wondering whether anyone was home. She looked tired. She looked straight. He'd also seen more real smiles on mannequins. But he was committed, if not to asking straight out what was wrong, then at least to getting a feel for it. Heading back to the car at that point would have been a way too obvious retreat.

"Hi. How's the ringee?"

"So far, so good," she said, letting him in. She headed for the rear of the house. "He's back here on the family room sofa. The doctor said he might have a mild concussion and that we're to watch him."

"Standard stuff."

"And he's not to play contact sports for two weeks."

Well, that was negotiable, but he knew better than to say so. "Yep. Same ol', same ol'," he offered instead. He stopped at the end of the sofa and met the gaze of one really smoldering, pajama-wearing kid. "Hey, Kyle. How you feeling?"

He threw one nasty look toward his mother in the kitchen and answered, "She says that I'm done playing hockey. That it's too *dangerous*."

Cat instantly, smoothly and firmly countered, "I'm sorry, Kyle, but we've been over this at least a hundred times already. Your head is more important to me than any cool points you might get for playing a macho sport. There's no discussion on this."

Oh, boy. Obviously the last few hours had been rough ones. No wonder she wasn't happy to see him. No sleep, a mom scare, a plane ride and then a battle of wills with a pissed off twelve-year-old. That she was still standing was a real accomplishment. Deciding that maybe he could help her deal with this, he sat down on the arm of the sofa and met Kyle's gaze again. "So how'd you get totaled?"

"We were scrimmaging and Jeremy Bancroft nailed me in

the corner while Todd Stallbaumer and I were digging for a puck. I had my back to him and my head down and then *wham*."

"Bancroft make a habit out of boarding?"

"He's an ass."

From the kitchen, Cat said, "Watch your language, please."

Kyle glowered for a second and then said, "He hates me and I hate him. He'll come after me even when I'm nowhere near the puck. Just to knock me down for the laughs."

"Is he a big kid?"

"Not all that much bigger than me. But he thinks he's hot shi—" He glanced toward the kitchen, took a deep breath and went on, saying, "Hot stuff. He owns the ice and everyone should bow down before him."

Logan nodded and was about to say he knew the type, when Cat said, "Bullies are a fact of life, Kyle. You just have to walk away from them. Stay out of his way and he'll pick on someone else."

In her dreams. Logan sighed, patted the kid on the foot and said quietly, "Let me see if I can work out a compromise with this, okay?"

Kyle didn't look too optimistic about the chances, but he nodded anyway. Logan got up and went into the kitchen. She was stirring something in a pot. "Cat," he began.

"No way, Logan," she shot back without looking at him. "Save your breath. I'm the mom. I'm the one responsible for keeping him safe. He can just find some other sport to play."

"Which one? Tiddledywinks?"

"That's a possibility."

"He could put an eye out."

"Not if he wears protective goggles."

He leaned against the bar and crossed his arms, determined to make the point as gently as he could. "Look, I understand wanting to make sure nothing bad happens to him. I really do. But you have to balance keeping him safe with letting him take some risks. He's not a tiddledywinks kind of kid. Geez, Cat, he could just a easily walk into a wall and end up with a concussion."

"I'll put curb feelers on his shoes."

"Yeah, and you can wrap him in bubble wrap and stick him in a closet until he's eighteen, too. But at some point, you're going to have to let him out and then what? You've got a kid who has no idea of where the line is between healthy risk-taking and outright stupidity. Is that what you want?"

She stopped stirring and her shoulders sagged. "No."

"Then you don't have much choice. You're going to have to hold your breath, cross your fingers and let him take some chances."

Wiping her forearm across her brow she asked, "What do you know about raising kids? You don't have any."

"I was eleven the first time I got knocked down hard enough to be hauled to the hospital. Playing baseball, by the way. Not hockey. My parents had this exact same conversation in the waiting room."

"Obviously, since you went on to sports fame and fortune, your dad won the argument."

"Yeah. In the end, he convinced my mom that he knew more about being a guy than she did."

"And being a guy involves asking for regular concussions?"

He ignored the hard edge in her voice. "Being a guy involves knowing how to avoid them," he explained quietly. "It involves knowing how to deal with bullies so they leave you alone."

She banged the handle of the spoon on the edge of the pot and then went back to her stirring. "That's really simple. You stay away from them."

"Cat, sweetie. How much experience do you have in dealing with bullies?"

"Unpleasant and nasty people are everywhere. The world's full of them. I go out of my way to avoid having to deal with them."

"Like you did with Billy in the Tucumcari Café?" he pressed. "And Mavis who wanted cash for the damages?"

"Not fair, Logan," she whispered, sounding like she might be on the verge of tears. "Not fair."

"Yes, it is. You don't back down. Expecting Kyle to do it is what's not fair." He gave her a couple of seconds to let that sink in and then went to stand beside her at the stove. He took her chin in his hand and tilted her face up. The worry and fear in her eyes made his chest ache. If Kyle hadn't been on the sofa, listening and watching, he'd have taken her into his arms and kissed all of that away. "How about a compromise? To make you feel better?"

She swallowed and took a shaky breath. "What do you have in mind?"

"I'll work with Kyle on the ice. One on one. I'll show him some ways to deal with the Bancrofts and shut them down. Once he owns a piece of the ice, he'll be a whole lot less likely to get hurt again."

"You want to make a bully out of him?"

"Wouldn't be possible even if I did. Which I don't. You're right, the world's got too many bullies already. Kyle just flat out doesn't have the mean streak it takes to be one of them."

She closed her eyes and sighed. "All right, you can give it a go. On one condition. If he gets hurt again, he's done."

"Okay."

Her eyes flew open. She pulled her chin from his grasp. "You agreed too quick. That was too easy."

He grinned and headed out of the kitchen. "You're such a mom."

"Logan!"

His hands on the back of the sofa, he looked down at Kyle. "Get up, get dressed and snag your gear, kid. We're going to the rink."

Kyle shot off the sofa and ran for the hallway like a bat out of hell.

"He might have a concussion!"

Logan turned back. Cat stood at the end of the breakfast bar, a haunted look in her eyes. "I'm not going to do anything to rattle his brain. We'll go nice and smooth."

She considered him for a couple seconds, then turned on her heel and yanked open the pantry door. He knew what she was thinking the instant he saw the purse. "No," he declared, closing the distance between them and taking it out of her hand. He dropped it on the bar. "You're not coming with us. This is a guys only deal."

If she hadn't been so damned tired, there might have been some fire in the look she gave him. "I'll take good care of your baby. Trust me, okay? I'm not just a pretty face. I actually know what I'm doing."

She blinked fast, like she was trying to keep from crying. "I'd really like to kick you in the shins."

"I have a better idea," he said softly, wrapping his arms around her shoulders and drawing her against him. When she looked up he kissed her—slowly and gently and thoroughly. She melted into him as she always did and made him feel good. And as always, the kiss held delicious promise. He didn't want to take an IOU, but the time and place weren't right for more.

He drew back and confessed, "I missed you on the flight home."

She buried her face in his chest. "I tried to pretend you were with me. It didn't work very well."

"Are you okay now?"

She gave him a little shrug for an answer, but any pressing for an explanation had to wait. Kyle wasn't a quiet kid. Logan let go of her and stepped back as the footsteps thundered into the family room.

Kyle zipped between them and wrenched open the garage door. "Please be careful!" Cat pleaded.

"I will," the boy promised, turning back to plant a quick kiss on her cheek. He was bounding down the steps when he added, "You're the best, Mom. The absolute best."

Yeah, right, Cat silently countered. That wasn't what they were going to be saying when they hauled her into court on charges of child endangerment. Logan gave her a kiss on the cheek—not nearly as quick as Kyle's had been—and then followed her son into the garage. She closed the door after them and then stood there, her exhausted mind trudging through inescapable reality.

It might be love. It might not. But there was no lying to herself about how drawn she was to him. She could be angry, she could be resentful, she could be afraid and it didn't make any difference to how she felt when he was near. And when he touched her, all the reasons to keep him at arm's length simply evaporated.

There was no getting off the roller coaster. Not right now. Maybe, in a few weeks, it would be a different story. But until then, she didn't have the strength to resist him. If she got burned, she got burned. The secret to surviving it was to minimize the fallout. She wasn't going to throw her heart at him. And she needed to make sure she was the only one who suffered because she couldn't say no.

Cat came out of the recliner in the family room as they came through the back door. She was wearing a pair of bright yellow flannel pajamas with SpongeBob Squarepants playing hockey on them. He grinned. How the hell she could look just as sexy in them as she did a couple of scraps of black see-through lace…?

"Ohmigod, Kyle," she said, one hand on her nose, the other pointing toward the hall. "The shower. Do not pass go. Do not collect two hundred dollars."

Kyle bounded to do as he was told, the same huge grin he'd worn all night still in place.

Logan watched Cat advance toward him and wondered how long it would take for Kyle to clean up. "Where's Millie?" he asked.

"Playing bingo with Florence's church group," she supplied as she stopped in front of him. "I thought you said you were going to take it smooth and easy."

"We did. It's his gear that reeks. Especially the gloves. He needs a can of shave cream."

"Excuse me?"

He put his hands on her waist. "You rub a little shave cream on your hands and it takes away the glove stench. And when he gets out of the shower, we're going out to the garage so he can have a lesson on the proper care of his equipment. Just unzipping the bag doesn't cut it."

She nodded and, deciding that they were done with the mom stuff, he drew her toward him. Her arms went up. But only to the center of his chest. He looked at the locked elbows and then into her eyes. They weren't cold. They weren't flashing fire, either. But they were an almost steely shade of blue. Okay, it was bull by the horns time. He could handle it. "Is there a problem, Cat?"

"I don't know how to say this."

"How about straight out."

She took a deep breath and touched her tongue to her lower lip. "Kyle's already been dumped by his father," she said. "When the season ends and you go back to your real life, I don't want him feeling abandoned again."

Shit. She was going to give him the heave-ho.

"I really appreciate the time you're taking with him, but I'd rather you kept some distance so that he doesn't get attached to you."

God, how stupid could a man be? How fricking blind? It hadn't even crossed his mind that Kyle might think of him as a father kind of guy. "Smart call," he said, letting go of her and taking a step back.

She nodded and crossed her arms across her midriff. "What's between us is just between us. It's better if it's not a family type deal. That way, when it ends, we're the only ones affected by it."

But she wasn't ending it now. She was willing to keep going. Or at least that's what he was hearing her say. There was only one way to find out if he was hearing right. He reached for her again. She twined her arms around his neck and brought everything back to rights.

"For someone who's never done the fling thing before," he teased, "you sure know the ropes."

She smiled. "I read a lot of women's magazines. Every issue has some sort of article on how to keep affairs from getting messy."

"You read a lot, don't you?"

"As recreation goes, it beats hanging out in bars."

Logan chuckled. "Well, I don't know about that. Do you own a fur coat?"

She laughed outright, her eyes sparkling. Relieved, he hugged her close. He was moving in for a kiss when he heard the front door open. He swore softly over Cat's resigned sigh and let her go again.

They were standing innocently on opposite sides of the breakfast bar by the time Millie rounded the corner. "Logan! How nice to see you here. Are you staying for dinner?"

Dinner had been almost five hours ago, but he rolled with

it. "Sorry, Millie. As soon as Kyle gets cleaned up, I'm going to show him real quick how to take care of his gear and then head out. I've made other plans for the evening, but thanks for asking. Maybe some other time." Cat mouthed *thank you*.

"Thanksgiving," Millie said, hanging her purse in the pantry. "We're having the entire team over for dinner."

"I'll plan on it." He made a mental note to bring Cat a bottle of Zin and to ask her if it was all right to bring Millie one of Merlot.

Cat looked over her shoulder and smiled at her son as he came into the family room. As usual, he hadn't bothered to comb much less dry his hair. And why he couldn't seem to grasp the general concept of a bath towel was beyond her. "Speak of the devil," she said, chuckling.

"Huh?"

"It's an expression," she explained. "We were talking about you and here you are."

He looked between the three of them. "What were you saying?"

"Nothing good," Logan teased as he opened the door to the garage. "This way, hockey man. Your gear is calling."

Kyle slipped out. "Bye, Millie," Logan said. He paused, gave Cat a kiss on the cheek, said, "See ya," and then left them standing in the kitchen.

"My, my, my."

Cat inwardly cringed. "It was a friendly kiss, Millie. Don't read anything into it that isn't there."

"Oh, I'm not," her sister-in-law assured her, beaming. "I've never seen Logan kiss a young lady before."

"Which tells me," Cat said as she headed for bed, "that you haven't been hanging out in the right bars."

Chapter Twelve

He was pitching his gloves into his locker when Nic came in.

"Jesus, Logan," he said, hanging his skates on the hook inside his own locker. "Who you trying to kill? Anyone in particular or all of them?"

Logan sat on the bench and started loosening his laces. "You know just as well as I do that stamina can make or break a tight game."

"Yeah, but you don't get long wind and iron legs in one fricking week. You're just taking your—"

Logan looked up. "My what?"

Nic scraped his hand through his hair. His shoulders sagged. "Look, why don't you take Cat out to dinner tonight. I'll crash at someone else's so you guys can have the house to yourselves."

"She's got some PR deal with the auction going this evening." Or something like that. He could bet on it.

"So, go with her," Nic suggested. "The meeting or what-ever has to end and then you can spend some time together afterwards."

He pulled off a skate and wiped the blade dry with a chamois. "I don't chase women. They chase me."

"It hasn't occurred to you that Cat's different?"

"She may be." He pulled off the second skate. "But I'm not."

Nic sighed and headed toward the door. Logan stood, put an overhand knot in his laces and hung them up.

"What you are," his friend said from the doorway, "is a guy who needs to get laid before he hurts someone. Swallow your stupid ass pride, call her and let her knock the sharp edges off of you. We'd all appreciate it."

Logan slammed the locker door closed and then stood there glaring at it. Yeah, he was frustrated. He was wound tight enough to explode. Drinking hadn't helped ease it one bit. Neither had pushing himself and the team to the physical limits. But spending a couple of hours with Cat in the nearest bed would, as Nic had so crudely put it, knock his sharp edges off, and that stuck hard in his craw.

No, he admitted, his teeth clenched, that wasn't the real problem. It was the fact that it wasn't simply a matter of finding a warm and willing body. He'd been out looking the past week. The bodies were there and free for the taking. But he hadn't wanted them. He kept measuring them all against Cat's. Kept measuring their smiles against hers. Their laughs. They'd come up way short on every single count.

And he'd felt like a louse for even thinking about stepping out on her. Which was beyond stupid. They hadn't made any commitments to each other past it being a short-term, no-strings-attached relationship. She had asked him to keep his distance from Kyle and he had. He'd played by the rules. Every single one of them.

But Cat had apparently decided that their affair was done…. Night after night, she'd had some excuse or another. Kyle had homework. There was a meeting on the damned auction. Or Millie needed to be driven somewhere for some geriatric social event of the fricking century.

He opened the locker door just so he could slam it shut again. Dumped. He opened it and slammed it again. He'd never in his life been dumped. She hadn't even had the decency to tell him straight to his face. And what was worse— *the worst!*—was that he was letting it bother him! Jesus, he was the catch of the fricking day. There were hundreds of women out there who'd jump at the chance to go to bed with him. And he was going to go find himself one. Today.

He'd shower and shave, get dressed and head to Old Town to start the serious bar circuit. And this time he wasn't going to measure any of them against Catherine Talbott. He was going to pick the first one who batted her eyelashes at him and haul her out and get on with his life.

Cat stood at her office window and watched the players head for their cars. Actually, they were kinda staggering along, barely able to move. Practice must have been a tough one, she decided. She'd have thought that after the back-to-back victories in Tulsa, Logan would have taken it easy on them. They were playing so much better these days. Last week they'd won every single game on their road trip. Last weekend they'd trounced the Austin Ice Bats fifteen-three in an interdivision contest. Even the radio commentators had noticed how much better the Warriors were. They'd laughed on air about the Ice Bats goalie not having the time for push-ups anymore. Right before they'd gotten all excited about there being a real chance for the team to make the play-offs.

But apparently Logan thought the boys needed pushing. Maybe she'd just head over to the ice and ask him about it.

As an opener for conversation, it would be a decent one. She couldn't very well walk up to him and ask him if he'd like to get a motel room for Saturday night. It might be honest, but a lot of water had passed under their bridge in the last couple of weeks. In the first few, rare nights the team had been in town, she'd been glad that she'd had plans and couldn't meet Logan for a quickie. She'd needed time to get her confidence back.

Last week... He'd been in town for one night out of the seven. And he hadn't been happy about a papier-mâché volcano being more important than sex. And she hadn't, either, by that point. She'd been perfectly willing say to hell with the emotional baggage that might come with wanting to be held and kissed and taken to the moon. But she couldn't tell him that with Kyle standing there with flour paste up to his elbows and listening to her every word.

But Logan was back in town now and wouldn't leave for another week. After tomorrow night's auction, her schedule was mercifully free of planning meetings. They were heading into Thanksgiving break and Kyle wouldn't have homework over the long weekend. She was going to have some free time and she couldn't think of anyone she'd rather spend a few hours with. Or anything else she'd rather do. Hopefully, he'd gotten over being twerked about the volcano deal.

If not... Well, she'd think of something.

Cat headed out of her office. Lakisha looked up from her desk. "Before you go anywhere..." She laid a pen on a stack of papers. "Your signature, please. Times four."

Cat flipped to the last page of the top packet, scribbled her name on the line above her typed name while asking, "What am I signing?"

"The first two are partial season contracts for Joey Kincaid and Michael Petrowski."

Cat froze and looked up to meet Lakisha's gaze. "Who?"

"They're Junior A players from Des Moines."

Logan was bringing in a couple of rookies? He hadn't discussed this with her. The roster was full. If two new ones came on, then— She shoved the top two packets off the stack and snatched up the bottom two.

"The others are releases for—"

"Tiny and Matt," she said, dropping them back on the desk. She stood there, vaguely aware that Lakisha was talking. She was the owner, dammit. She was the one who got to say yes or no to trades. She was the one who was going to have to look the players in the eye and hand them their severance check. Matt, with his missing teeth and charming, "Hey, Mizz Talbott." Tiny, the gentle giant who couldn't fight worth a damn but who always, always tried to defend his smaller teammates.

God! She'd agreed to the two weeks because she'd thought that Logan would never go through with it. Never in a million years. The trip to Des Moines had been a serious scouting trip, not just an excuse to go away for a weekend together. And he hadn't said one damned word to her the whole time. Not one. He'd been planning all along to let the boys go, to bring in new ones. The two weeks probation hadn't been for real. They'd been nothing more than a smokescreen. A little worthless, empty promise to throw the dimwit so she'd leave him alone to do what he wanted.

Furious, she threw the papers down on Lakisha's desk and stormed out the door. If she hadn't been so blindsided by ridiculous emotions and impossibilities in Des Moines, she'd have figured it out then. But, *nooo.* She'd been so wrapped up in Logan, in being a panting puck bunny, she'd just gone along and never looked past any of that.

And in the two weeks since she hadn't gotten her head one bit clearer. She hadn't learned a damn thing from Ben's bailing on her. She was still every bit as dumb, blind and unsuspecting as she'd been the day she'd stood at the airport ticket counter and been told that her husband had given her ticket to another woman and the plane was long gone. She'd thought her illusions and trust had been smashed to smithereens that day. Apparently not. Apparently she was pathologically, terminally, to-the-bone pathetically nice.

Nic was on his cell phone, standing with a couple of the boys, as she blew through the doors of the rink. They all stepped back and pointed to locker room number one. She didn't waste a single moment. And she didn't knock either.

Logan was standing in front of an open locker, wearing a pair of khaki trousers, a towel around his neck and nothing else. The look in his eyes as she came in spoke volumes. He wanted a fight, she'd give him one he'd remember for the rest of his life.

"You never intended to give Matt and Tiny a real chance, did you?"

"We had an agreement," he said coldly, turning his back on her and reaching into the locker for a shirt. "It's been over two weeks since Crockett's arrival. It hasn't made the difference you hoped it would. I told you right up front that's the way it would go. And I was right. A deal's a deal. I held up my end, and now it's time for you to hold up yours."

He'd held up his end? Ooooooh! She fisted her hands at her sides. "And what are Tiny and Matt supposed to do now?"

"It's not my problem." He tossed away the towel and pulled the shirt over his head. "They're grown men, they'll figure it out for themselves."

"Well, I can't just throw people away because they didn't live up to some grand and impossible ideal. What happens to these boys is my problem!"

"You're the owner of the team," he shot back. "Not their mother. This is a business, not some well-paying six-month camp for hockey orphans. You fired Carl Spady for nonper-

formance and didn't bat a fricking eye while you did it. This
is the same damned thing."

"Except I didn't like Carl. I didn't care what happened to
him. He was an ass. I do care about these boys."

"Great," he said sarcastically. "So you're a good person
with a generous heart. But you're also a businesswoman.
And the first lesson of Business 101 is that business has to
come before the personal."

Oh, yeah it did and she'd forgotten that little tidbit in Des
Moines. It was front and center now, though. "We're in the
black. We're doing fine, thank you very much."

His eyes flashed with cold fire. "The hell you are! You're
eking by and you damn well know it. Every hockey team
from Dunk Water Falls to Madison Square Garden is a break-
even operation until the last day of the season. Every single
one of them. The profit is in the play-offs. It's the hype and
hoopla and the hope for bragging rights that make the fans
delirious enough to throw wads of money at you. It's the
gravy. You *gotta* have it.

"Without that money you start the next season at zero. You
don't have the bucks it takes to buy the talent that you will
get you to the pot of gold the next time out. You run your team
like a charity and you're going to go nowhere. Your boys are
going to go nowhere."

God save her from the blind stupidity of male ambition.
"Maybe going somewhere isn't the point."

"Then why bother?"

"For the game! For the joy in playing. Remember the joy
part of this?"

"There's no joy in getting the hell beat out of you every
time you step on the ice. No joy when every muscle and joint
in your body aches and you can only hope to get somewhere
before anyone sees you cry. No joy in living in hotel rooms
and out of suitcases for the best part of your life. There's no

joy in drinking to make the pain bearable. No fricking joy in being absolutely disposable and always sliding on the edge of unemployed."

"Then why the hell spend your life doing something that makes you so miserable? Huh? Tell me why!"

"For the money," he snarled. "For the beer and the easy women."

Easy women? Oh. Oh. She'd kill him if she even tried to deal with that one. "In case you haven't noticed, there are easier ways to make money."

The veins on the side of his neck darkened and throbbed. "Not when all you know how to do is play hockey! Not when it's all that anyone and everyone has ever expected of you!"

"Maybe it's time you got a life of your own. Ever thought of that?"

"Maybe you should stay in your office and let me do what I know how! If you can't do that, you hire yourself another coach because I'm done fighting you every damned step of the fricking way!"

"Fine!" she declared, turning on her heel and grabbing the door handle.

"Fine!" He slammed the locker door closed.

She whirled back. "Just for the record… You can forget doing anything together Saturday night!"

His jaw dropped for a second. But that was all the longer the anger was checked. "You can forget the whole damned thing for all I care!"

"You got it!"

The door weighed nothing in her hand as she flung it wide and charged out into the rink. Nic sat on the bleachers a little bit away. The boys were gathered in a knot by the scorekeeper's box. She swept past them all, not caring that they were bug-eyed. Let them watch. It wasn't every day that they got to see the up-in-flames death of a fricking Pollyanna.

They'd have one hell of a story to tell their grandchildren some day.

The door to the office stayed on the hinges, but just barely. Lakisha blinked and rolled her chair back a bit as Cat came across the threshold. She backed it up a little bit farther as Cat headed to the front of her desk.

"Do you want to talk about it?"

"No," Cat declared as she snatched up the pen.

"If he comes in to apologize, do you want to hear it?"

She scrawled her signature on the second acquisition contract. "Hell will freeze before it ever crosses his mind."

"Maybe when you cool down—"

"Not in a million years." She signed the release papers, threw down the pen and stormed off toward her own office.

"I'll be hiding here at my desk," Lakisha called after her.

Cat spun back. "You can hide later. Take those contracts to Logan right now. And feel free to shove them down his throat if the urge strikes. Tell him I hope he's fricking happy!"

Lakisha's eyes were wide and her lips were puckered into an *O* as she slowly picked up the documents. Cat didn't bother to wait and watch. She went into her office and reached out to slam the door behind her.

No door. She stood there as a memory drifted through the haze of her anger. John Ingram had torn it off the hinges the day she'd fired him. She hadn't had the money to replace it so she'd just taken it all the way off and stashed it in the team storage room.

Damn, she really wanted a door to fling shut. She wanted the walls to shake and the windows to rattle. She wanted to grab Logan Dupree by the front of his shirt and…and… And what? The steam drained out of her. What did she want from Logan? An apology? For caring about whether or not she had the money for a new office door? For knowing way more than she did about the game and what it took to win? For the fact that she'd broken the rules and fallen in love with him?

She crossed to her chair and dropped down into it. She stared at the stack of Tom's napkins on the credenza. God, what had he been thinking when he'd left her the team? Logan had been right that very first time they'd met; she didn't have the grit to do this. He was right about everything. Nothing he'd just said had been off the mark. Not one thing. She was the one who owed an apology.

She turned to look out into the parking lot. Logan's car was already gone. Cat closed her eyes and sagged back. God, in the blinding heat of her anger, had she accepted his resignation? Was he on his way back to Florida? If he was… Tears welled up and spilled over her cheeks.

"Cat?"

Lakisha. In the doorway as usual. Cat brushed her palms roughly over her face and sat up. "I hope you really didn't shove them down his throat."

"He'd already gone by the time I got over there. Nic took them and said he'd track Logan down."

Cat nodded.

"Nic said to tell you not to drown yourself in a carton of Ben & Jerry's just yet."

Cat suppressed the bubble of teary laughter. "It'll take more than that to get it done."

"Well, life goes on. So does the auction from hell. Delbert at the Petroleum Club called while you were gone. If you're up to it, he needs to be called back."

Cat reached for the phone. "While I take care of Delbert's crisis du jour, get Charles Hollings's number for me, please."

"Why?"

"Oh, guess," she said, punching the speed dial button. "Hey, Delbert. If you tell me there's a strike in the kitchen, I'm going to slit my wrists. Right after I slit yours."

* * *

Logan chugged to the bottom of his third beer and watched Nic come across the living room, papers in one hand and two beer bottles in the other. The papers landed on the coffee table beside his feet in the same instant Nic dropped into the matching leather chair.

"They're signed," he said, twisting off a bottle cap. "You won. Congrats."

He hadn't won a damned thing. And there was no mistaking how Nic felt about it. "Not one more fricking word."

"Don't know that there's anything to say."

No, he and Cat had pretty much said it all. And there was no taking any of it back. "Shit."

"Well, there is that."

Nic drank. Logan set his empty bottle on the table and snagged the extra one Nic had brought. He opened it and took a good swig. It didn't taste nearly as good as the first three bottles had. Probably because he was beginning to feel the buzz already. He'd become such a lightweight. He worked his thumbnail under the edge of the label. "For two cents, I'd pack up and head back to the boat."

"Oh, yeah, leave me with the mess. Some friend."

Logan exhaled and shook his head. "I'm not going. I finish what I start. You know that."

"And the personal deal with Cat… Is it finished?"

He lifted his bottle in salute. "Deader than a warm puck on soft ice."

"Was it her idea or yours?"

He took another drink. "It was mutual."

"Better than being dumped, I guess."

He didn't need to be reminded about that dandy little slap shot from Cat. If he'd hadn't had a full head of steam up for nothing, things wouldn't have gone anywhere near like they had. And as much as he didn't need to be reminded, he wanted to talk about it even less. "Don't you have somewhere else to go? Something else to do?"

"No, not really." Nic leaned forward and rested his elbows on his knees. "Look, I—"

"Don't start, man. I don't want to hear it. I don't want to talk about it."

"Well, tough shit. You blew it today. Cat's the best damned thing that's ever happened to you and you blew it. Instead of letting her have some time to decide she was willing to take the risk, you shoved her away."

"How would you know?"

"The walls are only a foot thick. We heard every word. Hell, they probably heard you in Tulsa."

Aw, damn. And he'd thought this couldn't get any worse. He sighed and ran his fingers through his hair. "She pissed me off."

"Yeah," Nic countered dryly, "and you were trying so hard to be the king of peace. You owe Cat an apology."

He thought back. Yeah, he'd been angry, but he hadn't said one thing that could be considered even slightly less than honest. He shook his head. "Nuh-uh. It was time she faced up to reality. This is a hard game and a tough business. There's no place in it for soft hearts and pink fricking sprinkles."

"Well," Nic drawled, "I guess you showed her what you're made of, huh? Feel good for it?"

Anger flared. "Go to hell."

Nic tipped the mouth of his bottle at him. "Already there and watching the show." He took a drink and then added, "It's a lousy one, by the way."

"Enough, Nic. Leave it alone. Leave *me* alone."

Nic pushed himself onto his feet and headed for the kitchen, saying, "Pull your head out, man. You look stupid."

He felt stupid, too. He felt a lot of things, actually, but stupid was one of the few feelings he could name. That and a numb kind of sadness. "Nic!"

"What?" his friend answered from the refrigerator door.

"What risk was she thinking about taking?"

"A little late to wonder about it now, pal."

"C'mon, Nic. You owe me."

Nic stepped out of the kitchen, opening another beer. "No I don't. You wanna know, you go ask her." And then he turned and walked down the hallway, went into his room and closed the door.

Logan expelled a long hard breath. Go ask her? He remembered how she'd stood in the locker room, her hands fisted and looking like she'd come at him any second. He closed his eyes and swallowed. If only she had. He'd have had to wrap her up to keep her from hurting herself. And holding her…. God, he missed holding her. He missed everything about her.

Maybe he should go find her. And then what? he wondered. Make her mad enough to actually take a swing at him this time? Just bypass any talking and get straight to the physical? They were good together that way. Really good. Uncomplicated, perfectly natural and in tune with each other. It was when they put their damned clothes on that things got out of sync. It was like they were trying too hard.

He took a gulp of warming beer and winced. Too hard at what? Everyday conversation? No, that wasn't it. They'd had some great back and forths. Cat wasn't a shallow pool of intellect and she could hold her own with him. She had a quick sense of humor that could go wicked twisted in a heartbeat. He'd laughed more with her than any other woman he could remember.

He'd also had his heart nearly stopped more often, too. God, she was one surprise after another. As long as he lived, he'd remember how she'd vaulted out of that booth in Tucumcari and laid her principles right on the line. How she'd come across that hot tub and laid her desire on the line. No, Cat didn't have one cowardly bone in her curvy little body. When it came down to it, she stepped up. She was the kind of teammate a guy could go to the wall for. When you were caught in the corners, she'd muscle in and cover your back. No one would blindside you when Cat was there. He smiled. Cat would spend a lot of time in the box for being the third man in a fight.

His smile faded. He finished off the beer, leaned his head back into the cushion and stared up at the ceiling. So what had gone wrong? How had they gotten from easy and uncomplicated to yelling at each other across a locker room? Where had they lost the smooth edge?

The last two weeks had been hell. He'd been out of town for most of it, living out of the suitcase and moving from rink to rink, waking up at night and hating that he was sleeping alone, resisting the urge to call her every five minutes just to hear her voice, just to hear her laugh. When he had broken down and called, she'd been dashing somewhere, up to her eyeballs in being Cat and so, so far away. And when he'd been back in town, it hadn't been any different. He'd never felt so…alone. Alone and angry.

God, he was wallowing. He shoved himself to his feet and gathered up the empty beer bottles. He needed to be rational, he told himself as he carried them to the trash. Looking at emotions wasn't going to get him anywhere close to figuring out how to fix this. He dropped the bottles one by one into the pail and mulled that one over. Yeah, he wanted to fix it. Walking away would be harder than squaring up and dealing with it. If Cat didn't want to, though…

He got another beer out of the fridge. He slowly opened it, the sharp hiss mimicking the air leaving his lungs. Des

Moines. Everything had shifted in Des Moines. The edge had slipped out from under them while he'd been playing that pickup game. They'd been hit and mostly miss since the moment she'd come down those stairs to tell him she was going home. She'd created the Kyle Rule that night. And a few others she hadn't told him about—all of them designed to keep him at arm's length. He'd felt them, but hadn't put it all together to understand that's what she was doing. Not until now.

He needed to find out what had happened in Des Moines. Who had said what to her. That's where whatever risk Nic was talking about had cropped up; he'd bet money on it. There was a vague inkling in the back of his mind, a sense that he knew the answer already and that asking Cat straight out wasn't necessary.

If he hadn't had the better part of a six-pack in under thirty minutes... But he had and so his options were pretty much down to two. He could stop drinking and wait until his brain dried out enough to wrestle the answer from the closet on his own. Or he could get in the car and go over to Millie's and... Royally screw up any chance he might still have. Oh, yeah. Driving drunk. Showing up on the doorstep polluted and wanting to talk. Man, Cat was already ticked at him.

Okay, there was only one option. He looked at the clock on the microwave. Nope, back to two. If he stopped drinking now, he'd be sober enough to think straight about eight. How long to see the light after that...? Hell, it could be after midnight before he figured it out. And then what? Showing up on the doorstep at that hour wasn't going to be all that much more welcome than now and wasted. And no matter what time it was, Millie and Kyle would be there and he sure as hell didn't want an audience this time around with Cat.

Naw, he'd just keep on drinking. He'd think about it all in the morning. Cat probably could use the time to cool off, anyway. As sexy as she was when she was mad, getting her into bed wasn't the immediate objective. No, he just wanted to hold her so his world could come back to center.

Chapter Thirteen

He felt like hammered hell. His stomach was tight as a fist and his chest felt like he'd taken the butt end of a stick in the sternum. But he was a team player and he was where he was supposed to be. Dressed like a fricking penguin. The only consolation in that department was that every other man heading through the doors of the Petroleum Club had been talked into a tux, too.

It wouldn't have been worth it, and he wouldn't have bothered, if there wasn't a chance to see Cat tonight. He didn't have any idea what he was going to say to her once he did, though. Well, other than to say he was sorry for being such an ass the day before. After that, he was just going to have to wing it. And be ready to duck if she wasn't in the mood to be forgiving yet.

There were people milling around the area outside the dining room. Lots of tuxes, lots of spangled dresses. Everyone had a drink. He swallowed and decided that he'd be way better off without one. His head wasn't feeling any less abused than the rest of him.

The music coming out of the dining area was good, he realized as he waited to pass his invitation to the doorkeeper. A live R&B band. A female vocalist who sounded a lot like Bonnie Raitt. If it was supposed to be setting the mood for the party, it was going to be a rocker.

Oh, yeah, he granted as he walked in. Cat knew how to do it right. Which wasn't at all surprising. The bar was on the far side of the room. Three bartenders were hopping to mix and pass drinks. He grinned. Apparently Cat knew that a well-liquored crowd was a generous crowd. She also knew that the little touches mattered. Low overhead light. Candles and flower arrangements and glitter on the tables. Balloons everywhere, floor and ceiling. All of it in the team colors. Black, royal blue and silver. Classy. Really classy. The buffet was at least four tables long. Four groaning tables. No one was going to leave here hungry, that was for sure. Or rested. People were dancing everywhere. Even in the line to sign up for bidding paddles.

He looked around for a familiar face and saw Nic with Lakisha over in the corner by a chocolate fountain. Lakisha was holding a large, flat florist kind of box. Nic was feeding her dipped strawberries. Logan chuckled and threaded through the crowd.

"Eh," he said as he joined them and reached for a chunk of pineapple.

"Eh. I wasn't sure you were going to make it."

Yeah, at two that afternoon he wouldn't have put any money on it, either. "Hi, Lakisha," he said. "You look terrific tonight."

She grinned, shifted the box top to her hip so she could flip her beads—red metallic to go with her dress—back over her shoulder and wiggled her hips. "Honey, I always look terrific." She jerked her head in Nic's direction. "He's another story. Tell him how good he looks for a change."

Logan obediently gave his friend the once-over from top to bottom. Hair cut. A tie that was actually well tied. Nice tux that he hadn't slept in. Logan stopped and looked twice. "What happened to your patents?" he asked, staring at a pair of well-buffed, black leather laced shoes.

"She's holding them hostage."

"Way to go, Lakisha!" he said, holding his hand up. She took the high five with bracelets jangling. "You look great, Nic," he assured him. "You ought to fetch at least twenty bucks."

"Hah! I had my butt pinched twice between the door and the bar and over here."

"It only counts as one," Lakisha countered. "It was Mrs. Roman checking your goods both times."

Nic looked disappointed. Logan laughed and turned to face back into the room. "Which one's she?"

"The one with the platinum helmet hair over by the dance floor," Lakisha supplied. "The one with the, ah…package obsession and no inhibitions about it."

"Jeez," Nic said. "She own Fort Knox?"

More like a high-end jewelry store, Logan thought.

"Her husband's a biggy wig surgeon in town. Bucks is her middle name. Rumor has it that his middle one is Cheatin'."

And apparently tonight was a Revenge of the Wife deal. He slapped Nic in the gut. "Man, you could get lucky."

Nic looked like he might toss his cookies. "More like a disease."

Lakisha said something, but Logan wasn't paying attention. Cat was wearing that little off-the-shoulder black dress she'd worn in Albuquerque. Standing over by the windows, balloon streamers dancing around her head, a glass of water in her hand, the city lights twinkling behind her as she laughed and reached out to lay her hand on the sleeve of a tux. Logan checked the guy in it and went back to breathing.

And then gave up. God, she got more beautiful every damned day. He *had* to get things straight with her.

He looked back to Lakisha. "How's Cat doing?"

She arched a brow. "Well, she took the price off your head. But I don't know whether it's because she's forgiven you for being a first-class jerk, or because she's just up to her ass in alligators and doesn't have time to mess with killing you right now."

It wasn't exactly what he'd been hoping to hear, but probably what he should have expected. "I'll stay out of her way."

"And here I was thinking," Lakisha said, "that you didn't have two live brain cells left."

He managed a smile. "I have three."

"I have four," Nic bragged.

"Yeah, but they're on life support," Lakisha countered, laughing. She shifted the box on her hip. "I gotta go pin on boutonnieres. Stay away from Helmet Head," she said as she inched away. "She's a walking virus cloud."

Nic looked so damn relaxed and happy as he watched Lakisha shimmy through the dancers. "It's none of my business," Logan began.

"We're just friends." He reached for another strawberry. "Kish is cool."

Logan snagged a big marshmallow. "Sometimes being friends grows into something more."

Nic laughed and shook his head. "Her mama would kill her and mine would kill me. Neither one of us has a death wish."

"What mama doesn't know…"

"You ever meet an Italian mama?" Nic asked with a snort. He didn't wait for an answer. "They *know*. And I've met Kish's mama. She could teach mine how to do the evil eye thing. We're talking two peas in a fricking pod. Two *mean* peas in a fricking pod. Ready for a drink?"

Not for the next year. "Naw, but I'll go along for the change in scenery."

They worked their way to the bar and joined the line. The man in front of them glanced over his shoulder and then turned. "It's Logan Dupree, isn't it?" he asked, sticking out his hand. Logan shook it because it was the polite thing to do despite the hair prickling on the back of his neck.

"And Dominic Parisi?" the man went on, extending his hand toward Nic. He looked between them. "My name's Charles Hollings. I represent a group of investors interested in acquiring sports franchises."

A broker. Logan's stomach clenched tighter. "And?"

"I'm familiar with your background, Mr. Dupree. Yours, too, Mr. Parisi. You're both just the kind of partners the consortium seeks to include."

"Oh, yeah?" Nic drawled. "What franchise you currently looking to snap up?"

"The Wichita Warriors."

Of course. Why else would you be here? "I thought Mrs. Talbott declined the offer."

"She did originally," he answered, smiling.

Fricking shark.

"But yesterday she called me and indicated that she'd be willing to discuss a possible sale at the end of the season."

Christ! He'd screwed up bigger than he'd thought. He searched the crowd, looking for Cat while saying, "Well, we're not there yet and the road's a long one. A lot can change between now and then."

"We're prepared to make a substantial offer whenever she's ready to hear it."

"How much to buy in?" Nic asked.

"Given the number of current partners, and assuming you'd want to be on an equal footing, a hundred and fifty thousand apiece would be a fairly accurate ballpark figure."

"How many partners?" he heard Nic ask.

"Eight at the moment."

Logan ran the math in his head. One point five mil for the Warriors. Way too much for what it could earn out in a decent time frame. But then they weren't as much interested in earning back the investment as they were in having the bragging rights to owning a hockey team. A million and half would be impossible for Cat to turn down. And they knew it.

She was over at the auctioneers' table. Lakisha was with her, the box gone. Cat was handing her secretary a bidding paddle and laughing. A million and a half to buy her. It wasn't enough. Not anywhere close. There wasn't enough money in the whole damned world to buy Cat. She was priceless and that anyone would even think she wasn't…

His throat tightened and he clenched his teeth. No way was he going to let a sale go down. No *fricking* way. She wasn't going to get away from him.

He blinked and dragged a breath into his rock-hard lungs. Jesus. Aw, sweet Jesus. And then the tension drained out of him. His chest eased and his stomach relaxed. And into the calm flooded absolute certainty. His legs felt like he'd skated a hundred mountains. He swallowed, took another breath, and squared his shoulders. Okay, so he'd screwed up bigger than any man in the history of the world. If he had to crawl over glass to fix it, he would. The first chance he got. God, she had to give him a chance. She *had* to.

"Logan?"

It was a slow kind of start, a coming back from far away. "Huh?" he said, aware that Nic had a hand on his shoulder. He looked around. "Where'd the used car salesman go?"

Nic took the beer from the bartender, nodded his thanks, and answered, "You checked out and I ummed and aahed and he decided to go pick some other pockets."

"Good."

"Yesterday was just a really bad day," Nic offered as they moved away from the bar. "She'll rethink selling. You're not worried about it, are you?"

"Nope. If she really wants to sell, I'll double whatever they offer."

Nic stopped in his tracks and whirled around. "You're kidding me."

"Nuh-uh." He'd never been as sure of anything in his life.

"Why would you do that? You really think you can turn this into a hockey town?"

He wasn't going to do it for the money, but Nic didn't need to know that right now. Later. Cat had the right to know first. "Stranger things have happened," he said with a shrug.

"Like what?"

He managed a smile. "You're not wearing patent leather loafers tonight," he said as he walked off to figure out just how the hell he was going to salvage his life.

Cat leaned her shoulder against a window and lifted one foot slightly off the floor. The blood pounded in her toes as she wiggled them. Two more hours to go and she could climb back into some real world clothes and collapse. Exhaustion didn't even begin to describe what she was feeling. On the plus side, all the weeks of dealing with one crisis after another had paid off tonight. Not one hitch. Smooth as silk. And everyone was having a blast. They were laughing, eating, dancing, drinking and, most importantly, they were bidding through the roof.

Logan was definitely the odd man out. Every time she'd seen him in the last couple of hours he'd been standing by himself off in one corner after another, a glass of something in his hand. As far as she could tell, he hadn't taken so much as a sip of it all night long. He wasn't socializing. He wasn't eating. He certainly wasn't dancing. The high-spirited bidding seemed to be blowing right past him, absolutely unnoticed. Actually, he looked like he was a thousand miles away and wrestling with the problems of the world.

It was probably too much to hope that he was feeling miserable and guilty about their fight, but she did, anyway. It would make her attempt at offering him an apology easier. There wasn't a more handsome man there. Not another one she wanted to be with. Loving him wasn't something she was going to get over. And keeping her distance wasn't accomplishing a single thing except making her heart ache all the more. It didn't matter if he ever knew how she felt. In fact, it was probably better if he didn't. As long as he'd wrap her in his arms again, the ache would ease. She could be content with that.

"Ms. Talbott?"

She looked up. And up. "Hi, Tiny," she said, shifting her stance to wiggle the toes of her other foot.

"I know you're busy and all, but…"

"Yeah," she said, chuckling. "If I quit leaning on this window, the building will collapse. Who's the young lady who won the high bid on you?"

His face lit up. "That's Leanne," he said, sounding like he was talking about Venus de Milo. "She teaches second grade."

And she obviously owned the boy's heart. "She's a very pretty young woman. Just a gorgeous smile."

He nodded. "She's nice, too. And smart. And really, really good with kids." He sobered and glanced around them before leaning down to say, "Look, I need to tell you something so you know just in case there's a complaint or something."

"A complaint about what?"

"I've been wanting to ask Leanne out, but couldn't bring myself to do it, you know? But she started teasing me about coming here tonight and winning me and I figured that, well, it was a way around the having to ask, so..." He glanced over toward the ongoing auction. "I fixed it so she'd have a good shot at actually winning. I went to all the other teachers in the school and gave them money so they could give it to Leanne for tonight. Of course she doesn't know that I did that. She just thinks they donated it themselves."

Oh, what a darling! Leanne obviously knew a prize when she saw one. "Tiny, that's so sweet! But you can't afford to donate a couple thousand to the cause. I'll make sure you get it back."

He leaned closer. "That's not the point, Ms. Talbott," he said emphatically. "It wasn't a legit win. She bought me with *my* money."

And only he would draw such a fine line. "Tiny, don't worry about it," she assured him, patting his arm. "All is fair in love and hockey."

It took him a couple of seconds to think about it, but he eventually nodded. A smile came back to his face; this one soft and easy. "You know, I used to love playing hockey more than anything else. But I don't anymore. Getting cut loose was the second best thing that's ever happened to me."

Her happy bubble burst and she had to clear her throat before she could ask, "Logan's spoken with you about it already?"

He shrugged. His smile didn't falter, not for a single second. "Oh, yeah. Yesterday morning. I knew it was coming and it wasn't any big deal. I'd already started making some plans."

"Anything you can tell me about?"

"Oh, I'm going back to college," he answered, his tone suggesting that she really should have been able to guess that on her own. "I have maybe a year and half that'll transfer and count toward an elementary ed degree."

"You're going to teach?"

"You making us go out and volunteer was the best thing that's ever happened to me, Ms. Talbott. I never would have known that I was good at that. Or that it'd be more fun than playing hockey." His smile slid into a grin and his eyes sparkled. "And there is Leanne, too. I never would have met her in a bar or rinkside."

Oh, she could practically hear the wedding bells. "Well, if you're going back to school, you're definitely going to need a refund of tonight's expenses. I'll have a check cut for you first thing Monday morning."

He shook his head. "No need, Ms. Talbott. Coach is floating me the first semester. Until I can get all the student loan stuff together. He says it's a severance package deal, but I know what my contract says. I'll pay him back whether he wants it or not. Matt's gonna do the same."

She closed her mouth to moisten her lips. "He's floating Matt, too?"

"Yeah. Matt's been accepted into the police academy. Guess he was just eighteen hours or so shy of graduating when he got a contract offer to play pro. He's gonna pack all that he needs into next semester so he can go into the academy degreed when it starts up in June."

"Wow," was the only coherent thing she could get out of her brain and onto her tongue.

Tiny put his hand on her shoulder and leaned down to kiss her cheek. "Thanks for everything, Ms. Talbott. Playing for you has been good for me. I appreciate it."

"Bring Leanne to the Thanksgiving dinner at Millie's. We'd all love to meet her."

"Okay." Grinning, he turned and walked away, presumably to tell Leanne that she had not one, but two dates with him.

Cat covered her smile with her hand. She was going to cry. Matt and Tiny were going to be all right. They weren't destroyed by the end of the hockey. And they hadn't been thrown to the wolves. Logan wasn't the cold, all business, ambition driven monster he'd said he was. She sniffed, blinked back the tears. She wouldn't love him if he were all those things. Why hadn't he told her what he'd done for the boys? It would have taken every bit of the wind out of her sails in a second flat. The whole fight would have ended right then and there. She looked for him in the crowd. What she saw was Lakisha racing toward her, a panic-stricken look on her face. Cat took a deep breath and prepared herself to whip out the cell phone and dial 911.

"How much money do you have on you?"

Money? Thank God. "Twenty-three and some change."

"That's not enough."

"Tell me about it. If I'd had to buy a ticket for tonight—"

"Helmet Head's gonna bid on Nic!" Lakisha practically whimpered, clutching Cat's arms.

"Mrs. Roman?"

"I gotta do something. You gotta help me."

Not with what she had to offer. "There's only two people in this whole room who can afford to outbid her. One's the bid-*ee* and the other's—"

"Logan!"

"Yeah," she said as Lakisha took off like a shot. "Mr. Soft Heart."

She watched her secretary, saw Logan look up from his shoes as Lakisha came at him. He looked past her for a second and met Cat's gaze across the room. Direct as always. But the usual edge of confidence wasn't there. No, he looked a little lost, a little like he needed to be rescued.

"Catherine! Yoo-hoo!" a woman called on her right.

She smiled softly at him, silently promising that she'd make things right as soon as she could. And then she turned away to play the hostess again.

If he was reading her right… Logan rocked back on his heels as Lakisha's hands hit his chest and grabbed him by the lapels.

"You have *got* to help me."

"What's wrong?"

She let him go and whirled back toward the dance floor. Nic was out there striking a *GQ* pose. Logan closed his eyes, not willing to see any more of his friend's self-inflicted humiliation. "Helmet Head is going after Nic. We have to save him."

"He volunteered for this," Logan pointed out. "And he's had his shots."

He rocked back again and his eyes flew open as Lakisha crushed his jacket a second time. "If you'll loan me whatever it takes to buy him, I'll pay you back. Twenty-five dollars a week for as long as it takes."

"Go for it. The Bank of Dupree stands behind your bid."

She called as she took off, "Go tell the auction guys that!"

He glanced over at Cat as he made his way to the table. Her hand was over her mouth, but there was nothing she could do to hide the laughter in the eyes that met his gaze. It was going to be all right. She was going to give him a chance.

He took out his wallet and stepped up to the man with the clipboard. "I'm Logan Dupree and I'm sponsoring Ms. Lakisha Leonard in her bidding this evening."

"And the limit, sir?"

Logan grinned and tossed down a credit card. "The sky."

It would take a week for the feeling to come back into her feet. And that was being optimistic. Cat groaned and gingerly put them up on the seat of the chair directly across the little table. Yes, that was better. She looked around her. The lights were up and the party was over. The band was packing up, the banquet staff was breaking down the buffet tables. The auction people were putting all their stuff into lockboxes, and the clean-up crew was trying to herd balloons out a door over by the now almost depleted chocolate fountain.

Except for not having had a chance to find Logan for a quiet moment, it had been a successful affair if there'd ever been one. The bids had been so high it was almost disgusting to think that there were people who had that much money to throw away. But apparently, they not only did, but did it on a regular basis on all kinds of things. Long before the band's final set and the bar's last call, she'd had no less than three requests to plan parties for people. Big parties. With budgets that would pay the entire team for the rest of the season. Budgets that made party planning a high-profit enterprise.

It was nice to know that she was really good at something. If only she had the same kind of magic touch when it came to relationships with men. She was going to have to apologize to Logan twice. Once for the locker room debacle and once for not having made time for him this evening. That she'd been sidetracked every single time she'd headed his way was the absolute God's truth, but it sounded really lame anyway. Maybe she should limp on down to the parking garage, go home, put on some comfortable clothes and then see if she could find him somewhere. She checked her watch. Almost one. Kinda late, but maybe not too. He didn't have that much of a head start on her. She'd seen him talking to Nic and Lakisha at twelve-fifteen.

She inched her feet down off the chair. A hand holding a glass of Zinfandel appeared over her left shoulder. Logan. She knew it, knew there was a God. She took the glass as she looked up at him.

"Hi," he said softly. "You throw a good party."

"Thanks." She lifted the glass toward him. "And thanks. I really need this." *But not as much as I need to spend some time with you.* She took a sip and committed herself to opening the conversational door. "I didn't get to see the full battle.... Did you save Nic from the evil clutches of the doctor's wife?"

He gave her a lopsided smile that dimpled his cheek. "Yeah. But I'm not sure he's worth any twenty grand."

"Lakisha seems to think so and the team appreciates the contribution."

He stepped off to her side and picked her purse up off the table. "Are you holding this seat for somebody?"

"Please," she said, taking her bag from him and setting it out of their way.

He eased down into the chair, sitting sideways so that he faced her. With his elbows on his knees and his fingers loosely laced, he leaned forward and gazed up at her. "You have the energy to talk a bit?"

She wanted to tell him that she'd find the energy to do whatever he wanted, but apologizing to him needed to come first. "I think I can probably handle it."

"I'm sorry about yesterday, Cat," he said. "I went off the deep end and..." He sighed and slowly sat up straight. His eyes were dark and certain. "I screwed up big time and I'm really sorry."

Relief and wonder flooded through her. "And I'm sorry, too. I went a little crazy myself. I said a lot of things I shouldn't have."

"We both did. Can we call it even and put it behind us?"

Gladly. She nodded and took a sip of wine. "Are you re-signing?"

"It depends on whether or not you're selling the team."

Her heart jolted. How had—

"Some guy buttonholed Nic and me this evening wanting to know if we were interested in joining a buying consortium. He says the team's going on the block at the end of the season."

Okay, she needed to face this and not flinch. "I'm think-ing about it very seriously."

"Don't."

"Don't sell it?" she asked, incredulous. "But you told me I should. You told me the very first day we met that I didn't have the grit to—"

"That was then," he interrupted gently. "Now's a differ-ent set of circumstances. I have a stake in it now."

"In other words, it's pure self-interest."

His gaze met hers and held it. "Pretty much. But it's not business, Cat. It's personal."

Yes, it was. Deeply, intensely and achingly personal. She set her glass aside. "Can we be done with talking? Please?"

He didn't want to be done. Not yet. There was more to be said. So much more. He scraped his upper lip between his teeth and considered her. "You want me to go away?"

"No," she said softly. "I just don't want to talk anymore."

"What do you want?"

Her gaze dropped to his knees and her lips parted as she pulled one long, deep breath slowly into her lungs. He couldn't take it, couldn't stand the waiting, the not knowing what she intended to do to him. He had to move her off the dot. Get it over with. He reached out and gently laid his hands on her shoulders. "Cat?"

She looked up at him and the fine shimmer of tears tore at his heart.

"Would you hold me?"

He was the luckiest man on the face of the planet. "God, yes. Anytime," he said, drawing her onto his lap and wrapping his arms around her. She twined hers around his neck and bur-ied her cheek in his jacket. Logan closed his eyes and held her close. So what if she could hear his heart hammering ninety to nothing? He nuzzled his face in her hair, breathed deep the scent of island flowers and knew that he'd come home.

"I'm sorry that our timing was off," she said quietly. "That the only night you were in town last week was the night I had to help with the volcano project. I really wanted to be with you."

Ancient history, sweetie. "Being Kyle's mom is more important and I was being a self-centered ass that night. I'm the one who owes the apology."

She shifted in his arms so that she could look him in the eye. Her smile was so soft, so damn inviting. "I don't have any more projects going this evening."

"Are we back?" he asked, needing to be sure, knowing, that if he had to, he'd sell his soul for the right answer.

"I'd like to be. If you're willing."

Yes! He instantly tamped down his excitement. *Play it right. Take control. Slow and easy. Don't screw it up.* He reached to his hip and pulled his cell phone out of the holster. He handed it to her, saying, "Call Millie and tell her you won't be home tonight."

She opened the cover and then hesitated. "It's one o'clock in the morning."

"Old people don't sleep."

"True," she allowed and pushed a button. Again she stopped. "Where am I going to be?"

"With me."

"Yes, but I can't very well tell her that."

"Why not? If she needs you, you'll be at my place. She can call there." She didn't move and he cocked a brow. "You want me to tell her?"

She shook her head, but didn't punch another button. He moved to take the phone from her, but she quickly held it out beyond his easy reach.

"It isn't very discreet."

"Is there a shame factor in this for you?"

She looked stunned that he'd even suggest it. "Not at all!"

"Then let's be honest, okay? With each other and everyone else."

"You're right." She punched in the rest of the numbers and hit the send button. Not two seconds later, she said, "Hi, Millie."

Logan smiled, bent his head and pressed a slow kiss to her ear. "Yes, it went very, very well. I think everyone had a good time and the preliminary receipts look fantastic. The reason I'm calling—"

While she was listening to Millie, he shifted under her so he could nibble his way down her neck.

"Yes, he was," Cat said. A little bit distractedly, he thought. "Of course. Which brings me to the—"

She didn't make a sound when she sighed, but her breasts moved with it and they sang to him. He nipped his way down onto her shoulder.

"Yes, I know. I agree. The rea—"

Logan eased her back ever so slightly and kissed his way off her shoulder. She struggled back fully upright and threw him what he thought was supposed to be a *stop it!* look.

"Yes, Millie. I—"

He grinned and trailed his fingertips over the low edge of her neckline. She closed her eyes and sagged back. "Millie, I'm going home with Logan. I'm going to spend the night at his house. If you need me for—" A half second later she smiled and said, "Well, yes, he is. Hang on."

Distract her, would he? Well, it was his turn to endure. She handed him the phone.

"Hi, Millie. What's up?"

She undid his tie. He laughed silently, his eyes twinkling in a silent challenge for her to do her best. "Okay, Millie. No problem. I was planning to anyway."

She opened the collar of his shirt. "Yeah, I'm sure she does."

She undid another stud and stretched up to kiss the hollow of his throat. He tipped his head back and tightened the arm around her shoulder. "Sweet dreams to you, too, Millie. See you in the morning."

"What's no problem?" she asked, opening another few inches of shirt as he put the phone away.

"I have to bring you to the team Thanksgiving dinner," he said, catching her hand and gently stopping her assault. "Millie's invoked the serious girlfriend rule."

Serious girlfriend, huh? Maybe there was hope for down the road. But for right now, she was happy with just being back together. "And what are you sure about?"

"That you know how to make green bean casserole."

In her sleep. But having him so sure about her... Well, there was something to be said for keeping him guessing. "We'll have to stop at the deli on the way, pick some up and hope she can't tell the difference."

His jaw didn't exactly drop, but he did blink. "Really? You don't know—" He laughed, gave her a hug, and then eased her off his lap. "Anything you need to take care of before we leave? Anyone you need to talk to?"

"No." She picked up her purse. "If Delbert has a crisis, he's on his own. I am officially off the clock."

"Feet hurt?" he asked as he took her hand and they headed out of the club and toward the elevator.

"These shoes look great, but they're not meant to stand around in. Vanity won out over common sense as I was getting dressed and now I'm paying for it."

She punched the call button and the doors were opening when Logan swept her neatly up into his arms. She laughed and draped her arms around his neck as he carried her inside. "Are you thinking of carrying me all the way to the garage?"

"All the way to the car, actually. Don't think I can do it?"

"I think you can do anything you decide you want to do."

Yep, he could. He could find the speed to break up a pass when his legs were already burning. He could outmuscle a man sixty pounds heavier. He hadn't thought he could enjoy life after losing his eye, but Cat had forced him to accept and meet that challenge, too. Nic was absolutely right; Catherine Talbott was the very best thing that had ever happened to him. And before the night was over, he was going to convince her to think the same thing about him.

"My car's on level three," she said as he carried her into the garage.

Yeah, he knew. He'd parked no more than a dozen stalls down from her. "We'll take my car and come back for yours tomorrow sometime."

"It'll have to be early," she said as he gently set her on her feet at the passenger door and fished his car keys out of his pocket. "Kyle has a game at ten," she explained as he opened the door and assisted her in. "I'll need time to get home and change clothes before I haul him to the rink."

He mentally ran the roads and clicked off the time. It was going to be a really short night. Lots shorter than he wanted. "You don't stay off the clock for long."

She smiled up at him and fastened her seat belt. "And a possible companion for Millie is coming by the house at one-thirty. But, hey, I'll take what I can get, when I can get it, and be grateful."

Logan nodded and closed the door and went around to his side, thinking that, all in all, it was a pretty good attitude to have. He climbed in, put the key in the ignition, and cranked the engine over. He backed out, deciding that if it turned out that she couldn't give him everything he wanted, he'd take what she was willing and able to give and be grateful. And hopeful.

He slipped the gears into first just as Cat leaned forward, stripped off a shoe and pitched it over her shoulder into the backseat. The other one went winging as he was shifting into second and heading into the first curve of the down ramp.

He was holding the corkscrew turn tight and thinking that he'd have to carry her into the house so she didn't ruin her hose when she propped her foot on the dashboard and smoothed her hands up her thigh and under the hem of her dress.

His heart skipped and his blood sizzled. The engine revs kicked up. "You trying to get us killed?" he asked, easing off the accelerator.

"I'm not driving," she countered as they came out of the spiral and into the main level of the garage. "You are."

He braked, shifted into neutral and turned in the seat just as she rolled a stocking down her leg. There was absolutely nothing neutral about his reaction. "Want me to toss *you* into the backseat?" he asked as the little ball of nylon sailed back to join her shoes.

Her smile was wicked. "I wish you'd have thought of that while we were on the third level. It's a lot more private. Wanna go back up?"

Hell, yes and God, no. He opted for good sense and the larger goal. He rammed the car back into gear. "Just behave yourself until we get past the attendant booth, okay?"

The tires squealed on the concrete. And Cat threw her head back and laughed.

Chapter Fourteen

She'd pretty much decided that they were heading toward the pricey end of the west side when Logan hung a right off of Tyler and headed into the heart of a working-class neighborhood. She smiled. Her high school friend Lucinda had lived one street over.

"I should warn you," Logan said as he slowed to take the dip in the road. "I was busy and made Nic go house hunting. He didn't want to and said okay to the first one the Realtor showed him."

"It's a nice neighborhood," she assured him. "That house right there," she said pointing as they drove past a ranch with a chalet style front porch, "is where Janet Ast and I were busted for tee-peeing. Dad was *not* happy to see me standing on the front porch with an Officer Friendly at two in the morning."

"You were a wild child?"

"I wish I could say that I was. But that was the beginning and end of it. I was grounded for the next three years."

He laughed as he slowed and pulled in to the driveway of another ranch style house. The motion detection lights came on. She thought back as Logan came around the car to be the gentleman. Years and years ago, the Nickels had owned this house. It had been a really big deal in those days that a *professional* landscaper had done their front gardens. From the looks of it now, no one, amateur or pro, had done anything to it in at least ten years. They hadn't painted in recent history, either. The lower panel of the garage door was tilted at an odd angle that said that it would fall off if anyone actually tried to open it. A shutter was hanging loose on the front room window.

If the interior looked anything like the outside, the Realtor had probably wept with joy when Nic had declared it perfect. Logan opened the front door and held it for her. She slipped past him, into the foyer, and stopped. Lord, hopefully Mrs. Nickel had moved far away and would never see what had happened to her house. She'd really been into country decor and had had the talent to pull it off. Now…

"It's really…" She paused, searching for the right word. Barren?

"Early bachelor," Logan supplied, putting his keys on the low divider that separated the foyer from the living room. He shrugged off his jacket and tossed it over the partition, adding, "We just sorta camp here."

Obviously. A leather sofa, a matching chair, a coffee table, one end table and one lamp. All of it high end, but since that was all there was in the big living room, it just sorta sat there looking lonely. It wouldn't take ten minutes for Logan and Nic to move out. "More like nomad with money."

He stood beside her and considered it for a second before he said, "Yeah, which, when you come right down to it, is what we've been all our lives."

And nomads were nomads because they liked living that way. She had succeeded in dragging Logan to town, but there was nothing she could do to make him put down roots. There'd come a day when he moved on.

Man, she looked like she'd seen a dead puppy beside the road. He knew the decorating was terrible, but jeez, there wasn't any reason for her to cry over it. Time to move her on. He took her hand in his and backed toward the hall. "Wanna see my tent, little girl?"

She laughed softly. "I'd love to."

"It's not fancy. At least by female standards."

She rolled her eyes like hoping for fancy wasn't even in the realm of her hopes. "As long as it has a door, it'll do."

Yeah, well, he was going to turn on the lights just long enough for her to get the general layout so that she didn't stub her toe later. Fancy wouldn't matter for more than a minute of two. After that… "All rooms look the same in the dark," he reminded her as he flipped on the wall switch and drew her in.

"This isn't early bachelor," she exclaimed, standing at the end of his bed. "This is nomad with money and a sense of *yum*."

Score one for a good furniture salesman and the froufrou section of Wally World. "And a door," he said, pushing it closed. "With a working lock."

"Ah," she countered, laughing and climbing up on the bed, "but do you have a steam shower?"

"I haven't had anyone to share one with." He swallowed as she crawled on her hands and knees toward the nightstand. Jesus. She really needed to wear a warning label. Caution. Hot. "But I'm seriously thinking about having one installed tomorrow."

"Ooh, now there's a reason to come visit." She clicked on the bedside lamp and started to sit back on her heels.

He flicked off the overhead light, saying, "Don't move."

"What?" she asked, cautiously looking down at the satin comforter. "Is it a spider or something?"

Logan grinned and climbed up onto the bed. "Just what exactly do you have on under here?" he asked, running his hand up the back of her leg, under her hem and over the smooth curve of her bare hip. He stopped to finger a lacy edge at her waist.

"They're called foundation garments," she answered, sitting back and giving him a delightfully wanton look over her shoulder.

"Oh, yeah?" He followed the edge around to the center of her back. "Foundation for what?"

"Inspiration?"

"Well, it's working so far," he admitted. He let go of the lace so he could use both hands to pull the dress zipper. "Let's see just how…" The dress slipped down and pooled around her legs. A bustier. Tiny. Black. Lacy. "Oh, that is…" She'd been wandering around in public dressed like this? "Whoa."

She laughed, scooted around on her knees and put her hands flat on his chest. "You are so easy," she declared, pushing him down onto his back.

"No, you're just that incredible."

She laughed again, pulled his tie out from under his collar and threw it away. His shirt studs were her next focus of attack. He watched her face as she worked his shirt open. So beautiful, such a breathtaking mix of innocent and wanton. So open and genuine. No games, no hidden agenda.

"Cat?" he said softly, skimming his hands down her arms. She hummed in reply, but didn't look up as she ran her fingers up through the hair on his chest. "I love you."

Her hands froze and her head snapped up, her eyes huge as she met his gaze. Her lips slowly parted, but she didn't make a sound.

"I know we said this was just for fun and it wasn't going to go anywhere," he offered in her stunned silence, brushing his hands back up her arms. "And honest to God, Cat, I thought that's the way it would go. But it hasn't and there's nothing I can do to change it. I swear to you that—"

"How long have you known?" she asked on a ragged whisper.

"Truth?"

She nodded. He took her hands in his and laced their fingers. "It hit me when Hollings was pitching his consortium tonight. I looked over at you and I realized that you're worth more than all the money in the world. But it's been coming on longer than that. Looking back, I think it started when you handed me your little fuzzy-edged pink business card."

A tiny little smile touched the corners of her mouth. Taking it as a good sign, he continued, saying, "I've never known anyone like you, Cat. And I've been around the circuit enough times to know that I'm never going to find anyone like you again. I know this is sudden from your side of it and I don't want you to feel obligated in any way. I'm willing to—"

"Logan, hush a minute." She gently squeezed his hands. "Please."

His heart was pounding, trying to break through his ribs, but he kept quiet.

"When we were in Des Moines, at the rink…"

"Something happened there that derailed us for a while," he said, sparing her. "I don't know what it was, but we've moved past it, so it doesn't matter anymore. We don't have to go back to it."

"I derailed us. Deliberately," she said softly. "I went into this whole thing determined to play by the rules and keep things uncomplicated and I thought I was doing so well at it and then… Out of the blue. I was scared and I ran."

"What were you afraid of? Me?"

She smiled down at him. "I didn't intend to fall in love, either, Logan."

She loved him! He'd just scored the biggest, most important goal of his entire life! She gasped as he flipped her onto to her back, gazed up at him adoringly as he pinned their hands into the pillow on either side of her head.

"And you ran rather than tell me? Good God, Cat. Why?"

"I broke the rules. It wasn't just a brief affair for me anymore. I thought that if I put some distance between us, I could get over it and we could go back to the way it was."

"Has it worked?"

"No. But I have accepted the fact that I'm going to love you for the rest of my life."

That sounded perfect to him. "You're sure?"

"Yeah. Of course, I don't expect you to—"

"Too bad, Cat. You're stuck with me. For better or for worse."

"Really?"

He lowered his head and brushed his lips over hers. "Need convincing?"

She nipped his lower lip and pulled her hands from his. "No," she murmured, smiling up at him and tugging his shirttail out of his waistband. "But you can give it a shot just for the fun of it."

Yeah, he could manage that. Once for the fun. Always for the thrill, the bone-numbing satisfaction. Forever for love.

GAME OVER

* * * * *

Don't miss Leslie LaFoy's next release,
GRIN AND BEAR IT,
coming in December from Harlequin NEXT.

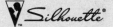

SPECIAL EDITION™

presents

the first book in a heartwarming new series by

Kristin Hardy

Because there's
no place like home
for the holidays…

WHERE THERE'S SMOKE

(November 2005, SE#1720)

Sloane Hillyard took a very personal interest in her work inventing fire safety equipment—after all, her firefighter brother had died in the line of duty. And when Boston fire captain Nick Trask signed up to test her inventions, things got even more personal… their mutual attraction set off alarms. But could Sloane trust her heart to a man who risked his life and limb day in and day out?

Available November 2005 at your favorite retail outlet.

Where love comes alive™

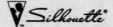

SPECIAL EDITION™

**Don't miss the latest heartwarming tale
from beloved author**

ALLISON LEIGH!

A MONTANA HOMECOMING

(Special Edition #1718)
November 2005

Laurel Runyan hasn't been to Lucius, Montana,
since the night her father supposedly murdered
her mother—and she gave her innocence to
Shane Golightly. Now, with her father's death,
Laurel has come back to face her past...and
Shane—a man she's never stopped loving....

Available at your favorite retail outlet.

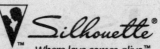

Where love comes alive™

From

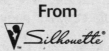

SPECIAL EDITION™

Come join the Walker family fun in

THE BORROWED RING

(SSE #1717),

the next book in the miniseries

HOME AT LAST...

by Gina Wilkins

**Available November 2005 from
Silhouette Special Edition.**

When private eye B. J. "Brittany" Samples tracked
down former teenage crush Daniel Andreas, more
than old flames threatened to consume her. Posing
as Daniel's wife in an undercover adventure to
uproot a fiendish operation, she was left with
unanswered questions like...was Daniel one
of the bad guys or the only man for her?

Available at your favorite retail outlet.

Where love comes alive™

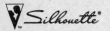

INTIMATE MOMENTS™

New York Times
bestselling author

MAGGIE SHAYNE

brings you

Feels Like Home

the latest installment in
The Oklahoma All-Girl Brands.

When Jimmy Corona returns to Big Falls, Oklahoma,
shy Kara Brand shakes with memories of a youthful crush.
He targets her as the perfect wife for him and stepmother
for his ailing son. But Jimmy's past life as a Chicago cop
brings danger in his wake. It's a race against the clock
as Jimmy tries to save his family in time to tell Kara how
much he's grown to love her, and how much he wants
to stay in this place that truly feels like home.

Available this December at your favorite retail outlet.

www.eHarlequin.com   SIMFLH

#1717 THE BORROWED RING—Gina Wilkins
Family Found
Tracking down childhood friend Daniel Andreas was an assignment
close to P.I. Brittany Samples's heart. But things took an unexpected
turn when "B.J." caught her quarry—who dispensed with reunion
formalities and recruited her to pose as his wife! Soon their dangerous
new mission had B.J. wishing the husband-and-wife cover wasn't just
an act....

#1718 A MONTANA HOMECOMING—Allison Leigh
When Laurel Runyan returned to Lucius, Montana, after her estranged
father's death, she had nowhere else to go—she'd recently broken off
an engagement and given up her job and apartment. But having her first
love, sheriff Shane Golightly, as a neighbor reopened old wounds. Was
Laurel ready to give her hometown—and Shane—a second chance?

#1719 SECRETS OF A GOOD GIRL—Jen Safrey
Most Likely To...
While at Saunders University, coed Cassidy Maxwell and teaching
assistant Eric Barnes had put off romance until Cassidy got her degree.
Then she hadn't shown up at graduation, and Eric was crushed. Now,
years later, he'd gone to London to woo her back. But Cassidy wanted
to keep her childhood friend—and her own dark Saunders secrets—in
the past....

#1720 WHERE THERE'S SMOKE—Kristin Hardy
Holiday Hearts
After her brother died fighting a blaze, Sloane Hillyard took action,
inventing a monitor to improve firefighter safety. She found a reluctant
test subject in Boston fire captain Nick Trask—who warmed to the task
as his attraction for Sloane grew. But after losing her brother, would
Sloane risk her heart on another of Boston's bravest?

#1721 MARRIAGE, INTERRUPTED—Karen Templeton
Cass Stern was on edge—newly widowed, saddled with debt, running
a business and *very* pregnant. Things couldn't get weirder—until her
first husband, Blake Carter, showed up at her second husband's funeral.
Blake wanted more time with their teenaged son—and he wanted Cass
back. Cass's body screamed "Yes!" but...well, there were a lot of
buts....

#1722 WHERE HE BELONGS—Gail Barrett
For Harley-riding, smoke-jumping rebel Wade Winslow, it was
tough going back to Millstown and facing his past. But former flame
Erin McCuen and her financial troubles struck a chord with the bad
boy, so he decided to stay for a while. The stubborn and independent
woman wouldn't accept Wade's help...but could she convince him to
give their renewed passion a fighting chance?

SSECNM1005